Butterflies Don't Lie

B . R . M Y E R S

NIMBUS
PUBLISHING
nimbus.ca

Nimbus Publishing Limited
3731 Mackintosh St, Halifax, NS B3K 5A5
(902) 455-4286 nimbus.ca

Printed and bound in Canada

NB1122

Design: Sari Naworynski

Library and Archives Canada Cataloguing in Publication

Myers, B. R., author
Butterflies don't lie / B.R. Myers.
Issued in print and electronic formats.

ISBN 978-1-77108-162-7 (pbk.).— ISBN 978-1-77108-163-4
(html).— ISBN 978-1-77108-164-1 (mobi)
I. Title.

PS8626.Y358B88 2014   jC813'.6   C2014-903199-8
C2014-903200-5

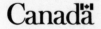  

Nimbus Publishing acknowledges the financial support for its
publishing activities from the Government of Canada through the
Canada Book Fund (CBF) and the Canada Council for the Arts,
and from the Province of Nova Scotia through Film & Creative
Industries Nova Scotia. We are pleased to work in partnership with
Film & Creative Industries Nova Scotia to develop and promote
our creative industries for the benefit of all Nova Scotians.

For Cynthia, for planting the first seed years ago,
suggesting I write a book someday.
And for Ken, for everything else.

ONE
• • • •

I shifted my butt, trying to unglue the backs of my sweaty thighs from the vinyl seat. The cheap chair made a squelching noise. One of the moms sitting across from me looked up from her iPhone.

"Pardon me," I said. She smoothed out her flower-print sundress then went back to her texting. *Holy geez*, I thought, *why anyone would want to dress like a tea cozy is beyond me.* I bet she was posting all kinds of flowery dresses on Pinterest.

Pace yourself, busy lady!

I scooted forward, perching my jean cut-offs on the edge of the chair. It was harder to write sitting this way, but Chet was almost done. The librarian's voice drifted down the hallway, soft and lilting, as she encouraged the class to sing the goodbye song. Chet's voice was one of the loudest. I chuckled. That kid cracked me up.

I turned my attention to the last question of my quiz, "True Love or True Dud?"

> **How do you know when you're in love with the right guy?**
>
> A. You think about him constantly and mention him in every conversation you have with your family and friends.
> B. When you reminisce about your dates together, your heart beats faster and you smile automatically.
> C. No matter how awful you feel, seeing your guy always makes you feel better.

I circled my answer, and with the lightning speed of someone who does a quiz each week, I had my score tallied faster than you could say, "sweaty palms." It was moot, actually. I *was* in love with the right guy—he just didn't know it yet.

When I daydreamed of Blaine Mulder, the first things I pictured were his perfect shoulders. He's not so much a muscle-dude like the rest of the jocks he hangs out with, but more like a chiselled model. His T-shirts always fit the same way, with the seams lining up with the tip of his shoulder joint. Blaine is one hot, walking mannequin of perfect proportion.

And I should know. I've spent hours in grade ten math class staring at the back of those magnificent shoulders, hence the C I got on my final exam. I'd nibble the eraser end of my pencil, daring myself to tap his above-mentioned perfect shoulders and whisper, "Hey, what question are we supposed to be on?" Or how about this icebreaker: "Did Mr. Miller say 5.6 or 6.5?"

Yes, I am lame—even in my fantasies.

Francine was more upset about my math mark than my academic parents were. My best friend is an organization fiend—she'd made a study timetable up for me and everything.

But on the day of the exam, Blaine's girlfriend, the equally beautiful and perfectly proportionate Regan Baxter, broke the news she was moving halfway across the country. Yup, the M-word.

Don't get me wrong—seeing Regan in tears wasn't a wish come true. But the timing of Blaine's sudden singleness was a sign. How on earth could a girl think of quadratic equations knowing the shoulders in front of her were potentially touchable?

That night Francine and I lounged in my pale blue bedroom, sitting on my twin beds with the matching Holly Hobbie bedspreads. She blew a red curl off her forehead while I lamented over Blaine with my usual agonized, "It's never going to happen," followed by the predictable, "I might as well call up Glen Fairweather."

Francine looked up from her laptop and eyed me without sympathy, "Why do you think hooking up with Mr. Gummy Worm is going to help?"

Glen was the only guy I'd ever kissed in the swapping-mouth-fluids kind of way. If you could call it kissing. His fat lips had moved against mine like a fish dying in the air. And don't even get me started on the tongue action. I had no experience, but I'm pretty sure no girl ever felt her heart skip a beat in Glen Fairweather's arms.

I preferred to imagine kissing Blaine instead of suffering through the disappointing reality of what I actually attracted. I'm terribly average—well, except for the C, which makes me below average I guess. Therefore, I was content to enjoy making up fantasy makeout sessions every math class, sometimes with clothes and others totally in the raw (x=X-rated).

But that night Francine had heard enough. "Our summer break officially starts next week," she announced like I was as stupid as my math marks indicated. She turned her laptop toward me and I read the title of her latest spreadsheet.

"Operation Tongue?" I rolled my eyes. "Fran, you can't be serious. You're psycho."

My God. There were rows of specific tasks with columns for the check marks. She'd covered everything—from places where I would most likely bump into Blaine, down to which summer job I should apply for.

She pointed her pencil at the row titled "Employment." My stomach dropped.

"What the heck am I qualified to do at the yacht club?" I asked, trying to hide my shaking voice. Before Francine could list off her reasoning, I had a stroke of genius. "What about the Queen's Galley?" I offered. The seaside restaurant overlooking the harbour also happened to be right beside the above-mentioned yacht club, where Blaine would be teaching sailing lessons all summer long.

Francine's lips did that funny puckered thing. She considered my suggestion, then with a few taps on the keyboard, the Employment column now said, "Queen's Galley."

My heart settled back down my throat as she continued showing me the spreadsheet. I hated lying to my best friend, but fear is a strong motivator.

The kids' voices echoed down the hallway, growing louder. I rolled the magazine up and craned my neck around the corner. A parade of kids bobbed toward the lobby. Chet was in the back, as usual, holding Ms. Kranston's hand, also as usual.

A little girl dressed like a miniature tea cozy ran straight to her matching mother.

Gag.

Chet let go of Ms. Kranston and made a beeline for my legs, making me stumble. Chet's hugs were like the leg-binding curse from Harry Potter, but I loved it. He looked up at me and smiled. His eyes disappeared into thin slits behind his thick glasses.

"*Fwog and Owed,*" he told me, showing the book he'd chosen.

"Frog and who?" I teased.

"Owed!" he repeated. Listening to him speak was like listening to someone under water. When he was younger we used sign language, but I've grown so accustomed to his speech I don't need it, plus the little stinker is getting smarter everyday.

Ms. Kranston smiled at us, but not in the demeaning way most people do when they see a kid with Down syndrome, as if his extra chromosome exists purely to make them feel all soft and warm inside. The truth is that Chet does make everyone feel that way, but that's because he is pure kindness rolled up in a cute package—not because he has special needs. As his older sister, I tend to be overprotective.

"So, Kelsey," Ms. Kranston started, brushing a stray bang off her dewy forehead. "Chet tells me you'll be working at the Queen's Galley this summer."

"Yup," I said. "I'll be in the dining room."

She frowned. "Aren't you too young to be a waitress?"

"Busgirl," I shrugged. "But I still get a percentage of the tips."

Ms. Kranston glanced up at the ceiling. "Oh, the stories I have from my waitressing days," she sighed. Then she hit me with a serious look. "Serving the public will be a good prelude to real life."

I batted my thigh with the rolled-up magazine. "Yeah, I guess so," I said, not wanting to mention that she's still serving the public in the library.

She smiled. "It sounds like you've got your summer all planned out."

I pictured Blaine with his back to me, pulling his T-shirt off and exposing those perfect shoulders, a bottle of sunscreen in my hands ready to massage into his glistening bare skin. I wet my lips and smiled. "Oh yeah, Ms. K., I've got big plans."

TWO
. . . .

"Owed wanded to weave, but Fwog makes him keep twying," Chet said.

"Uh-huh." I pulled on Chet's sweaty hand, leading him down the stone steps. The library, like most of the buildings in Mariner's Cove, is two hundred years old, giving the town a time-capsule feeling.

In October, the town does a graveyard walk for weekend tourists. They eat up the pirate stories of bloody dagger fights and long-lost treasure. There's also a rumour that the rambling brown house beside the bank used to be owned by a self-taught apothecary. Francine told me that when the owners renovated they found glass jars of brains.

Gross.

Every time I leave the library I feel like I'm walking out of a gingerbread house. But the charm of centuries-old buildings ends with the aesthetics; you have to get used to sitting in front of a fan in the summer and wearing extra sweaters in the winter.

The steps are long and shallow, and Chet's short legs took two extra strides than mine. Walk two steps, leap, and then repeat. I checked my watch.

I had to be at the Queen's Galley in an hour. Showing up late for my uniform fitting wouldn't be the best way to start my summer job. I imagined Francine's spreadsheet glaring back at me with its one pathetic check mark. I took a little bit of comfort in the fact that she'd be offline for the next three weeks, and unable to track my progress on Operation Tongue.

"Den da kite wend high in da sky." Chet squeezed my hand when I didn't reply. "Fwog hewped Owed." He gave me his pudgy smile.

"Chetter-cheese," I said, picking up the pace. "We're going to be late."

"Kowsey," he muttered under his breath, unimpressed with my impatience. (When Chet had first started saying my name Dad thought it would be cute to shorten it to "Kows." Mom and I talked him out of it, thank God.)

We hopped off the curb. I focused on my mom's car, parked across the street. Most kids would think it was pretty sweet to get the keys to a brand new car—even if it's a nerdy hatchback—but I only get to drive when I'm chauffeuring Chet to his various activities. I'd already been told that I would be biking back and forth to the Queen's Galley.

Francine hadn't even flinched when I told her that latest parental bombshell. "A windswept French braid," she'd simply justified, "will be perfect for chance encounters with Blaine."

Sometimes I hate how she never lets me complain. That's a smarty-pants problem solver for you.

I clicked the button on the key, unlocking the doors. I was lucky to park so close. Now that the summer was officially here, the summer people, or, as Francine and I call them, the stunned-er people—"Stunders" for short—were arriving in droves and taking over the village.

We haven't seen you in ten months, but of course you may move back into your sprawling mansions on the beach and let us serve you. We love how your money keeps the village alive for another year.

It sucks when the weather gets colder and school starts, but it is always a relief to get Mariner's Cove back to ourselves.

"Kowsey!" Chet practically ripped my arm out of my shoulder as he pulled me back. I screamed as a black blur raced into the corner of my vision. I threw my arms around Chet and pushed us both into the side of the car, squeezing my eyes shut.

Someone swore and there was a loud crunch. Chet started to cry. "Oh my God," I said, frantically patting him all over. "Are you okay?" my voice cracked.

Chet nodded and then pointed behind me.

A guy was on the road, untangling himself from his bike, the rear tire still spinning. A vicious scrape ran the whole length of his calf and was already bleeding.

A mop of neon blue hair poked through his bike helmet. He stood up and winced, but then quickly shifted his weight to his uncut leg. Then he hit me with a stare. "Are you crazy?"

Usually I take the less aggressive course of action—you know, like the river? Big stone? No problem, just go around. But seeing my brother almost get hit by this Stunder launched me into Protect Chet mode.

"Me? You're the asshole that was racing down the street." I could see my reflection in his sunglasses. I definitely had my lemon face on.

The colour grew high in his cheeks. "I'm on a bike!" he said. "I'm watching out for cars, not idiots wandering into the streets."

I glared back. His face became hard, like he was ready to push our spitting battle to epic proportions. Then Chet whimpered behind me.

The guy took in a sharp breath, and his expression suddenly fell. "Oh," he said. "I'm sorry, little dude. Are you okay?"

I stood in front of Chet, blocking him from this maniac. "Not as sorry as you're going to be. My dad is a lawyer, and he'll sue your ass." I lie brilliantly when I'm in Protect Chet mode.

He turned back to me, and his jaw became rigid again. "But you walked him right in front of me."

I opened my mouth a few times.

Bacon turds! He's right. Stupid Stunder.

But I wasn't going to let being wrong get in the way of my argument. "Lucky you're only on a bike," I spat out. "If you were driving a car we'd be dead!" And then I added for good measure, "Asshole."

The guy gripped the handlebars of his bike, but he didn't say anything else. By this time, I'd noticed some passers-by had started craning their necks.

Hey, what do you expect? It's a village.

Mr. Reckless Biker apologized to Chet again, but I ignored him and pulled Chet to the other side of the car. My hands were shaking so badly it took a few tries to buckle him into his booster seat.

I managed to get myself behind the wheel and waited until my heart wasn't hammering an SOS against my rib cage. When I finally checked the rear-view mirror, the guy had started down the road toward Main Street, limping alongside his bike.

BUTTERFLIES DON'T LIE   15

"Asshole," I muttered under my breath.

"How-hole," Chet copied softly.

We only live a five-minute drive from the library, but it's a twisty path. It's like that old song—"*Over the hills and through the woods to Grandmother's house we go...*" There's a joke that when they established Mariner's Cove, after the houses and business were built on the waterfront, all the other roads were made by following a meandering cow.

Today, the curves and twists seemed especially foreboding. I was taking the corner before our road when I noticed Chet mop his eyes with his arm. A stone dropped in my stomach. God, I hate guilt.

"Hey, don't cry. It's okay. No one was hurt," I said, feeling calmer now that my hands had stopped shaking.

Chet caught my eye in the rear-view. His voice dropped to a whisper. "You said *how-hole*. Mom will be mad."

I rolled my eyes at that one. "I get angry when someone almost hurts you. *And Mom has no right to be mad.*" I bit my tongue to keep the second part inside my head. Chet doesn't need to know the real deal between me and my parents. I wiggled uncomfortably. "Besides, that guy *was* a how-hole."

"But he said he was sowwy." His voice was thick.

"Sometimes being sorry isn't enough," I said, fighting off visions of what could have been. "We don't have to tell Mom and Dad," I reinforced. "Like you said, the guy apologized. So we can leave it at that."

Chet looked out the window. "Weave it at dat," he repeated.

THREE
· · · · · ·

I slammed the microwave door shut and ripped open the popcorn bag. "Ouch!" The bag dropped, spilling popcorn on the kitchen counter. Geez, those little suckers really do heat up.

"Kelsey." Mom said my name with a long, exaggerated sigh. "Please eat something real." She hovered over a baking dish, turning chicken breasts meticulously with a fork, making sure the marinade was soaking up evenly. She was wearing her usual skort thingy: half skirt, half walking shorts. Mom was a walking advertisement for Sears—from the seventies.

I rolled my eyes at her back, then began shoving the popcorn in my mouth. "This is real," I insisted, through a mouthful of chemically prepared kernels—make that *deliciously* prepared kernels. I hadn't eaten since breakfast and the salty, fake buttery goodness was making my mouth water.

After another handful, I grabbed my Kipling shoulder bag hanging off the kitchen chair. I'm not exactly a trendsetter in the style department, but my Aunt Bea lives in New York, and she sends me the coolest stuff. It's bright yellow and has a little fuzzy gorilla dangling from the key chain. I love that little guy. When I feel crappy, I stick its plastic thumb in its little O-shaped mouth. Call me cuckoo, but it I find it soothing. Like the little guy is sharing some of my pain.

Mom glanced over her shoulder and said, "You're going to ruin your supper."

That was a total joke. Supper probably wasn't for at least another three hours. My parents were adamant about eating late in the evening. I knew it had to do with how long it took those two academics to make a decision. They could never figure out a menu quickly. My mom is an overachieving English professor who marks tests from kids all over the world, and my dad has a job teaching history at Dalhousie, the closest university to Mariner's Cove, with a forty-five-minute commute.

Francine and I called them "Academia Nuts." If they had been on the *Titanic*, they would've been drawing a seating plan for the lifeboats while the water rose up their legs. They're all talk and little action. Hence, I'm their gofer for all things that need action. Like Chet.

Chet came into the kitchen rubbing his tummy. "Hey, Chetter-cheese." I held up my half-eaten bag of popcorn as an offering. "I'm outta here. Finish this, okay?"

He took my snack and grinned wide enough to make his eyes disappear. It must be nice to be so happy that your smile takes over your face. We both ignored Mom's disapproving glare.

She tapped the fork on the edge of the glass dish and slid the marinating chicken into the fridge. "When will you be home?"

"I don't know," I shrugged. Mom's car keys poked out of my capris. She'd strongly suggested I not show up at the Queen's Galley in my jean cut-offs.

The patio door slid open and Dad walked in.

Hello, Mr. Socks 'n Sandals.

He noticed Mom's car keys. "I didn't think you started until tomorrow," he said to me. He was wearing the barbecue apron his undergrads gave him last year, the tacky one with the slogan, *Old Teachers Never Die, They Just Lose Their Class.*

"It's just to pick up my uniform," I sighed.

God, get me out of here.

They both gave me a nod, as if taking the car to do something for myself was a heavy burden on their evening of discussing how to spend their summer vacation. Ah, the lives of teachers.

I couldn't get out of the driveway fast enough. I rolled down the window and turned up the radio, letting Taylor Swift's voice wash over me. Nothing is better than hearing your favourite song when you need it the most. It was like the spiritual world heard my request or something. I shook off my funk and started to concentrate on Operation Tongue. I smiled as visions of Blaine's shoulders filled my head.

Francine had made sure to give me easy goals so I could check off something on her spreadsheet every few days. She told me this was positive reinforcement, which would be good for my confidence.

She was right. Even though all I had to do was pick up my uniform, I was looking forward to checking off the "Pick up uniform" box. Each completed task would bring me one step closer to Blaine...and to the very last box: "Have a simply amazing, neurotransmitter-firing, stomach-full-of-butter-flies kiss."

Here's the thing: Francine is kind of geeky, but she's also super smart and she managed to snag one of the school's hottest guys. Tanner had been in danger of being kicked off the basketball team if he didn't pass physics. His coach teamed him up with Francine for tutoring.

Imagine a six-foot-three jock taking orders from a curly haired redhead who barely tips the scales at one hundred pounds. I guess all those times hunched over a textbook rubbing shoulders, mixed in with some dirty talk about $E=mc^2$, was all the chemistry it took.

Pun intended.

Everyone said their names together super fast, *FrancineandTanner*, and eventually they became known as *Franner*, like one entity. But Francine didn't jump into her superjock's arms and race toward the rainbow in a dew-soaked field. Not my Fran-man. She tackled her new social calendar with her usual precision: she made a spreadsheet scheduling an equal amount of time spent with Tanner and me. She even had overlapping times so that Tanner and I could be friends too.

God love that smarty-pants.

However, for all her preparedness, this time Francine had left one crucial loophole: aquaphobia. Specifically *my* aquaphobia, or rather, my fear of anyone finding out I have aquaphobia. Tough when you live an arm's length from the ocean, but I'd managed to adapt and keep it a secret. Even Francine was ignorant to my terror of the wet stuff. She moved here in grade six—two years after "the incident." I never talked about it with her, and since Francine isn't much of a swimmer our friendship blossomed on dry land perfectly.

Mariner's Cove may be right on the water, but it's not an island, thank God. Francine had wanted me to teach alongside Blaine at the yacht club, but since boating requires being in the ocean, I had to cough up the idea of the Queen's Galley. I'm so good at lying about it she hadn't even blinked. But like I said, I never talked about what happened the summer I was nine, and I was pretty sure everyone else had forgotten too, even Mom.

The hatchback coasted down the steep, tree-lined road that eventually levelled out in front of the restaurant. It was easy to find a parking spot since the Queen's Galley wasn't opening until the next day. I checked my watch and then hopped out of the car. Across the quiet intersection, the roof of the yacht club peeked up from below the road. The rambling white building was built on the slope leading down to the shore, where several wharves stretched out butted with sailboats.

I squinted, trying to will Blaine's perfect mop of blonde hair to come up the stairway to the road. A bunch of guys were gathered at the gazebo at the top of the stairs, but there was no one I recognized, only the usual Stunders.

The Queen's Galley was built by Captain Bowsky over two hundred years ago. I bet that rich and fancy naval officer never dreamed his home would someday boast "the best fish chowder this side of the coast."

Gardeners were putting the finishing touches on the grounds as I walked up the stone path to the red wooden door. Wedding pictures are a common scene here, but today it was just me and my bright yellow Kipling bag.

The foyer was dominated by a huge vase of fresh flowers. A sweeping staircase led to the second floor. Everything was perfect. Perfectly quiet. "Hello?" I called out.

I checked my watch again, and then rubbed the fuzzy arm of my yellow gorilla. I poked my head into the dining room, but it was empty too. Above the fireplace, Captain Bowsky's portrait stared down at me. His eyes did that creepy follow-you-around-the-room thing.

I walked to the back of the room where the long windows overlooked the harbour. Sailboats drifted along and I imagined Blaine standing behind the wheel, wind rippling his hair, the first five buttons of his shirt undone—or maybe it was completely off. Yeah, completely off.

CRASH!

I jumped and turned to the white door on the other side of the room. One panel near the top was replaced with glass. I sneaked up and peeked through the window and into the kitchen.

A gangly dude in a wrinkled T-shirt was bent over a large sink behind a long counter. His black ball cap was on backwards, hiding most of his neck. Someone's voice boomed, followed by another crash, making me jump again. But the guy at the sink stayed bent over with both arms submerged up to his elbows.

"Hey, we don't open until tomorrow," someone said from behind. A large woman in a white smock leaned against the doorway, watching me.

My cheeks grew warm. "I'm just here to pick up my uniform," I said. She wiped her hands on a cotton hand towel, looking me up and down. "I'm…I'm one of the busgirls," I stammered.

"Uh-huh." She motioned to the kitchen door. "Well, let's get you introduced, then," she said. "I'm Loretta." Her hand engulfed mine and gave it two strong shakes. I mumbled my own name, then wordlessly followed her through the swinging door.

The booming voice belonged to a man with a moustache that looked like it had been drawn on with a thin marker. He was taking large chunks of ice and dropping them into another sink.

CRASH!

"Joe Jeezer!" Loretta said to Mr. Moustache. "What are you doing, Clyde?"

Clyde ignored us, and began hacking at the mounds of ice with a knife. I flinched with each stab, but T-shirt guy was unshaken, still bent over his own sink, working something with his hands under the running water. His cargo shorts ended just at the knee. My eyes trailed down and saw a long white bandage on his calf.

A low buzzing started inside my head like a warning signal. Loretta's voice broke through my building terror. "Clyde, calm down. You're going to scare away the new staff before we even open."

Clyde continued to stab, apparently lost in his world of appetizer apocalypse. T-shirt guy straightened up, and then turned to me. Neon blue hair poked out from under his ball cap.

How-hole!

His mouth dropped open, and I'm sure his "Holy shit!" expression was a perfect mirror of my own face.

Loretta put a heavy hand on my shoulder. "Kelsey, this is Luke," she said. "He's going to be working here all summer, just like you."

FOUR
· · · · ·

> When faced with the guy you'd like to kill, you...
>
> A. waste no time and throttle him like he deserves.
> B. point a finger and rat him out so he can get fired.
> C. play it cool and attack him later when there are no witnesses.

I stood frozen. Loretta's voice echoed from far away, prompting Clyde to at least look at her.

Clyde, proud owner of the perfectly straight, thin moustache, pushed down his shoulders and waved a hand at the mess of ice chunks and little blobs of pink. "He wants this shrimp ready for appetizers for his private party tonight!"

Loretta stared at the sink, then wiped a hand over her red face. "Don't get your 'stache in a knot," she told him. "The four of us will have them thawed in no time. Are you steaming or pan-frying?"

I scanned the room and my heart dropped—even I could do the math. "Um…" I started. "I'm not kitchen staff. I'm a busgirl." Then I added, to clarify any further confusion, "And I don't start until tomorrow." This made sense in my head, but it came out in a shaky voice, like I wasn't even sure.

Loretta snorted. I'm certain she could smell my fear. "Listen babycakes, around here everyone is kitchen staff. The new owner is having a cocktail reception in the bar tonight, and if he doesn't have his shrimp appetizer, the first one to get fired is the uppity new busgirl."

Uppity new busgirl?

How about the ready-to-pee-her-pants-because-she's-so-angry-and-scared busgirl?

My Kipling bag still over my shoulder, Loretta pushed me in front of the stainless steel sink. Her big red hands worked the taps, and soon I was elbow deep in ice and beady-eyed shrimp.

Clyde put a hand on one hip. "Each summer it's the same thing," he began. "A new owner waltzes in thinking he knows how to run this place and ignores all my suggestions." In his other hand, the knife made sweeping motions in the air. "Then by the end of the summer, he realizes how clueless he really is, and sells it." Clyde paused and looked up at the ceiling. "No one ever listens to the chef."

Loretta was nodding thoughtfully through Clyde's speech. Her fingers worked to separate a shrimp from the bed of ice. She brought it to her face, staring down her nose at its pathetic little face. Then she twisted off its head and threw the body into a huge bowl on the counter.

Everyone craned their necks and looked at the lonely headless thing at the bottom of the bowl.

Clyde's moustache stayed in a hard, straight line. "One," he counted, in a deadpan voice.

Loretta flicked the water from her hands, then began bustling around the kitchen, clanking pans on the stove, grabbing a block of butter from the industrial fridge, and asking Clyde about produce deliveries. Soon Clyde was by her side, babbling about sauce and a new recipe he picked up last fall in California.

I stared down at my sink of lifeless shrimp and began to decapitate those poor little suckers. It took me a whole minute to snap apart the first one. I tossed it into Loretta's bowl.

Plop.

My fingers were already numb. I glanced at my watch. Somewhere in the harbour, Blaine was feeling the warm sun on his face. Did he miss Regan? They'd only dated for a few months, but to ease my conscience I'd checked his Facebook page the night before and been thrilled to see he'd changed his relationship status to "single."

Plop. Plop. Plop.

I glanced at How-hole. He'd already gone through most of his pile of shrimp. Show-off. His chin turned toward me and I snapped my gaze back into my sink. He shuffled closer, the tip of his Converse inching closer to my flip-flop. His laces were undone and tucked inside. I snorted. That was so elementary school.

"Hey," he said. I ignored him, instead choosing to take an immense new interest in the fascinating practice of shrimp thawing. I twisted off a head.

Plop.

"Okay, Kelsey." He cleared his throat like my name choked him up or something. "I'm sorry I scared your brother. He's your brother, right?"

Twist. Rip. Plop. Repeat.

I stayed quiet, continuing my assault on the shrimp.

Twist. Rip. Plop. Repeat.

Clyde and Loretta's voices floated over from the stove, totally ignorant of my turmoil across the room.

"Look," he tried again. "If we're going to be working together all summer..." He left the sentence hanging. Then to my horror he reached into my sink and started to work on MY shrimp.

Who did this How-hole think he was?

A ball of heat rose up my chest. My fingers came to life.

TWIST. RIP. PLOP.

I was in hyper mode now, determined to show him up. Shrimp heads were flying across the sink like I was a Las Vegas blackjack dealer.

"You can't ignore me the whole summer." There was a long pause. "Kelsey?" Then he sighed. I stopped mid-rip. He sounded just like my mom.

That did it. I turned and gave him my best dagger-eyeball glare. The last time we had a staring contest, he'd been wearing sunglasses and all I could see was my reflection. But this time, a pair of blue eyes blinked back at me. Piercing blue eyes. Just like a tropical ocean. Ocean. Water.

Gulp.

A cold flush ran down my spine.

He leaned back a bit, and his blue eyes grew even wider.

"Looks like Luke's got the hang of it." Loretta's head suddenly poked between us. She noticed his empty sink.

I waved toward my bowl, fishing for a compliment.

Loretta's face fell. She tilted up the bowl and showed me a glossy pile of shrimp heads. My insides crumpled a bit.

"We're not serving the heads," she said. Then she slid a tall white bucket across the floor with her foot. "Put all those heads in here," she ordered. "Then finish your sink."

She looked at Luke and motioned to a workstation in the corner. "You come with me. You'll be expected to help with salads and desserts." He tried to catch my eye, but I refused to give him the satisfaction. I had a plan: play it cool, then attack him when there were no witnesses.

Still, this was hardly the beginning I had been envisioning for Operation Tongue. Francine had none of this on her spread-sheet. I couldn't exactly check off "Decapitate shrimp" when I got home. My hand went to the Kipling bag, searching for my fuzzy yellow gorilla. I went to put the little plastic thumb in his mouth, then stopped—my gorilla was covered in shrimp slime.

FIVE

s I dug through the shrimp heads, a memory surfaced: In grade two, Trent Fraser had thrown up in the afternoon, right before creative writing. I'll spare you the gross details, but let's just say he had hotdogs for lunch that day, a lot of hotdogs…and grape juice, apparently.

Nothing causes a stampede of screaming kids like someone barfing. Ms. Ritter almost lost her cameo brooch, she ran so fast to get the janitor. While all the kids stood clear with our backs up against the wall, Blaine stayed with Trent, patting his back.

Even as a little kid, Blaine had the makings of a nice guy. I looked into my bucket of shrimp heads wishing he were here now, certain that he would be comforting me.

The back door to the kitchen slammed open. "*I'm back,*" a voice sang out. I recognized the most popular girl from high school at once. Chloe Rhodes glided into the kitchen looking windswept and smelling of fresh flowers and sunshine.

I'm not sure how someone can smell like sunshine, but she did. Her long, black hair was in a slick ponytail. She always wore something gold, and she was always smiling—seriously, a toothpaste commercial could break out at any moment. She was a real-life version of Princess Jasmine from *Aladdin*.

She was fashionable, chatty, and rumoured to have several college guys vying for her heart. In short, the exact opposite of me. She was also a grade above, which, according to the high school social rule book, meant I knew everything about her and she didn't even know my name.

Clyde's face broke into a smile, transforming him into a friendly, approachable, almost completely sane guy. "Chloe!" With his hands full of utensils, he gave her a one-armed hug. My mouth dropped open at the transformation. Loretta even grinned. Then she said, "Our favourite busgirl returns."

Chloe laughed and tossed her sleek ponytail over her shoulder. Her gold hoop earrings dangled. She smiled at How-hole, then reached up and playfully flicked a piece of blue hair poking out from under his cap. "Wow!" Her eyes sparkled. "Your eyes are so blue they're almost the same colour as your hair!"

Loretta and Clyde nodded with amused expressions, as if this struck them as charming news. How-hole actually blushed. Chloe giggled, and then she turned, finally noticing me.

"This is Kelsey," Loretta started. "She's one of the new staff this year."

"Busgirl," I blurted out. "I'm supposed to be one of the busgirls."

It was quiet for a few dreadful seconds. Chloe simply lifted a shoulder, but there was a hint of a smile. I stuck out my hand, hoping she couldn't tell it was shaking. Her eyes trailed down and her expression froze. A shrimp head was stuck on my pinkie.

"Oh," she said, still looking at my finger, as if she were talking to the shrimp. "When you're finished here, you should come pick up your uniform." She backed up a bit, probably worried my fish smell would drown out her sunshine. She left through the swinging door into the dining room.

I looked pleadingly at Loretta. Even she could tell I was no help in the kitchen. She waved her cotton towel. "Get out of here, babycakes."

I wiped my hands on my capris and sped out of there faster than you could say "sushi platter."

I followed Chloe's ponytail through the dining room until she disappeared between a pair of French doors at the far end.

The mid-sized room off the main dining area served as the restaurant's old-fashioned bar. It was lined with mahogany wood and brass trim. Framed pictures of schooners were hung all around for that fresh-from-the-sea feeling, I guess. Round tables with curved leather chairs dotted the floor space. It smelled like stale beer and furniture polish.

Several other girls were already sitting at a few of the tables. They were slightly older, and I didn't recognize any of them. They greeted Chloe with hugs and cheek kisses. I sat in a chair closest to the window, painfully suspicious of how I must smell like dead fish. A set of double glass doors led to the patio.

I rubbed the fuzzy gorilla, pretending to look outside as I eavesdropped. It was soon obvious these girls were the waitresses, and that Chloe and I were the only busgirls.

"I thought you quit for good last year," Chloe teased one of the girls.

The blonde twirled the end of her hair and snapped her gum. "Two weeks of late shifts at the gas station was enough for me. Besides, there's a new owner. Things might be different this summer."

Chloe and the other girls looked unconvinced. A few bits of gossip about the new owner began to be shared.

"Divorced," the blonde offered.

"Scandalous playboy," someone else added under her breath with a hint of a giggle.

"I heard he won the restaurant in a poker game in New York."

"Hard-ass," a dark-haired waitress said. She was wearing a white tank top with a bedazzled skull on the front. There was a black widow spider tattooed on her ankle.

After two minutes I was envisioning the prime suspect in every *Law & Order* episode. I looked down at my Kipling bag and realized the gorilla was already sucking his thumb. Panic started to rise in my chest.

Stupid aquaphobia! I should have been volunteering to check Blaine's shoulders for sunburn, not sitting by myself, the odd girl out, as the debutantes compared notes.

I thought about Francine, and a small ache grew in my stomach. She'd only been on her family vacation for three days and I already missed her. But if Francine had been there, she'd have told me to focus and concentrate on my goal.

I imagined the spreadsheet. No matter how sucky the day was, I was determined to check off the uniform box. Last year the employees wore white blouses with black pencil skirts. With a push-up bra and some altering, I could make it a snug, sexy fit.

I had to take Francine's advice seriously; after all, she was the one having awesome kissing sessions with Tanner. She described it as every synapse firing double the amount of neurotransmitters, thereby creating throbbing fireworks in her thoracic cavity.

Smarty-pants.

I squinted out the window. It was almost sunset. Most of the boats had their sails down and were tying up to their moorings. A couple walked hand in hand along the edge of the restaurant's lawn.

"All right, girls!"

Ahoy, Skipper!

Through the French doors, a man strolled in wearing a white turtleneck and blue blazer. And, I'm not kidding, the guy even had on a white captain's hat. If he'd had a beard, I'd swear I was looking at the High Liner Foods mascot.

He clapped his hands like a Sunday school teacher, signalling for our silence, which was useless since we'd all been rendered speechless by his outfit.

He introduced himself as Omar Deveau and then proceeded to give a five-minute history lesson about the restaurant. How this would help us serve chowder to tourists, I wasn't sure. My stomach growled, making him pause. He narrowed his gaze at me. I coughed in my hand, then gave him a small smile.

Mr. Deveau took a moment to smooth down one side of his already-slicked-back hair. "I want the Queen's Galley to really stand out this summer. A trait all the most successful establishments have in common is a...?"

He looked at us expectantly. Some of the girls wiggled in their chairs, crossing and uncrossing their already tanned legs. The dark-haired waitress twirled her earring.

"A *theme*," he finished, disappointed with our lack of business savvy. His finger played with the brass buttons on his blazer. "The rich nautical history here makes Mariner's Cove the perfect summer destination for thousands of tourists each year."

My stomach threatened to growl again. I wished I had eaten the whole bag of popcorn earlier. Mr. Deveau's voice droned on. I snuck another look outside, wishing I was relaxing on the patio watching people stroll by—in particular people who worked at the yacht club.

Suddenly, a wonderful image began to form in my mind: *I'm carrying a tray of tall drinks across the patio, looking all sexy in my tight black skirt and fitted white blouse. Blaine happens to stroll by...*

"The tourists want colonial history." Mr. Deveau's voice was full of expression. "Imagine you've been transported back in time..."

I catch Blaine's eye, then take an ice cube from one of the glasses and slowly run it along my throat. (I got that idea from the "Are You Naturally Seductive?" quiz in the May issue of *Modern Teen*.) *Blaine stops in his tracks. He stares back at me, then a smile slowly curls at the edge of his mouth. I lift my hand to wave him over...*

"For the full effect, I'll need one of you to model," Mr. Deveau finished with another clap. "Yes, you there."

It was suddenly quiet. I left my patio fantasy and saw that everyone had turned in my direction. My arm was still stuck in the air from waving at a pretend Blaine.

Uh-oh.

Visions of seducing Blaine from the patio vanished in a flash of *Little House On the Prairie*. Mr. Deveau was holding up what I really, really hoped was NOT my uniform.

SIX
• • •

changed in the bathroom. The flowery wallpaper and antique sconces didn't make the scene any prettier. I put everything on except for the hat. Oh, dear God, the hat.

It took every ounce of strength I had to walk back into that bar. I tripped on the skirt a few times. How was I going to carry a tray dressed like this? I pushed through the French doors. Chloe actually gasped. Mr. Deveau clapped his hands together, then rushed over to me, primping and tucking material. He made me twirl around for him.

The dark-haired waitress with a tattoo turned a shade of pale that would rival a zombie. A pink bubble popped and stuck on the blonde's face. I stood before my co-workers like the Ghost of Christmas Yet to Be: I was their future, and it scared the crap out of them.

"How," the dark-haired one said, staring and pointing at my skirt, "are we supposed to navigate the stairs to the upper floor?"

Mr. Deveau was busy trying to make the sleeves of my peasant blouse fluff up more. "There's a dumbwaiter, Julia," he said, matter-of-factly. Then he hit her with a sidelong glance. "And every lady knows to lift her skirt when she walks up stairs."

I didn't have to look at Julia to feel the heat from her stare. Instead, I studied my floor-length brown skirt, pleated for extra puffiness. I probably could have worn a pair of snow pants underneath and still looked the same. A long white apron was tied around my waist.

If Blaine ever did walk by while I was on the patio, I would hide under the nearest table.

"Are You Naturally Seductive?"

No. I'm a natural nerd.

And when I didn't think it could get any worse, Mr. Deveau noticed what I'd try to hide in my fist. I played dumb, but he finally took it from me and plunked it on my head.

"Holy—" the blonde one started.

"Quaker!" Julia interrupted. "She looks like a pioneer!"

Actually, I thought "Laura Ingalls Wilder's nightcap" would be a more accurate description. But yeah, a long brown skirt, paired with a short-sleeved peasant blouse and topped with a white nightcap screamed, "I'm from the past, would you like rolls or crackers with your chowder?"

Chloe's lips were pressed together like she was trying to keep from laughing. Then Mr. Deveau dropped the bombshell. "You'll soon see how easy it is to work in this because I need staff for the private party I'm throwing in an hour."

Mouths fell open all around the room. In the end, Mr. Deveau decided that considering I was already changed that I should stay, especially since I was the newest staff member and should start training right away.

Chloe volunteered, and Julia, whose lip did a weird, curled-up thing when she was handed her uniform, was tonight's waitress.

She also had to sub as bartender, since she was the only one old enough to serve alcohol. The others, including the gum-chewing blonde, were allowed to go home. I watched them leave and wished I could go too.

We met in the small holding bar, just off the main foyer, waiting for the guests to arrive. Back in the day, when the restaurant was super busy, this room was actually used by people who lounged around on the red velvet cushions drinking cocktails until their table was ready.

Tonight, with our white nightcaps and forced smiles, the vibe was less elegant.

I kept telling myself that it would be worth it when I checked off "Pick up uniform."

I'm so pathetic.

Julia was texting her boyfriend and basically ignoring me and Chloe. Now that I was closer I could see her earrings were little diamond skulls. I guess she likes a theme just as much as Mr. Deveau.

Chloe, I had to admit, made the silly uniform work. She looked like an extra in a Jane Austen novel or something. She would be the lowly maid who catches the eye of an earl and consequently finds out she's the long-lost daughter of a duke.

Are You Naturally Seductive or an Uppity Busgirl?

"You know," I began, hoping to turn things around, "the uniforms aren't that bad." I paused but no one said anything. "I mean, when Mr. Deveau started talking about the history of Mariner's Cove, I was worried he was going to make us dress like pirates."

Julia didn't even look up from her phone. "We look like brothel wenches. Pirates would have been cool. I was a pirate for Mardi Gras, and I was dead sexy. We'd get better tips dressed as pirates."

I shared a look with Chloe. I snorted, but she only smoothed out her skirt.

Great.

The guests arrived slowly. Mr. Deveau ushered everyone through the dining room and into the bar. As Julia served the wine and beer, Chloe and I headed to the kitchen, ready to be loaded down with trays of finger foods.

Loretta laughed so hard when she saw our uniforms, she turned a slight shade of purple.

"Go ahead," Chloe said in a light tone. "Tell us we look like brothel wenches."

Clyde wrinkled his nose. "Don't give yourselves that much credit. You look like the girls who empty the brothel wench's chamber pot."

Loretta didn't breathe for another minute. How-hole's ball cap was turned around the right way so the brim was hiding most of his face, but his shaking shoulders told me all I needed to know.

Blaine would have never laughed. He would find something positive to compliment us about—especially Chloe, because she was totally selling the thing.

I reminded myself of the one and only reason I was putting up with this, and I used the image of Blaine's perfect back to help get me through this horrible night.

I picked up my tray of sautéed garlic shrimp wrapped in pea pods. My training consisted of copying Chloe. She smiled, told people what the food was, and then gave them a napkin.

I tried my best to smile, hoping it didn't look as fake as it felt. Then I dropped the toothpicks when I had to push my cap back up on my head. Chloe managed to glow the whole night.

I recognized some local business owners, but Mr. Deveau spent most of his time with a George Clooney look-alike. You know, older but still kind of good-looking.

"Shrimp in a pea pod?" I offered, showing off my Chloe-esque smile.

Mr. Deveau was still wearing his captain's hat. He smiled at me like I was his favourite girl in the world. "Kelsey," he said, "I'd like you to meet someone very important." He waved his hand toward the man. I was impressed he bothered to introduce me at all. "This is Mr.—"

"Just Edward," the man interrupted. He smiled. I noticed even the tiny wrinkles around his eyes were handsome. "No pretences here," he told me.

My cheeks flushed and my brain went blank. The chair beside me had more personality.

Mr. Deveau sensed my inability to speak. "These are absolutely to die for," Mr. Deveau informed Edward. "The chef bought them fresh from the fishermen on the wharf this morning."

I envisioned the white bucket full of half-frozen shrimp heads still thawing in the kitchen.

Edward frowned. Even I knew we didn't catch shrimp anywhere near here. Mr. Deveau realized his mistake and pulled at the white collar of his turtleneck. "I'm sure everything will work out well in the kitchen."

Edward's gaze hardened, turning Mr. Deveau an even more interesting shade of red. He nervously touched his lips with his napkin. "Please try one," he urged.

On cue, I thrust the tray closer to Edward. I kind of liked that he made Mr. Deveau nervous. He took a shrimp and winked at me. My knees turned to water. "Thank you," he said.

"With a smile like that, you'll make lots of tips this summer."

I could feel the heat move up my neck, filling my cheeks. "I'll do my best," I said.

By the time I returned to the kitchen I had started to feel the floor under my feet again. There's a reason women flock to George Clooney. Well, besides the fact he's a movie star and super rich. One word: *Suave-a-licious.*

The party was only two hours long. Julia had washed down the bar, put the empties in the basement, and was on her boyfriend's motorcycle before you could say, "Play us a jig on the fiddle, Pa."

Chloe barely gave me a smile in the bathroom. She changed back into her sundress and gold hoop earrings in silence. I guess the rules of high school count in the summer, too. Cool older girls don't chum around with the younger nerdy ones.

I clutched my stomach. The ache wasn't hunger. I missed Francine. Maybe she was wrong this time.

I shouldn't be here at all. Why did I ever think I had a chance with Blaine?

A morbid cloud of self-pity hung over me.

I was sticky and gross. Instead of putting my capris on, I stayed in my brothel look, except now I had my yellow Kipling bag as an accessory. The front door was closed, so I went into the kitchen.

Loretta was wiping down the counter. Clyde motioned to several white buckets on the floor. "Empty that into the flower beds," he ordered. He read my expression, then explained. "It's the leftover dishwater. I hate waste. And in my restaurant, fresh flowers go on the tables every day."

This was the perfect end to my miserable shift. I pictured myself giving him a salute, then taking the bucket and dumping it over his head. That would wash off his pencil-thin moustache.

Here's the thing about being mad—it gives you a lot of strength. I adjusted my Kipling bag, grabbed the white bucket, and pushed out the back kitchen door.

The screen door slammed behind me. I marched down the steps, and swung that bucket with the strength of ten angry busgirls. Slowly, painfully, I watched in silent horror as a wave of shrimp heads scattered over the flower bed.

"Once the mopping is done, you can leave." Clyde's voice echoed from the screen door. I could see his silhouette. The bright tip of a cigarette lit up. He exhaled smoke through the screen. I slunk back, even though I was sure he couldn't see me—or the pile of shrimp I'd just bombed the flower bed with.

The bushes close to my feet rustled. I clamped a hand over my mouth, swallowing a scream. I hate the dark. I hate little critters. I hate things that can run up my leg. I tucked the skirt between my thighs, trying to make pants.

What would Laura Ingalls Wilder do? Smack it over the head with a frying pan and have it for stew, I guessed.

This was useless. *I* was useless. And I was trapped. Clyde mashed his cigarette butt into a sand-filled pot by the door and finally disappeared.

I left the bucket hidden in the bushes and decided to make a run for it. There was no way I was going back in the kitchen to face How-hole. He'd probably thought up a load of insults about my uniform.

Mr. Deveau's voice coming from the kitchen stopped me in my tracks. "Excellent, Edward." His voice was sickeningly sweet. "You won't regret it." He ended with a clap. He probably writes with lots of exclamation points, too.

Clap! Clap! Clap!

It was like being around someone who sets off popguns randomly. I envisioned a summer of frayed nerves and fingers permanently stained with fish guts.

. My good pal, Edward, turned to talk to whoever was behind them. "Make sure you do a good job," he said. His patronizing tone was unmistakable.

I felt slightly sorry for Clyde. I had a suspicion Edward was going to be a big influence on the summer. But it wasn't Clyde who came to the door after Edward and Mr. Deveau had left.

How-hole swished the mop back and forth over the floor. The screen door creaked open. Instinctively, I backed up into the bushes. He turned and poured the old dishwater over the railing. The old dishwater I was supposed to dump. He stared in my direction. I stopped breathing. He took off his ball cap and ran his hand through his hair a few times. Then he went back inside.

I looked guiltily at the white bucket, but only for a few seconds.

What's done is done. I can't fix it now.

Besides, what harm could a little seafood do to a flower garden? The plants might actually benefit from all the extra enzymes or whatever.

I ran to the car, my fuzzy yellow gorilla bouncing off my hip the whole way.

SEVEN
......

D ad was watching TV when I dragged my sweaty, stinky self home. "Mom had to pick up some bread and run a few errands," he told me. Chet was asleep, tucked into Dad's side. *The Sound Of Music*, Chet's favourite, was still playing.

It was the scene where Liesl secretly meets Ralph in the darkened garden. They danced, they sang, and then finally, as the rain ran down the walls of the glass gazebo, they kissed. My heart broke a little.

"How are things in the colonies these days?" Dad asked. I still had my stupid cap on. I explained the new owner's "vision" for the summer.

"It could be worse, Kelsey," he said softly, running his fingers through Chet's hair. "You could be a pirate."

"I'd get better tips as a pirate," I said. I watched a bit more of the movie. When Julie Andrews hit the last note of "My Favorite Things," Chet stirred awake. He blinked at me a few times, trying to focus, then he did his famous squint, making his eyes disappear.

"Time for bed, Chetter-cheese," I said, pulling him up to stand. His arms wrapped around my waist and he buried his face in my apron. "Pwetty," he said.

"Pretty gross," I mumbled.

God love that little stinker. Only Chet could make me smile right now.

After my shower, I climbed into bed and flipped open my laptop. Francine's spreadsheet was glowing. I was exhausted, my feet were swollen, and I couldn't think of one person at the Queen's Galley who liked me. But when I checked off the box labelled "Pick up uniform," I felt a little endorphin release.

I read down the list to the next box. "Spontaneous chit-chat #1."

According to Francine's plan of Blaine domination, I would have to bump into Blaine for a "spontaneous chit-chat" two more times before advancing to the next box, labelled "Party." We all know what happens at parties, right? Making out. My neurotransmitters were more than ready.

THE NEXT MORNING, Mom knocked on my door. "Kelsey?"

I rubbed my eyes and pushed myself up in bed. She knocked again.

"Yup," I said, blinking at the blurry alarm clock. Why was she waking me so early?

Her face appeared in the crack of the door. She hesitated for a second, then came in and stood at the foot of my bed. She looked at the pile of clothes on my floor, and the disapproving expression I know so well surfaced. "I get so tired of telling you to pick up your clothes." She frowned at the brown skirt.

"It's my awesome peasant uniform," I said, hoping she might feel a bit sorry for me.

"Your dad mentioned something about pirates." Her hands cupped her mug of coffee. "I need you up and dressed in ten minutes."

I picked out an eye booger. "Huh?" I was praying I hadn't heard her correctly. Summer is for sleeping in. Especially if you're having awesome dreams about kissing under a gazebo.

"Chet's swimming lessons start today," she said brightly. She read my confused expression. A long, exaggerated sigh, her speciality, came out, and she told me her news, which pretty much dropped a bomb on Operation Tongue.

She had decided to take this summer to write her thesis. A thesis she had been working on for the last year but was really going to buckle down and complete. And since Dad was tutoring three days a week at the library reading program, I would have to take Chet to his swimming lessons.

"My whole summer is going to be spent watching Chet at the pool and working!"

Mom did the long sigh thing again. "Kelsey." She dragged my name out. "I will be there to pick him up. All you have to do is get him there and wait until I arrive. It's perfect, really—you can go straight to work afterwards."

"Perfect if I don't want to have any kind of a life this summer!"

Or any time of the year, for that matter.

She gave me a look that was a cross between a huff and a challenge. "And what big plans do you have that this is interrupting?"

"Operation Tongue" didn't exactly roll off *my* tongue with my mom standing in my room with her cup of coffee waiting for a rebuttal.

How Do You Argue?

When in an argument, you often:

A. bring up past mistakes made by the other person to win the argument.

B. use "I" statements to explain your feelings and encourage your partner to do the same.

C. stay quiet or try and change the subject.

Mom sensed victory. "Chet is really starting to blossom, Kelsey, and I don't want him to miss this opportunity. The more exercise the better, and he'll meet new kids…"

I softened as the list went on. How could I deny him this? I didn't want Chet growing up with aquaphobia too.

"Yeah, sure," I finally said—as if I even had a choice. The irony of me taking Chet to swimming lessons was enough to make my stomach turn.

She doesn't even remember.

Mom disappeared into her home office. I pulled on a T-shirt and shorts, combed my hair into a ponytail, and packed Chet's swim bag.

Chet chased me to the car, wearing his new shark goggles. As I drove, he sang his version of "The Sound of Music." Then he disappeared behind his latest library book. He said, "Owed's baving soup is funny."

"Uh-huh," I nodded, cramming a stale cranberry muffin in my mouth. Gross. I'm usually a toast-with-a-lavish-layer-of smooth-peanut-butter kind of girl, but whatever errands Mom went on last night she'd totally forgotten to pick up the bread. "What is Frog wearing?" I asked, already knowing the answer.

"Naked!" Chet screamed.

I laughed, spraying crumbs all over the dashboard. I remembered reading that as a kid, and it freaking me out that Frog would go skinny-dipping with his best bud.

The local pool, or lido, as we all called it, happened to be on the same green slope as the yacht club. I dropped Chet's swim bag and sat on his folded towel on the bleachers. His instructor was an older girl I recognized from high school, whose name I couldn't remember. That happened a lot in Mariner's Cove. It was a village on the cusp of becoming a town: small enough so that everyone looked familiar, but big enough to not know everyone's name.

I leaned forward, feeling anxious. Chet was probably older than the other three kids in his class, but he was small for his age. The instructor gave him a high-five. I smiled automatically and my shoulders relaxed.

Everybody loved Chet, especially me.

I had been one of the older kids in my first swimming lesson too. Academia Nuts don't put a lot of emphasis on summer sports. When I was Chet's age, I spent most of my time in the library. Which was okay until I'd read everything in the middle-grade section.

(Goosebumps, anyone?)

Bored, I'd stopped by the magazine rack, and that's when everything changed. I started doing quizzes, analyzing not only myself but my parents as well. Soon everyone I came in contact with was categorized and labelled before you could say, "lonely only child."

Those magazines were like the older sister I never had. Just as the fairy godmother had appeared before a bewildered Cinderella at her most desperate moment, quizzes were my saving grace when I finally got my first period. They opened a whole new world for me. It was like I had my own hotline to an advice guru. Magazines always had the answers I was looking for.

I couldn't imagine approaching Mom with my love life problems. She was all grammar and proper tense. Words like "crush" and "style" weren't even in her vocabulary. It's not like Mom neglected me or was mean, she was just *there*; necessary but kind of boring—like oxygen. She was the one who'd sat me down for the sex talk, but she made it sound so dull it was an effort to even be embarrassed let alone interested.

Chet was knee-deep, blowing bubbles. They do that to get you used to putting your face in the water. And if you can put your face in the water, everything comes easy after that.

Except if you're me.

I checked the clock by the lifeguards' shed. Chet had another twenty-five minutes of class. All around me, moms were on their iPhones or chatting with other parents. I looked at Chet again. He laughed and splashed with another boy in his class. The kid had green hair—a sign of a cool mom.

I thought of the next empty box on my spreadsheet. The yacht club was next door. It would be silly not to take advantage of this opportunity. I left the pool and crossed the parking lot. *"Spontaneous chit-chat #2," here I come*, I thought.

I redid my ponytail, trying to make it look more like Chloe's. I pinched my cheeks and wiped a few muffin crumbs from my lips and T-shirt. I made up a story in my head as I walked past the gazebo and down the stairs.

Francine had told me that Tanner was working at the yacht club as well, scraping barnacles and overturning motors or something mechanical like that. It wouldn't be peculiar if I came down here looking for *him*. We were friends, and I could ask if he'd heard from Francine.

Ironclad story. Totally legit.

My heart started to thump against my chest. I crammed my fists into the pockets of my shorts. I wished I had brought sunglasses. I turned the corner and smacked into someone's chest.

"Oh, hey." Blaine smiled.

"Hey," I said. Then I kept walking.

What? Wait! Stop!

But my body wasn't listening. I kept walking around the porch, one foot in front of the other. I didn't stop at the end, either. I went into the marine shop, then out through the other doorway, bringing me right back to the foot of the stairs.

"Oh my God," I whispered. My face turned into a goofy grin. I replayed the way our chests had smacked against each other. He'd put a hand on my elbow. He'd smiled at me.

He. Smiled. At. Me.

"Oh, hey," he'd said. As if bumping into me was a pleasant surprise. My heart was exploding with fireworks. I ran up the stairs, barely feeling my feet hit the steps, and then hid in the gazebo.

Spy much?

Blaine was taking his class out on lasers in groups of two. The kids were probably early junior high. I bet a few of the girls had mad crushes on him.

I leaned against the gazebo's railing, scenes from *The Sound of Music* drifting into my mind.

"I am sixteen going on seventeen..."

The lasers took several turns. Laughter and screams echoed up the slope. Blaine was great with kids. Chet would love him to death. I lingered a little while longer, waiting until my cardiac cells had stopped doing the tango, then headed back across the dusty parking lot.

Mom was standing at the edge of the parking lot near the steps leading down to the lido, her hand shielding her eyes. She tilted to the side as if to look around me. "Where's Chet?" she asked.

Geez, she can't even recognize her own son. I pointed at the pool. "He's wearing his new shark goggles," I told her. I hope she picked up on my attitude. I felt slightly gratified in a weird way.

"No, he's not," she said. Her scared voice sent a chill down my spine. I scanned the pool deck. I couldn't see Chet. The kid with the green hair was already towelled off and having a snack. I looked at the clock on the lifeguards' shed. My stomach dropped. His lesson had ended five minutes ago.

Chet was missing.

EIGHT
· · · · ·

"Hﾐ is class ended five minutes ago!" Mom's voice got lost in the wind. I raced down the bleachers. Chet's swim bag was still where I'd left it, along with his folded towel. I looked back up to Mom, but now she was gone, too.

A bubble of panic was building in my chest. I ran up to the green-haired kid. "Hey there," I began, my voice trembling and scaring me even more. "My brother was in your class, he had the shark goggles."

"Oh." The kid smiled widely. "You mean Chet?"

"Yeah, did you see where he went after class?"

The mom looked worried, then a flash of disgust crossed her face. "I think he went straight up the steps," she said. Then she cruelly added, "I assumed someone would be watching him."

Her tone did nothing to upset me, though the terror building inside made me unable to speak. I had to push down the panic—*I won't be able to find him if I'm a crying and screaming mess.* I hustled around parents and kids, swerving my way back up the steps. I frantically looked in every direction, but there was no sign of him. For the second day in a row, I'd put Chet at risk.

If he'd gone down the steps to the yacht club, someone would help him, I reasoned. So I took off down the road that edged the harbour. I scanned the beaches, hoping to see him making a sandcastle or chasing a seagull.

Oh God! What if he chased it right off a wharf?

"Kelsey!"

High on the green slope, close to the Queen's Galley patio, How-hole was waving at me. Chet was beside him, staring intently at one of the shrubs.

I started up the lawn. A wave of relief swept through me, cooling the goosebumps on my arms. *Thank you, God*, I kept repeating in my head.

How-hole turned back to Chet, then crouched beside him, pointing at something on the bush. My mom came out of nowhere and zoomed past me. She rushed to the pair and squeezed Chet into her chest. How-hole stood up and brushed his hands on the back of his shorts, smiling at their reunion.

I could imagine her speech of gratitude to the kindly stranger. Their body language told me everything. Her head bobbed up and down as she peppered How-hole with compliments. He held his hands behind his back, like he was humbled. Then he gave her a big smile, and even a laugh.

Great, they're pals.

I trudged up the slope, the dread burning a hole in my gut. Mom stopped talking and they both turned my way. I gulped. My two enemies had made an alliance—had he told her about me walking Chet in front of his bike the other day?

I was rescued by Chet as he ran up to me with his goggles still in place. "Buddifwy," he said. A monarch was on the shrub, slowly fanning its wings.

"Did you chase it?" I asked him, imagining that's how he ended up here.

Chet nodded. "How-hole," he whispered, pointing to Mom's new best friend. His whisper was loud enough for them to hear.

I laughed weakly.

Mom narrowed her eyes. I could almost see her mind doing a phonics check on "How-hole," but it only lasted a second before her good manners kicked in. She smiled at him again. "It was very lucky you happened to be on the grounds when Chet came running down the street."

How-hole snuck a quick glance my way. "I was called in early to work today," he said. "I recognized him from the other day," he added cautiously.

Now it was Mom's turn to be surprised. "Oh?"

There was a hint of a smirk on his face. I guess he'd figured out that my family wasn't going to sue him, since I hadn't even told my mom. He then added, "I ran into Kelsey outside the library yesterday."

If I were a cartoon, smoke would have been pouring out of my ears. My only choice was to stay quiet. (The guilty have a tendency to blab, that's why they always get caught on *Law & Order*.) Mom looked suspicious, but thankfully Chet was a distraction. He was more interested in trying to catch the butterfly flitting around the shrubs.

But How-hole wasn't finished torturing me yet. "So I guess that's two lucky days in a row for Chet and Kelsey," he delightedly informed my mom.

Dagger eyeballs on the sly are hard to do, but I think I managed to convey, *PLEASE, SHUT UP!*

Mom took notice of his clothes and asked, "You do lawn maintenance?" He was wearing mud-caked work boots and his T-shirt was smeared. I was grateful for the switch in topic, but the longer she chatted with How-hole, the more likely it was that Chet would spill the beans about yesterday.

"I do whatever is necessary," he answered, and then he gave Mom a smile so charming he reminded me of Edward.

She actually laughed, and then tucked a strand of hair behind her ear. *Oh my holy bacon turds!* My mouth almost filled with my own vomit—Mom was flirting with How-hole.

I guess a younger guy can seem charming to an old bag, just like a mature rich dude can seem attractive to a young loser like myself. Great, maybe we could double date. Poor Dad with his socks and sandals.

Mom took Chet by the hand, then turned to me. "Call if you need a drive home after your shift," she instructed curtly. I could tell from her tone that a speech about responsibility would be waiting for me tonight. She passed me my Kipling bag, bulging with my uniform. Then she and Chet walked hand in hand over the green slope, disappearing around the corner toward the lido parking lot.

How-hole crossed his arms and hit me with those blue eyes. I was all too aware of my plain face and messy ponytail. I took a few breaths, fighting the embarrassment of once again screwing up in front of him. I had to at least acknowledge how grateful I was. "Um…thanks for finding Chet," I managed to choke out.

"Sure." Then he slouched down to me, looking serious. "But is your dad going to sue me for finding your little brother?" he asked, his voice thick with drama.

I refused to take the bait. Besides, having the wits scared out of me had hardly put me in the mood for confrontation. He wasn't wearing his baseball cap today, and I could see about two inches of dark roots before his neon blue hair started.

I took the witty approach. "You need a touch-up," I said, motioning to his head. "Like three months ago."

He didn't even flinch. Those piercing blue eyes kept staring. I shouldered my Kipling bag, already feeling exhausted. "This is hilarious, fun times," I declared, "but I've got to get ready."

He made a grand gesture of stepping out of my way. I noticed his knees were caked with mud.

Clyde's voice bellowed through the kitchen window. I picked out a few delightful curse words. "Looks like another awesome day at the Queen's Galley," I mumbled, making sure to take a wide step around How-hole.

I scrunched up my nose. He stank! What the hell was that smell? At least I managed to get a shower this morning. It was like he'd washed with the old dishwater from last night.

Old dishwater.

A bad feeling tickled the back of my brain, sending a chill down my arms. I hurried my pace and rounded the corner. The flower bed—Clyde's meticulous flower bed—was a carnage of holes and wilted stems. I snuck a glance behind me at How-hole.

I blurted out, "Geez! Did you do this?"

Clyde came bursting out of the kitchen door. He stood on the porch, glowering at me. "Hurry!" he ordered. "Inside, now!"

I was ushered through the kitchen and into the dining room, where Julia and the blonde waitress from the other night were bent over a long table. It looked like arts-and-crafts hour for frantic florists. Tiny white vases and several larger ones were all in a row. Bouquets of plastic flowers littered the table and the floor underneath.

Clyde was red faced, and his thin moustache twitched and hopped like a conductor's wand. "Plastic!" was all he could say. He pointed at the table, then gave me one last push before he disappeared into the kitchen. There was complete silence for three seconds. Then a loud clang of pots slamming down made me jump.

"Hey, kid," Julia sighed. "Pull up a chair and start making pretty."

"Huh?" I let my Kipling bag drop to the floor.

The blonde blew out a pink bubble, then slowly sucked it back in and began to chew again. "She means start filling these vase thingies." She held up her latest creation of white tulips as a visual demonstration. "I'm Veronica, by the way," she said. "But everyone calls me Ronnie."

She handed me a vase. "Start with a big flower," she instructed, "then fill in the spaces with the tinier ones. It's easy, you'll get the hang of it."

Julia grunted while trying to shove a handful of yellow roses into the too-small vase.

"Sometimes less makes more of an impact," Ronnie smiled at Julia. Then she daintily picked out a few stems, leaving a perfectly sized bouquet.

"Works for me," Julia said. She slid the vase to the end of the table.

Ronnie scanned the table for her next creation while blowing another pink bubble.

I couldn't help but feel a bit of hope. If this were a magazine quiz, I'd bet Ronnie would score as the kind of girl who was most helpful. I needed someone like that at Queen's Galley. At that moment, I decided to make Ronnie the buoy I would cling to for the rest of the summer.

Julia cracked her back and looked around the dining room. "Oh, man. Like, *every* table," she complained.

"At least we only have to do it once," Ronnie pointed out.

Yup. Definitely the helpful type.

She continued, "These little plastic suckers are good forever— or at least until the world ends." She smiled as she said this.

Julia twirled her left earring. She was sporting plain silver studs today. "Not if Clyde gets his way. I've never met anyone so passionate about fresh flowers. When I came into work this morning I thought they'd discovered a body or something. But it was only Clyde crying over his ripped-up flower bed."

I thought of How-hole covered in dirt. "Why would anyone do something so vicious?"

Ronnie and Julia both stopped and gave me a look.

"It was a dog," Julia said.

"There were huge paw prints all through the dirt," Ronnie added. Her tone had an ominous lilt. "For some reason it came along last night and ripped up all the flowers."

Oops.

"A dog?" I echoed, hoping I'd heard incorrectly. "Like a big one?" I saw the flower garden; it looked like someone had attacked it with a backhoe. One dog could do all that? A shiver made the hair on the back of my neck stand. To me, big dogs were like sharks on dry land: fast-moving hunters with massive jaws. *Real Life in the ER* even had a segment on security-guard dogs gone berserk.

"And no one knows why?" I asked, the carnation in my hand beginning to shake.

Dogs like garbage. Dogs like stinky garbage. Dogs like stinky shrimp heads.

"The kitchen guy—" Julia began.

"You mean Luke," Ronnie interrupted with a smile. "I love him! He's so nice. The guy we had last year moped behind the counter all the time." She put on a serious face. "He would glare at us when we brought in trays of dirty dishes. Like it was our fault we didn't serve on paper plates."

Julia put down a vase with one huge orange lily in it and grabbed another. "Anyway," she continued, "the dude got a blasting from Mr. Deveau, something about being the last person here last night and leaving the garbage improperly bagged."

I swallowed dryly, fighting off mental images from the movie *Cujo*. Plus, the added layer of guilt wasn't making eye contact easy. I focused on my plastic carnation, nodding along, playing the innocent bystander.

"Poor Luke," Ronnie said. She held up a tiny vase with three daisies. "Maybe a nice flower arrangement would cheer him up."

Julia scoffed at this. "Don't feel too sorry for him. He lost his license when he smashed up his dad's car."

Some of my guilt about the shrimp heads began to melt away. If this dude was already bad, my little slip-up was hardly worth being sorry about. "Was he drunk?" I asked, disgusted. I replayed the scene when he had almost hit Chet with his bike.

"Worse," Ronnie said, lowering her voice. "He's crazy."

My head snapped in her direction.

Ronnie's eyes lit up. "Oh, yeah. Loretta let it slip she had to fill out some kind of work form for his shrink or parole officer or something."

Julia twirled her left earring again. I could almost read the thought bubble above her head. Ronnie wasn't exactly the queen of details.

I craned my neck and saw How-hole bent over the sink, scrubbing something hard. If he was so crazy and reckless, why had he helped Chet? And why did he cover for me and take the blame for the flower beds?

NINE
.....

After being on the job for one week, I discovered the only good thing about being a busgirl is the period between serving warm rolls and clearing away dirty dishes. I usually snuck in a magazine quiz or two while killing time in the pantry.

The days dragged by in a boring blur; I would work the lunch or evening shifts at the Queen's Galley, then take Chet to his swimming lessons the next day. Then repeat.

Fun, fun, fun.

Since the terrifying morning Chet wandered away, I was scared stupid into staying glued to his adorable little side at the lido until Mom showed up. However, this cut into my chances of bumping into Blaine for spontaneous chit-chats. Honestly, that empty spreadsheet glowing back at me each night was too depressing. It was like Francine was staring at me, unblinking, waiting for an explanation.

> ### Are You Relationship Ready?
> Your BFF wants to set you up on a blind date. You feel...
> A. doubtful: I resist getting my hopes up about a guy for fear I'll be disappointed.
> B. excited: I have a lot to offer someone and I love meeting new people.
> C. hesitant: getting too committed to one guy will take away my independence.

I considered the options, then blew the air out of my cheeks, totally confused. I wanted Blaine. I was ready for Blaine. Why was the universe conspiring against me?

The only person who seemed more miserable than me was How-hole. The guy spent his days slumped over a sink of dirty dishes, ball cap turned backwards, only talking when Clyde or Loretta asked him something. This guy was seriously a downer. But here's the weird part: he never ratted me out for the shrimp-head thing, which we both knew was my fault.

I wondered if he was holding it over my head, waiting for the right time to blackmail me. I started going through my old magazines looking for personality quizzes; instead of answering for myself, I was trying to think like How-hole. But after two hours I was still stumped.

Who was this guy? A reckless thrill-seeker? A depressed delinquent? A patient predator waiting to blackmail me into helping him hide a body? I had to find out his angle, and this meant, of course, talking to him.

WHEN I ARRIVED to work the next morning, I had a plan. I waited until Mom's hatchback disappeared up the steep hill with Chet singing in the back seat, fresh from another swimming lesson. He was having an awesome time, but it was obvious to me he probably wasn't going to pass this level. I meant to talk to Mom about it, but since her lengthy lecture last week on how I needed to take my responsibilities more seriously, we'd only been exchanging a few sentences here and there.

It made me angry sometimes, how she just expected me to pick up and take care of Chet when she decided to take on more work. Wasn't she the parent? Shouldn't she be noticing that he needs more help in the pool if he wants to pass? Shouldn't I be doing more fun teenage stuff instead of working and babysitting my little brother?

This thing with Blaine couldn't start fast enough. And once he noticed me, I was certain, my real life would begin.

I paused in front of the Queen's Galley, where a flower delivery truck was in the driveway by the kitchen. A fresh load of guilt knotted my guts. I groaned, imagining all those vases needing to be filled again with real flowers. Julia would be so pissed if she knew I was the reason for all the extra work. She'd never been mean to me, but she had a tough kind of confidence that made me shrink a little bit every time she walked by.

A car blared its horn. From under the canopy of maple trees, a bicycle zoomed down the hill. The rider was sitting straight up with his arms dangling by his sides. He flashed by me, perfectly comfortable even though a single pebble could jar the handlebars and send him sprawling to the asphalt.

He coasted to the end of the street, then made a full circle through the intersection and slowly pedalled back. His blue hair peeked out from underneath his helmet. I rested my elbow on the front gate of the picket fence, watching him. The bike slowed down as he got closer. I went over the script in my head, preparing myself, trying to ignore the weird way my stomach was flipping over.

"Hey!" I said to him, motioning to the hill. "You could have died. Don't you watch *Real Life in the ER*?"

"No. Should I?" He stopped right in front of me. One foot skidded on the ground, taking all his weight. He took a few deep breaths, his face red with exertion. I wondered how far he'd biked. Where he lived.

"Well, yeah," I said. "Or, I mean, at least you'd know the risks if you saw all the banged-up accident victims."

A bead of sweat started to trickle from his left temple. He blinked back at me, staying quiet, waiting for me to continue.

I looked at the steep hill, hoping for a wave of inspiration. Dammit! Why had I started on such a stupid topic? My elbow suddenly felt ridiculous resting on the gate, but I couldn't move. It would seem totally unnatural to move right now.

The trickle of sweat slowly curved along his cheekbone. He was perfectly still.

"Um…" I started. "For instance, a show from last season had this kid who was biking and he skidded on some gravel and ended up with really bad road rash. Like, all over his face and stuff."

How-hole's expression was like stone. The sweat trailed down past the corner of his mouth.

Focus, Kelsey!

"Yeah, so. Just be careful." I stared at the handlebars of his bike to further emphasize my point—which by this time I had completely forgotten.

He said, "Maybe I don't care about my face." Then a quick grin played on his features. "Or my stuff."

His stuff?

The blush rushed to my ears. I replied with a very dignified snort-laugh followed by an arms-crossed-in-front-of-the-chest manoeuvre, clearly showing him that I was unaffected by his stab at sexual innuendo. "Whatever," I said, impressed I managed to get out a multisyllabic word. "It's not my business if you want to show off."

Satisfied I managed to get the last word, I turned and pushed through the front gate, heading up the flower-lined walkway to the Queen's Galley.

"And who should I be showing off for?" he called out.

I glanced back. The grin had taken over his whole face. I opened my mouth but no words came out. He only chuckled, then shook his head.

He pushed his bike along the fence and headed toward the side entrance. I stayed on the walkway, still watching him. He whistled while he locked his bike to the railing of the back kitchen porch. I kept staring with my mouth hanging open like an idiot.

He caught my glance. But instead of another smirk, he only gave me a nod, then sauntered up the steps and into the kitchen like he owned the place.

"Close your mouth." Loretta appeared in the front doorway, leaning on one hip. "You look like a broken fountain." There was a dishtowel in her hands. "Shake the lead out, baby-cakes," she said. "Lunch starts in ten minutes." Then she disappeared back into the restaurant.

I looked back at the bike. My burning ears now had their own heartbeat. No. Not How-hole! We were totally wrong for each other. He was NOTHING like Blaine. And according to every quiz I'd ever taken—and my hormones in math class—Blaine was the perfect match for me.

How dare How-hole assume I was flirting! All I was trying to do was be nice and tell him to be more cautious. Nothing overly bizarre or flirtatious about that, right?

"What a how-hole," I muttered. Like no one else had ever ridden a bike downhill without holding on.

Okay, I never had. But that's not saying much since I'd never been in the ocean past my knees, either. But at least I knew what kind of guy he was now.

Reckless thrill-seeker. Definitely.

And we all know what happens to girls who hang out with reckless thrill-seekers, right? Yes, road rash and a starring episode on *Real Life in the ER*. No thanks.

This new development called for a change of tactics. I had to stay on How-hole's good side and therefore escape blackmail from my shrimp fiasco. But I still had to let him know loud and clear that I was unavailable in the dating department. I needed to keep things friendly, yet formal.

Francine would like that logic.

I could do this. I had to do this. Francine had given me a mission, and unlike math—and everything else lately—I wasn't failing this test. I would kiss Blaine by the end of the summer. Which, to me, seemed much more thrilling than riding down a steep hill on your bike without holding on to the handlebars.

LUNCH WAS SLOW, so Mr. Deveau let one of the waitresses have the afternoon off. Chloe and I were paired up with Ronnie to handle the dining room.

There was one elderly couple having fish chowder with iced tea, and a woman with a backpack and map spread over a table for four; she had ordered an avocado salad and kept asking for coffee refills. I wondered about caffeine overload as I went into the kitchen to put on another full pot of the Queen's Galley dark-roast blend. I pictured her heart full of the stuff, pumping erratically.

The percolator started to make the gurgling sound it makes when it's close to finishing. How much coffee did Mom drink every morning? I couldn't remember the last time I'd seen her without a mug nearby.

I frowned at my reflection in the coffee pot. I hadn't seen much of Mom this past week at all. She was mostly squirrelled away in her office, and then at night she always had something to run out and get. Anyway, I wasn't going to focus on that anymore. I had a mission to pursue and the sooner I could check off another box on Francine's spreadsheet, the sooner Mom and her affair with coffee would fade into the background of my thoughts.

I purposely waited until the kitchen was quiet—Loretta had trained How-hole to make a few salads and now used her extra time to sneak out back for a smoke.

He stood at her workstation, ball cap on backwards, in his usual T-shirt and cargo shorts. The long bandage on his calf hadn't decreased in size over the past week. It had become my daily reminder of our first encounter.

Stainless steel bowls were neatly lined up on the counter while tiny piles of freshly cut herbs were organized on the other side. I was surprised that How-hole seemed to know what he was doing. He took a garlic clove and crushed it with the flat of a knife.

"Um…hey," I tried. He tilted his chin my way. I took a deep breath and held it, then the words tumbled out. "I wanted to thank you again for helping with Chet last week."

He lifted a shoulder in a bored shrug. "Your mom already said thanks," he said. He broke an egg into a bowl, added the crushed garlic, then started to whisk. *Clink. Clink. Clink.*

He said nothing else. I grew warm wondering if he wanted me to blab about the shrimp heads. I wanted to say thanks for that too, but the words were stuck. And so were my feet. I hated how I couldn't walk away. I wondered if he could pick up on my awkwardness and was letting the painful silence linger, enjoying my lame attempts at conversation.

I glanced at his calf again. I thought it would have started to heal by now.

I wonder if it's infected?

"Have you seen a doctor about that yet?" I asked.

He stopped working and looked at me. I was never prepared for those eyes. I took a step back. "This one episode of *Real Life in the ER*, a guy came in and his leg wound was so gross it had maggots." I shivered. "So, yeah…"

How-hole stuck his leg out, then flexed his foot a few times. "I'm good," he said. "Thanks for being so concerned though."

"I'm not concerned," I defended. "You're working around food. I'm just thinking of the general public."

He started to whisk again. "You need to stop watching that show."

"A girl needs to be informed," I said. I stuck my chin up in the air a bit.

"A girl needs to have some fun."

I snort-laughed again, my speciality today, apparently. "Oh, I have fun," I lied.

Yeah, buckets worth.

He focused on his work. *Clink. Clink. Clink.*

I wasn't fooling him. Reckless thrill-seekers aren't tricked easily. I stayed quiet trying to come up with another opener. A whiff of garlic hit me.

He noticed my reaction, and the corner of his mouth curled up. "Loretta's Caesar salad dressing is a *Queen's Galley favourite.*" He said the last part with a flare that perfectly imitated Mr. Deveau.

I couldn't help but smile, but I fought the laugh. I could not and would not laugh at How-hole's jokes. I had to be friendly, yet formal.

Mr. Deveau burst into the kitchen, which was no surprise to me. He'd been hovering more than usual that afternoon. I had no choice but to suspend my interview and move into the next room, trying to stay inconspicuous. You could never be busy enough for Mr. Deveau. His greetings were always questions.

"Polish the silverware yet?"

"Are the linens folded for this evening?"

"Do we need to dust the upper moulding?"

Seriously, this guy thought he was Carson from *Downton Abbey.* But today he was especially tenacious. "She'll be here at one o'clock!" he kept saying. He checked his watch a million times, just like Alice's rabbit in Wonderland.

I nestled up next to Ronnie, who was rearranging one of her perfect bouquets. "You could do this, like, professionally," I told her.

She beamed back at me. Mr. Deveau stalked by, his fingers fidgeting with the brass buttons on his blazer. Ronnie gave me a tip. "He's super anxious today," she whispered. "A fancy cake decorator is coming. He's trying to convince her to put one of our summer weddings on her show."

"Wow," I said. "No wonder he's freaking. There's only three people in the restaurant. Who'd want to promote this place?"

"Just look busy," she said. "As long as you're tidying something he'll leave you alone."

I snuck a quick glance over at Chloe. She'd been folding and refolding linen napkins, but was making it look totally natural. Since Chloe had the dining room cased out, I decided I could top up all the salt and pepper shakers in the pantry. The "pantry" was just a row of shelves along the back of the kitchen that connected to a short hallway leading to the holding bar.

I was very familiar with this area as I used it as my personal hangout with its never-ending supply of wrapped peppermints that the waitresses put on the tray with the bill. I probably consumed a pound of peppermints my first week.

I hefted the huge bag of salt Clyde kept on the bottom shelf. Loretta had returned from her smoke break and was humming along to the radio. I could hear the whisk beat a few times. I scanned the shelves for another make-work project. I wiped out a few sugar bowls and lined them up on the counter.

Mr. Deveau's high voice signalled something grand was happening. I peeked out the glass window of the swinging kitchen door. Mr. Deveau was seating a woman at a table by the window overlooking the harbour. He was all smiles and red cheeks. I could see him sweating. And wow, the chick was hot. Ronnie and Chloe appeared instantly, making Mr. Deveau beam.

I looked at the empty sugar bowls again. I was running out of make-work projects so I decided to wait until Mr. Deveau was wandering around the kitchen to fill them up. No point in looking busy if no one's watching, I reasoned. I took another glance out the door's glass panel. Everyone was smiling. A good sign.

Ronnie and Chloe had the dining room covered, and since I couldn't prod How-hole for details about my possible upcoming blackmail, I sauntered into the small holding bar.

I needed a fix.

A long counter jutted out from the wall. I slipped behind and reached under the shelf for my Kipling bag. I pulled out the July issue of *Modern Teen*. I reached into my apron pocket and unwrapped two peppermints.

Are You a Fearless Flirt or a Helpless Romantic?

Your new boyfriend is shy about starting a kiss, so you...

A. dump him because you don't have time to babysit.
B. grab him by the collar and lay one on him.
C. sit on the couch and talk for a while, hoping he builds up the courage on his own.

I smiled, picturing Blaine and I hanging out by our lockers. I sucked and chomped on three more peppermints as I whipped through the rest of the questions with my usual lightning speed. I tallied my score and was pleased to read that I am indeed, a fearless flirt.

Then I froze. Someone was right behind me—someone who smelled a lot like garlic.

TEN
....

How-hole's arm reached over my shoulder from behind, pointing to the magazine. He read out loud, "*You are the girl that guys love to be around. You build up their ego and make them feel desirable with your smiles and attention. You know what you want, and are fearless in your endeavours to make that special love connection.*"

I flicked his arm away and pressed the magazine to my chest. "Excuse me! This is private."

"Do you really believe that stuff?" he asked. His voice wasn't condemning, it was more confused.

I spun around and gave him my best lemon face, a useful tactic when I have no desire or clue how to answer.

He waited for me to say something, then took another route. "Well," he said, waving a hand at the magazine, "it's probably hard to get an accurate answer when you're cheating. Tends to mess up the results, I imagine."

This I could not ignore. "I'm not cheating!" I said indignantly.

He studied me through squinted eyes. "Really? I guess I better watch myself, then. I never had you pegged for the fearless flirt type." He leaned his elbow on the counter. There wasn't much space between our bodies and the wall. I'd have to push past him.

"You don't know anything about me," I said. His blue eyes bored into me, and I dropped my gaze, hating how my face had grown hot. "Besides," I said, throwing the magazine down on the counter, "just because I'm dressed like Laura Ingalls Wilder doesn't mean I'm boring."

He gave me a hint of a smile. "I never said you were boring. I just think someone who's afraid to tell the truth isn't exactly…" He took the magazine and read. "'The fearless type: always ready to try something new, no matter what others think.'"

"I'm extremely fearless!" I said. "Just because you ride without holding on to the handlebars doesn't make you some kind of brave hero."

He handed me back the magazine, then folded his arms in front of his chest. "Prove it."

"What?"

"Prove that the magazine is right."

I snorted. "How? By driving like a maniac and smashing up my mom's hatchback?"

It was suddenly dead quiet. I could actually see my words, typed, in the air between us.

His jaw tightened and he rubbed the side of his chest. "Never mind," he said. "You wouldn't have the guts to go through with my idea, anyway." Then he disappeared around the corner.

An invisible thread pulled me along. I told my feet to stop, but they followed How-hole back into the pantry. My empty sugar bowls looked at me accusingly.

I thought of Francine's spreadsheet. I was tired of being scared. If I did this stupid thing How-hole had planned, I knew I would be brave enough to walk up to Blaine and kiss him full on the mouth—just like a fearless flirt would do.

I caught up to How-hole and stepped in front of him, blocking his way. "All right," I said. "I'll prove it."

A few minutes later we were at the top of the steep hill overlooking the Queen's Galley. How-hole was on the seat. And I, the extremely fearless flirt, was sitting forwards on the handlebars secretly shitting bricks. Every episode of *Real Life in the ER* was coming back in horrific detail.

"Nervous?" he asked.

"No." My hands shook as I tightened his bike helmet over my head. It was only fair that I got the helmet, since I was the one who would probably hit the pavement first.

I balanced, then placed a death grip on the handlebars beside my thighs. My feet were tucked under my knees, and my long skirt was bunched between my legs.

Real ladies always lift their skirts when they ride a boy's handlebars.

How-hole pushed off. The bike wobbled a bit, then he pedalled strongly and straightened out. He was making it go faster? It was like climbing that first hill of a roller coaster—you know you're going to scream, but there's no way to get off the ride.

We slowed for just a second, then the front tire—and my face—tilted downward. The shadows of the trees blurred past me, the wind blasted through the helmet and messed up my hair. I screamed. The pavement looked ready to jump up and eat me.

My skirt blew into my face, blinding me, but I didn't dare let go of my death grip on the bike. So there I was, careening down the hill with a convicted felon who might be crazy, with my skirt over my head. We were going so fast I couldn't feel the wheels on the road. It's like we were flying. Oh God, were we flying!

Suddenly I could see again. My skirt settled back down as the bike slowed. We levelled off at the bottom and glided past the restaurant. How-hole started pedalling again, making the circle through the intersection. We got a few beeps from startled driv-'ers, then came to a stop in the driveway by the kitchen.

He held the bike steady while I unclenched my knees. My heart was racing. I took off the helmet and handed it back to him. "See?" I said, acting all tough and macho. "Definitely fearless." I couldn't help but notice I had left out "flirt."

The edges of his blue eyes crinkled in a smile. I walked ahead of him, trying not to trip on my shaky legs. I marched into the kitchen with my head held high and caught my reflection in one of the glass cabinets. My hair was windswept, my cheeks were red, and I was smiling. Like, hugely smiling.

I put my cap back on, tucked in a few stray wisps of wild hair, and hummed all the way to the pantry. Mr. Deveau boomed through the swinging door, almost knocking me over. He patted his red face with his silk handkerchief. "Sugar!" he demanded. "She wants sugar with her coffee."

I stared back at him blankly.

I thought his eyes would burst out of his head. He motioned to the cake decorator by the window. "Hurry, girl! She wants sugar!"

Jolted into action, I poured several scoops from the open bag into one of the empty sugar bowls I'd just cleaned. He stared at me all the while, making me glad I'd at least tidied up back there. I rushed out after him, and then placed the bowl on the table. I was so nervous a few crystals spilled onto the linen. Mr. Deveau's face contorted like he was in silent labour.

"Oh, pardon me," I said.

She barely glanced up. I watched as she put not only one, but three heaping spoonfuls into her coffee. She played with the spoon for a bit, letting it tinkle the side of the cup. Mr. Deveau grimaced each time. Then he gave me a signal to leave, which I obeyed wholeheartedly.

I escaped back to the pantry, resting against the shelves. I could smell yummy bread. Someone had put rolls in the warmer. I smiled, feeling more energized and hopeful than I had in a long time. I'd dodged a bullet from Mr. Deveau, and I had survived How-hole's test. Hopefully this would make us even for the shrimp-head thing.

I felt in my heart that this moment was the turning point in Operation Tongue. I was sure Blaine would come into the restaurant that very afternoon. I grinned like an idiot. My luck had finally changed. This was the start of my new, awesome life. This summer something amazing would happen for me, I just knew it.

Then I heard someone gag. Mr. Deveau shouted.

I glanced at the sugar bowls lined up beside the bag of salt. My eyes grew wide and my stomach dropped to the floor.

ELEVEN

M r. Deveau burst through the swinging door, veins bulging on the side of his head. He leered at me and leaned in close. I thought going down the hill on How-hole's handlebars with my skirt over my face had been terrifying, but at this very moment, I really thought I would pee my pants.

"You!" Mr. Deveau started. "How could you be so stupid?" The veins throbbed violently, threatening to burst all over my face.

"I…I'll fix it," I whispered. My insides turned to water. I clenched my thighs together, wishing I could disappear.

"All you had to do was bring out one simple thing." His voice was harsh. I'd never seen him this upset. The kitchen became very quiet. Out of the corner of my eye, I could see that Clyde and Loretta had frozen, as if any movement might bring them into the argument.

"Can't you read?" He held up the salt bag and pointed at each letter. "What does this say?" he asked.

My lips trembled.

"S—A—L—T." He stabbed each letter with his perfectly manicured finger. "Is this a salt bowl?" He slammed the glass bowl on the counter.

I shook my head, not daring to open my mouth. I had managed to prevent incontinence—so far—but the tears were right there, brimming on my lower lids. I dug my fingernails into my palms, trying to concentrate on the pain.

Ronnie came through the swinging door with the poisoned cup of coffee. I caught her look of sympathy before she glided back out with a fresh cup. It was that look that made the first tear come. I tried to blot my face with the crook of my arm as I began to scan the shelves. Mr. Deveau was breathing harshly. Then, finally, on the bottom of the cupboard, I found it. My hands fumbled with the bag of sugar, the stress making me clumsy.

Mr. Deveau grabbed the bag from my hands and slammed down a bowl. He ended up spilling sugar all over the counter, onto the floor and my foot. I didn't bother moving. I was afraid I'd empty my bladder or really start to cry. I focused on the pattern of spilt sugar on the floor.

A timer dinged. Chloe appeared from around the corner. She must have been listening. She only held my eye for a couple of seconds before dropping her gaze. She stepped around Mr. Deveau's mess over to the bread warmer and took out the rolls, placing them in a napkin-lined basket.

"Thank goodness *someone* knows what they're doing," Mr. Deveau said, staring back at me. "If I could, I'd fire you on the spot, you clueless little thing."

He smoothed back one side of his hair, then stormed out. His excuse for my dumb mistake floated back to me. Chloe followed him with warm bread for their table. Ronnie glowed with her usual sunny disposition as she rhymed off the specials.

I inhaled shakily—it felt like I'd been holding my breath since Mr. Deveau's entrance. I got down on my hands and knees and started to clean up the sugar. A few pots clanked, and slowly the kitchen came back to life.

"Here." A dustpan and brush appeared over my shoulder. Loretta looked down at me. Her face showed its usual unimpressed frankness. I wondered how many busgirls she'd seen get yelled at. "I'm busy making crêpes for tonight's dessert special," she told me. "When you're finished, go help Luke."

I waited until she'd turned her back, then I glared across the room at How-hole. This was all his fault. If I hadn't let him tease me into doing that stupid bike stunt, I wouldn't have messed up the sugar. The floor had never been cleaned with such violent strokes.

Stupid handlebars. Stupid shrimp heads. Stupid salt. And lastly, stupid Kelsey. I was sick of being such a screw-up. I hated this job. I wished Francine hadn't left me alone this summer. She must have known I'd never be able to handle the spreadsheet by myself.

I concentrated on getting every last speck of sugar. I didn't want to face anyone until I was sure I'd blinked away all the tears. Images of Blaine and I making out vanished with every sweep of the broom. Soon, the only sign of my disastrous mistake was the burning of the tips of my ears, still throbbing from humiliation.

I made my way back to the prep table, where How-hole had made several piles of chopped vegetables. The knife flew swiftly in his hands, creating perfect little diced pieces of red pepper. He was like an infomercial or something.

I stood with my hands in my apron pockets. I waited for an order but he stayed quiet, content to slice and dice. He kept his head down, concentrating on his work—or maybe he was so embarrassed for me he didn't know what to say.

I doubted that. He seemed like a guy who would always tell you his opinion—you know, one of *those* guys.

I glanced at the windowsill and saw a little vase with three daises. I rolled my eyes. *God, am I the only one here who doesn't have a friend?*

I thought of Francine, but instead of the usual lonely ache, I felt a punch. She was off having a fabulous vacation with her family at their cottage, and I was stuck in this colonial hell, desperately trying to check off her little boxes like it was some kind of science experiment.

Maybe that's all it was to her—one big science experiment. And I was failing miserably.

Ronnie waltzed in and gave the lunch order to Clyde. He nodded while slapping a slice of butter into the frying pan. Loretta leaned over from her crêpe station and grinned at the order. "Escargot for the lady," she sang out. "And a Caesar salad for the captain."

Clyde snorted at the nickname.

"Do up that salad, Luke," Loretta ordered, flipping a perfect crêpe. She stacked it on a plate that was already a tower of thin wraps.

How-hole quickly changed gears. He wiped his hands on a tea towel, made space on his cutting board, and then he began ripping apart a few romaine leaves.

"He's flirting with her," Ronnie said behind us. My face flushed. "I'm not sure if it's because she's so attractive or if he thinks it will convince her to showcase the wedding."

I stayed quiet, wishing Ronnie would think of a topic that didn't involve the guy who had just chewed me out in front of everyone. I hoped someone would at least call him a snot-nosed dirtbag or something, but everyone seemed happy to accept it and move on.

I didn't know any of them very well, but I did feel a bit betrayed.

I imagined how awesome it would be if Blaine were working here. He wouldn't have stayed quiet and watched Mr. Deveau humiliate me. He would have stood up for me. He would have put his arm around me and declared that I was the best girl in the world. And that if Mr. Deveau couldn't see that, then he was a true snot-nosed dirtbag.

But this was a pointless fantasy because if Blaine *were* working here, I never would have made that stupid mistake with the salt in the first place because he'd never ask me to ride on his handlebars.

I paused, realizing how sad that made me.

"Garlic." How-hole nudged me.

I blinked a few times, still stuck in my daydream. "What?"

He waited to see if I would clue in. "Pass me the garlic, please," he repeated.

I frowned as he smashed several cloves with the flat blade of the knife. He added the pulpy mess to the dressing, then whisked it in and started to hum. I didn't recognize the tune.

"I thought you already made the dressing," I said.

"Garlic," he said again.

I picked up a whole bulb and raised my eyebrows. He nodded and took it from my hand. He looked over his shoulder at Ronnie. "How is the captain at flirting?" he teased her. "Maybe I could learn some tips."

Ronnie giggled. Everyone, including me, automatically smiled. It was like angels were ringing bells. *I bet she's never had to keep a spreadsheet*, I thought.

"Keep your mind on the food," Clyde chastised, but I could hear a lightness in his voice. I would love to know what the kitchen staff gossiped about. I was slightly jealous of How-hole.

He whisked in the last bit, then dipped the tip of his pinkie in to taste. He smacked his lips together. "Needs salt."

I gave him a look. His blue eyes only danced back at mine. My stomach swooped a bit. Well, it only made sense since I hadn't eaten anything since breakfast. I needed to remember to pack a snack for myself in Chet's swim bag from now on. Two stomach swoops in one day was too many. I dipped my hand into my apron pocket for a peppermint, but all I felt were empty wrappers.

Ronnie took out the salad and escargot. I peeked through the kitchen window and watched as Mr. Deveau scoffed down How-hole's super garlic-infused Caesar salad.

The effect was brilliant. Slowly, over the main course, and through a dessert of blueberry cake with real whipped cream, the cake decorator kept moving her chair further away from Mr. Deveau's eager conversation. I dared to walk through the dining room. The smell of garlic was enough to turn the air green.

But my thrill at secretly embarrassing Mr. Deveau was short-lived. As soon as she left, he found me, and the blaming started. Thankfully, this time I wasn't alone. Ronnie was beside me, needlessly polishing the silverware. My heart warmed at her show of allegiance.

"No contract!" he spat at me. I held my breath—the fumes were almost visible. I waited for him to blame me for the garlic too. "No TV appearance! Do you know how much that would have helped us?"

I shook my head. Why did he keep asking me questions I had no clue how to answer? And why didn't someone give this guy a mint, for freaks sake?

"And to make matters worse," he continued, "we have an especially important wedding coming up with NO wedding cake!"

> *How Do You Argue?*
> When in an argument, you often:
> C.) stay quiet or try and change the subject.

A glob had formed in my throat. I wanted to swallow it down, but I was afraid any movement would trigger a ballistic reaction in Mr. Deveau. I had to wait this out.

"Do you know any wedding-cake caterers?" he asked me in a baby voice that made me want to vomit.

"No," I said quietly. At least I'd found my voice. I wanted to mention that it was only salt, and surely the whole mess couldn't be blamed on me. And if he didn't dress like Fred from *Scooby-doo* or talk like an English butler then maybe, just maybe, she would have said yes.

The witticisms were great inside my head, but the comebacks never seemed to get all the way out.

He smoothed his ascot and looked out the window at the harbour. He let out a long sigh. "Edward is going out of town, and has left this extremely important task up to me. He can't rearrange his schedule for every little screw-up."

Someone cleared their throat. "Excuse me, Mr. Deveau," Chloe said hesitantly. "I know a caterer you could use."

Mr. Deveau cocked his head, trying to gauge the likelihood of one of his busgirls having an idea worth considering. "Are they well known?" he asked suspiciously.

Chloe nodded. "She has years of experience, and she was just on a local cable show giving tips on how to throw the perfect backyard barbecue."

Mr. Deveau cringed when she said *barbecue*.

Chloe sensed his hesitation. "She can give you a huge list of satisfied clients," she said. "And she's friendly, and makes the best egg salad sandwiches." Chloe paused to give Mr. Deveau one of her winning smiles, and then added, "But best of all, she can be here tomorrow."

Ronnie and I looked at Mr. Deveau. I could hear the cogs turning in his head. "All right," he finally agreed, as if he were doing Chloe a huge favour. "Ask her to meet me here tomorrow. Make sure she has a portfolio. And let her know, this is not a free lunch date." He shot me a look. "We can't risk another fiasco like today."

I closed my eyes and pictured my yellow gorilla sucking his thumb.

TWELVE
· · · · · · ·

I sat on the front steps of the Queen's Galley, daydreaming of ways for Mr. Deveau to get hurt.

Maybe he should ride on How-hole's handlebars.

I was under the shadow of the massive oak that dominated the front lawn. I ran a hand through my hair, trying to lift it off my sweaty neck. I closed my eyes and remembered the way it had flown straight back when I went zooming down the hill. A warm breeze carried the smell of the ocean up from the harbour. My stomach twisted. I could almost taste the salt water.

I checked my watch, then dug out my magazine. Dad wouldn't be here to pick me up for another half hour. I went over my flirty quiz twice, rethinking all my answers. Each time I got a different result.

Dammit!

How does a strange guy who barely talks to me know me? I thought. *And why do I care?*

"I don't," I answered myself. Besides, How-hole was the least of my worries. I'd probably get fired for whatever screw-up I had next. In addition to Chet's swimming lessons, I was his babysitter whenever Mom and Dad both happened to be working or out of the house, which seemed to be happening much more frequently these days. This job, miserable as it was, was my only bit of freedom this summer.

I rubbed the back of my neck. The only thing that gave me comfort was knowing this day couldn't get any worse. Things could only improve, I wistfully reasoned. I glanced over at the gazebo, hoping for an appearance by Blaine, but it was empty.

"Hey." Chloe's perfectly creamed legs walked past me. I grunted. She stopped at the second-last step and turned around. "Look, try not to let Mr. Deveau bother you," she said.

"Thanks," I said tiredly. Then I added inside my head, *easy for the favourite to say*.

Chloe could apparently read my mind. Her expression changed. "I don't get you," she said.

That was a weird thing to say. I straightened up. "Excuse me?"

"Sorry, that came out rude," she said. "I mean we've worked together for a week now, and I don't think I've heard you say three sentences in a row." She laughed lightly, like my shyness was hilarious compared to her effortless charm. "You're squirrelled away with a magazine all the time. If you talked a bit more, people would notice you."

I pictured Mr. Deveau's veins popping out of his head. "I think I've had enough attention for one day, thanks," I pointed out.

She gave me a pitying look, then said, "Never mind." She put her ear buds in and started to walk away.

The unfairness of her assessment felt like a slap in the face. Was it my fault the most popular girl in school didn't understand that I was intimidated by all the older, much cooler girls at work?

I might be a confused flirt, and maybe I'm a dork in the romance department, but I sure wasn't taking advice from Ms. Perfect on how to roll with the punches. I jumped up and ran after her, ready to plead my case.

"Yeah?" She took her ear buds out, waiting for me to say something.

I wanted Chloe to know I wasn't as big a loser as she saw at work. I wanted to seem cool, likeable, or at least interesting. I needed proof I wasn't a total social dunce. Francine's spreadsheet blinked behind my eyelids. "I have a friend," I blurted out. I did a mental facepalm. Only people who have no friends insist they have friends.

Chloe's gaze shifted away, probably too embarrassed to keep eye contact.

"I have a friend," I repeated. "She's tiny with big red hair. Um…she dates Tanner Kaizer."

Chloe's face changed into a smile of recognition. "Oh, yeah. I know Tanner."

I smiled back and tried hard not to roll my eyes. Of course she'd know Tanner. The hot jocks are popular no matter which grade they're in.

"Her name is Fran, right?" she asked.

Franner.

Francine would be pissed if dating Tanner was her only way of being recognized by other students at school. She prided herself in getting top marks each year. Some girls date guys like Tanner just to get noticed. But Francine isn't like most girls.

"She seems like a real sweetheart," Chloe added.

That little hollow part of my stomach began to ache. I nodded then motioned to the yacht club. "She's super smart too. She suggested I work at the yacht club this summer, but I wanted to come here instead." I gave a shrug. "No wonder I'm screwing up so much. Francine is always right. I guess I should have listened to her."

Chloe stayed quiet, rolling the ear buds in her fingers.

I tugged on my Kipling bag. "She's gone for the whole summer." I tried to fake a laugh. I hadn't meant to ramble on like this, especially not to supercool Chloe. I paused and let out a breath. "The worst part is that I can't even text her to tell her she was right."

Yup. The teen version of asphyxiation: no texting.

Chloe's mouth fell open at the horror of not being able to text. She looked a lot like a gaping Glen Fairweather at that moment. I thought I'd finally gotten to her. That she may have some clue what life is like for the ordinary people.

"She told me—" I stopped mid-sentence as Blaine's pickup truck drove by. I caught a glimpse of his left shoulder, but he didn't see me. He was staring straight ahead.

What next, dear God? Kill me now.

I dragged my eyes away from the spot Blaine's truck had just been, and turned my attention back to Chloe. "Francine told me I would have an amazing summer even without her," I added dully. "She promised this job would make so many things happen, but I don't think she meant being yelled at in front of the entire staff."

Chloe looked pained.

A horn blew and my dad waved out the car window from across the street. Chloe started to say something, but I walked around her and down the front path.

I pushed through the front gate and across the street, my stomach clenching with guilt. Chet was in the back seat, giving me his huge grin. I'd have to be all happy and talkative on the drive home. My evening was already planned out. I pictured us watching a movie or playing soccer in the backyard after supper.

Here's the thing: everyone else sees me as a failure or a screw-up, but not Chet. To him, I'm a rock star. That's why the guilt kills me the most, because sometimes I wish he didn't need me so much.

I SLEPT HORRIBLY that night. Francine's spreadsheet loomed, the size of a billboard. The empty boxes waiting to be checked stared me down accusingly. It leaned forward and landed on top of me, flattening me out.

I woke up flailing my arms against the bed sheets. I rolled out of bed, rubbing the aching spots. Carrying trays and standing all day wasn't good for my posture or my ego. Mr. Deveau's words echoed inside my head, stuck on repeat.

Chet ambled in wearing his shark goggles. He was humming something that sounded suspiciously like "Edelweiss."

"Okay, Kowsey?" he asked. His eyes were wide with concern. My heart melted. He was the only one who asked me that anymore. I took his hand and looked deeply into his shark goggles.

"I'm worried, Chetter-cheese," I confessed.

He frowned at this. I pressed my lips together. God, the little stinker looked cute even when he was scared.

I gripped his hands tighter, pulling him closer to me. "I'm worried that the fart I can't hold in any longer is going to knock you unconscious!" Then I let one rip.

Chet screamed and laughed, struggling to get away from me. "I blasted you with my farticles!" I announced—unnecessarily, of course. The barbecued sausages Dad had eventually served for supper last night had been festering in my gut.

Chet put his hands around his throat, pretending to choke on the fumes. The door opened and Mom stood there, one hand on her hip, the other holding a mug of coffee. Chet stopped choking and gave her his famous squint.

No one, even Mom-the-serious, can resist his charm. I wished I could take him to work with me. She tapped her watch. "Swimming," she announced, like she didn't have a driver's license.

"We're already in the car!" I said, too tired to hide the cheekiness in my voice. The truth is I wanted to get a little reaction out of her. The only time I saw her was in between Chet's activities. She hadn't been home last night either. But maybe it was for the better. She'd probably take Mr. Deveau's side about me being "irresponsible" with the salt, and I'm pretty sure she wouldn't want to hear about my bike ride with a convicted felon.

After a lightning-fast shower, I put my wet hair in a pony-tail and slipped on my cut-offs and flip-flops. I growled when I saw Mom had still forgotten to pick up bread. Dad had left me a banana and yogurt smoothie on the kitchen table. Instead, I grabbed three granola bars and a bottle of water.

I sat beside the green-haired kid's mom on the bleach-ers that day. She was actually pretty nice. "You have a lot of responsibility," she said to me. I sat a little straighter. It was nice to hear someone say that out loud.

"Nah," I said. "Chet isn't work." *But my parents make him seem like that*, I added inside my head.

I could have stayed there all day—lying on a towel, eyes closed, my music on, dreaming about me and Blaine—but since I'm so responsible, I had to go to work.

When Mom arrived to pick up Chet, I wanted to crawl under a rock and hide: her hair was in the same messy bun as earlier, and she was still wearing her slippers.

Geez! Embarrass much?

When I pointed this out, she only huffed as a reply. Why couldn't she be like the green-haired kid's mom?

I crossed the intersection and walked along the white picket fence of the restaurant. Chloe was standing just inside the door-way. The flashback of my confession about missing Francine made me wish there really was a rock to disappear under—like forever. I must have sounded like a complete basket case, or at the least, a desperate loner looking for attention.

It would be awkward trying to avoid her all day. (Yes, I like to avoid conflict. I learned that from a quiz in the March issue of *Cosmo Chick*.)

I put my head down and decided to enter through the kitchen. The garden had undergone a total makeover. It looked like something out of *Martha Stewart Living*. There were tall blooming foxgloves, delphiniums, lilies, a huge daisy bush, and a few lavender bushes I recognized from some of my dad's old gardening magazines. (Plus, I once did a quiz called "What Type of Flower Are You?" For the record, I'm a tiger lily: delicate, yet strong.)

The kitchen door closed behind me. I stopped and listened for a few seconds. Someone was singing, and it wasn't Loretta. I tiptoed around the corner. How-hole had his back to me; instead of his ball cap, a set of Beats rested on top of his head. He was using a ladle as a microphone. I put a hand over my mouth, trying to muffle my laughter.

He let loose like it was the finale of *Canadian Idol*. I didn't recognize the tune and the lyrics weren't anything I'd heard before. It sounded like one of those "life-is-so-unfair" songs. Geez, it could've been my summer anthem.

The spontaneous choreography sent him into a spin with a side-step on the end. He froze when he saw me. My eyes darted around the room. I started to play with the zipper on my bag. He slid the headphones off his head, letting them wrap around his neck. His hair was kind of curly today. It didn't look so bad. *Must be the lighting.*

"What…um," I started. "I mean I didn't recognize the song."

How-hole cleared his throat. "It's old…like, eighties stuff." He realized he was still holding the ladle. His arms fell to his side, then he crossed them in front of his chest. The ladle poked out from under his arm like a bad joke no one could forget.

I smiled. He was nervous, and I liked that I had something to do with that. After all, he was usually the cool one. I said, "You're here early."

He blew a wisp of blue hair out of his eyes, then motioned with his thumb toward the back kitchen door. "I had to help with the garden," he explained. "Plus I had to make up a new batch of Caesar dressing."

My eyes grew wide. "You didn't get in trouble with Mr. Deveau, did you?"

He placed the ladle down and leaned against the counter, his suave attitude resurfacing. "No." Then he added, in a more serious tone, "Don't worry about him, okay? He can't fire you."

My cheeks grew warm. The horrible scene replayed in my head, the words just as sharp.

"The truth is," he began, talking faster, trying to lighten the mood, "he can't fire any of us. He's not the owner."

"Oh."

"Besides," he added. "Chloe got another caterer to come in."

And now we're suddenly talking about Chloe. Isn't that sweet. I guess I knew who he was showing off for. "Yeah," I said, curtly. "Must be a nice feeling to save the day instead of ruining it. I bet she doesn't have to worry about getting yelled at."

"Interesting." He squinted back at me. I hated how he seemed to be reading my mind. "You're the only one I've heard say that about her." I squirmed under his stare. He pushed off the counter and started washing mixed greens in the sink. "Anyway, Mr. Deveau is meeting with the caterer on the patio."

"When?" I checked my watch, determined to not screw up today.

"Right now."

I was still in my cut-offs.

"Oh geez! I have to change!" I headed for the bathroom, unzipping my bag as I ran.

I pushed open the door and smacked right into Chloe.

THIRTEEN
. . . .

Chloe and I were in some kind of silent movie, where the actors stared at each other while their mouths moved but no sound came out. The heat swelled up and set my cheeks on fire. My armpits were sticky. It was a long, tortuous three seconds.

"Oh," I finally said. Holy bacon turds, for a chick who spends most of her time reading, my vocab today was *el sucko*.

Chloe looked just as uncomfortable. "Hey," she said.

I stated the obvious. "Maybe this year for Christmas someone can buy us a thesaurus."

She let out a shaky breath. "I'm sorry about your best friend," she said.

My eyes darted around the washroom, wondering if this was a joke. Considering my public berating by Mr. Deveau, it made no sense for her to bring up Francine. "Why are you sorry?" I asked slowly.

Chloe's white cap was bunched up in her hands. "My best friend is away for the summer too." She gave me a sad smile. "And yeah, it sucks."

"Is she having an awesome time at her family's beach house?" I asked, a little sarcastically.

Chloe shook her head and said, "It's kind of a long story." She motioned to the uniform poking out of my bag. "Get changed and meet me in the holding bar, okay? There's a pile of linen to fold for lunch."

Even though she didn't say very much, I felt like Chloe and I had started to build a bridge, like we'd crossed some invisible line.

Chloe wasn't kidding about the huge pile of napkins to sort through. "That's for you," she said, pointing to a glass of Coke on the bar.

"Oh, thanks," I said, surprised. Although the thought of having Coke at ten in the morning made my teeth ache.

Chloe folded a napkin in thirds then doubled it over, running her hand along the seam to smooth it down. "When we set up for lunch," she said, "I'll show you how to make a flower and a fan."

I copied her actions the best I could. Five minutes of silent folding and pressing went by. Then, out of the blue, she started. "My best friend," she paused and caught my eye, "is Jesse Collins."

"Oh right," I said, trying to sound surprised. Of course I knew who her best friend was! She and Chloe were the top of the food chain at our high school. This was the total opposite of our conversation yesterday.

That's the interesting thing about popular people like Chloe. They have no clue that people they didn't even know existed (like moi), knew everything about them and their friends. Chloe was the beauty queen and Jesse was the tall athletic phenom—or at least she used to be.

My heart sank. I knew where this story was going. Everyone in Mariner's Cove had talked about it for months.

"Well," Chloe began. "You remember about her dad, right?"

I did. It was even in the papers. I nodded sadly.

"She dropped out of track and gave up on a scholarship after he died." Chloe took a long sip of Coke. "It's hard to see someone you love feel so horrible. She wasn't herself at all."

"It must have been a nightmare." My parents are beyond frustrating sometimes, but I don't know what I'd I do if it were just Chet and me.

"Yeah." She let out a little puff of air. Then after a long pause she said, "But here's the thing. She really needed to get away this summer, and escape all the gossip and staring."

"Little community, big gossip," I said automatically. I cringed inside. I felt like an idiot, but Chloe relaxed her whole body.

"Exactly," she agreed. The indignant huff was hard to miss. "So, Jesse is at camp, working as a counsellor, meeting new people—people who don't know about her dad. And she can have some fun, get recharged. And I'm totally happy that she's done it, but…"

Chloe closed her eyes. She took another long gulp of Coke and finished off the glass. "But I really miss her, and I hate that I couldn't make her happy, you know? I wanted to be the one who could bring her around." She sat down. I could tell she was unloading a lot of guilt at my feet.

I didn't know what to do. I took a long swig of my Coke. A pain built up in my chest. Chloe had been missing her best friend too. Maybe she had big plans for this summer and had no one to make sure she was checking off her spreadsheet.

"Hey," I started—then, without warning, I let out a humongous belch. I clamped my hand over my mouth. "Oh my God, excuse me. I didn't know that was there!"

Chloe started to laugh, and then let out her own burp.

"Huh," Julia stood in the doorway, looking impressed. She was still in her leather chaps. Her boyfriend's motorcycle rumbled off in the distance. "This place just got a whole lot more interesting."

By the time the tables were set with mine and Chloe's beautiful napkin fans and fresh flowers from the new garden, Mr. Deveau was wrapping up a deal with the new caterer. The woman was middle-aged and stylish, but not over the top. Some moms dress like they're trying to look young, but it comes off cheesy. She wasn't like that, she was classy. She also had a nice smile.

Chloe and I watched from the kitchen. She nudged me in the ribs with her elbow. "That's Jesse's mom," she said, proudly. "She needs all the extra jobs she can get. With Jesse dropping track, the scholarship isn't possible anymore."

My stomach clenched with guilt. "That's how you know her," I said, seeing her suggestion from yesterday in a whole new light.

"Come on." Chloe tugged playfully on my apron. I followed her through the dining room and waited by the doorway as Mr. Deveau sealed the deal with a handshake. He didn't even make eye contact as he whisked by me to the bar.

The woman gave Chloe a beaming smile, and pulled her into a hug. "Heard from Jesse?" she asked.

Chloe giggled. "I got an e-mail yesterday. Sounds like her cabin is a hoot. And there's—" Chloe paused. "Some good-looking guys…sort of."

Jesse's mom squeezed her shoulder. "You don't need to tell me everything, Chloe." She smiled and it was almost a look of relief. "I'm so happy she decided to go." Chloe nodded and they both got misty-eyed. The intimate scene didn't need my nose poking in, so I slipped away.

A petite woman with grey hair was frowning up at Captain Bowsky's portrait. Her hands were clasped behind her back. The tables in this area were empty; most of the customers had decided to dine on the patio today. I smiled at her as I walked by.

"Creepy," she said.

"Excuse me?"

She nodded her slightly spiky hair toward the painting. She said, "His eyes do that weird thing where they follow you—"

"Around the room!" I finished.

Her bright red lips stretched into a smile. "Thank goodness," she said. "I thought I was the only one he was haunting."

I laughed. "Have you ordered yet? Can I get you anything?"

Folded linen napkin? Sugar bowl? Peppermint that's been warming in my pocket?

She smoothed out her long white tunic. Her ballet flats had daises on the toes. I immediately thought of Ronnie. "Oh, no, thank you," she said. "My daughter was meeting with the manager about a wedding cake. She's a caterer." Her voice went up at the end, a sign of pride. I wondered if my mom told people I was a busgirl. I imagined her voice going down, keeping it low, like a secret.

I did the math and peeked out at Chloe and Jesse's mom, still talking. The elderly woman said to me, "Chloe has a strong link to my granddaughter. When I'm around her, I don't miss Legs so much."

"Legs?"

"That's my nickname for my granddaughter, Jesse." She smiled again. It was genuine. Again I pictured the tall, popular girl from high school. You think you know everything about someone, but we all have secrets, apparently. She tilted her head and studied me. "Is this a nice place to work?"

I plucked at my apron. "It could be worse. I could be a pirate."

"Actually, I think you make a rather cute Little Bo Peep," she declared. "Are you having a good summer?" she asked.

"I guess it depends on your definition of good." I stopped and gave her an apologetic smile. "Sorry, that just kind of came out."

"It means you're honest," she said, matter of fact.

I thought of all my quizzes and I suddenly felt tired. "I'm not sure what I am these days."

We stayed quiet for a few seconds, then she reached out her hand to mine. "May I?" she asked. The question on her face softened. "I read palms," she explained.

My hand reached out to hers like it had a mind of its own. With two academics for parents, palm reading wasn't high on the list of belief systems. Still, I liked how her fingers traced the lines on my hand as if decoding an ancient prophecy that started in the womb. Or maybe it was just nice to have someone paying attention to me.

Her bangles tinkled. "Oh, dear." Her well-shaped eyebrows furrowed together. I leaned closer as if *DANGER!* were written on my palm. "It's inevitable," she sighed. When she let go of my hand, I instantly missed her warmth.

I searched her eyes. "What?" I asked.

She clasped her hands behind her back again. "You're in for an unexpected romance," she said. My eyes flicked to Captain

Bowsky, certain I would see him wink. I snorted and followed her gaze to the main foyer, where Chloe was saying goodbye to Jesse's mom.

"All right," she sighed. "I better give Scarlett O'Hara a hug. That's my nickname for Jesse's friend Chloe," she laughed. "The boys hover around her like bees to the hive, but that's because she's such a honey. You can't say that about most beauty queens."

"I wish I knew her secret," I said. It seemed honesty was trickling out of me uncontrollably. Hey, the woman had seen my future, there were no secrets between us girls now.

Jesse's grandma looked at me like I had two heads. "It's easy," she said. "Chloe loves herself." She leaned in closer and dropped her voice, ready to deliver a delicious bit of gossip. "A girl can't sparkle unless she knows which bits shine."

I tried to come up with something in me that shone. She could tell I was struggling. "Everyone has something that makes them glow," she insisted.

I knew what made me glow—thinking about kissing Blaine. "What if you can't get the thing that makes you glow?" I asked her.

She thought for a moment, then said, "When you stop chasing the thing you *want*, you give the thing you *need* a chance to catch you." She ended the sentence with a wink, like it was a secret signal or something. "See you later, Bo Peep." She made her way to the main foyer, where she enveloped Chloe. It was comforting to watch them.

The rest of the shift went smoothly. Each time I went into the kitchen, How-hole gave me a friendly nod. I guess we were sort of friends now. When you walk in on someone's audition for *Canadian Idol*, you bond.

Mr. Deveau was in jolly good form, with his red polo shirt and white pants. I couldn't believe the guy dressed that way on purpose. He paused by the window, studying the harbour. "With the sun sparkling off the water and the sailboats breezing by," he sighed, "it makes my heart leap."

I caught Chloe's eye and had to bite the inside of my cheek to keep from laughing.

He let out another loving sigh, then clapped his hands. "The cake is ordered and the wedding photographer is scheduled to come by for a preliminary shooting. We will leave nothing to chance on the special day." He gave Chloe and Julia a thumbs-up.

As if Julia, or anyone else, was losing sleep over the stupid wedding. It's not like it was the royal wedding or anything. Now that would be totally awesome. Still, even though Prince Harry is a hottie, he's no Blaine Mulder.

Chloe and I walked down the front stairs, dragging our swollen feet, glad to be finished another shift. We'd already changed out of our uniforms. She told me about her plans to go to the beach the next day with a few friends and invited me to tag along.

My heart soared. I didn't bother trying to hide how excited I was. She gave me a wave goodbye, then popped in her ear buds and left in the direction of the yacht club.

I hung out by the front gate. I checked my watch. Dad was usually late getting supper ready. I wondered if I had enough time for a quick trip to the yacht club. I couldn't very well have a spontaneous chit-chat with Blaine if I didn't bump into him. A heaviness settled in my chest. If it was this much work to check off a spontaneous chit-chat, it would be Labour Day weekend by the time I worked my way down to the kissing box.

I unwrapped my last peppermint for the day. How-hole pedalled by, his neon hair poking out of his bike helmet. He flashed me a grin, and I imagined his blue eyes were crinkling at the edges. I laughed out loud and watched as he leaned forward, practically standing on the pedals, to get up the steep hill.

"Work it, dishpan hands," I called out.

I kept watching the spot where his bike disappeared over the slope. *"When you stop chasing the thing you want, you give the thing you need a chance to catch you."*

Little Bo Peep, has lost her sheep...maybe I have been chasing the wrong thing.

I slowly sucked on my peppermint. Jesse's grandma had put me in a philosophical kind of mood. I started to think about all the fuss with the upcoming wedding. Is that what love was really about? Why was it so important to have a fancy caterer, and flowers grown specially, and a photographer who has to show up for light tests? Does the amount of money you spend equate the amount of love you feel?

It made no sense to me. My parents had been married in the afternoon, had a buffet reception at a colleague's house, and that was it. And they were still happy...right?

I crunched down on the peppermint, breaking it in half. Goosebumps covered my arms. I tried to remember the last time I'd seen my parents smile at each other.

A horn beeped. Blaine's truck rumbled through the intersection. Without thinking, I pushed off the front gate, my legs propelling me to the edge of the road. Francine's spreadsheet loomed in my mind. If Chloe's best friend was trying to make a new start at camp, I could certainly wave at Blaine. We were math buddies, after all.

I stood on my tiptoes and waved, "Hey, Blaine!" My heart was thumping out a tribal message.

Go. Go. Go.

Blaine turned his head. His face was blank. Time froze. Then he smiled at me.

He. Smiled. At. Me.

Suddenly weddings and flowers and cakes were beautiful and wonderful and fabulous. And everyone should be in love because it makes you leap to your feet.

I was busy waving at him and he was busy smiling back. Neither one of us noticed the bike racing down the hill, or the rider with his hands down by his sides.

FOURTEEN

A flash of blue caught my attention. I turned my head. There was no time to warn him. I saw everything happen in slow motion. The scream was trapped inside my head. I almost choked on my peppermint. How-hole gripped the bars and swerved to the side at the last second. Blaine didn't even brake, he hadn't seen How-hole at all. The truck and bike passed each other as if death wasn't leaning against the picket fence, smoking a cigarette, just waiting for the blood spill.

I almost got How-hole killed!

I was the only one having a coronary, though. Blaine was now looking forward, driving away from me. How-hole, ignorant to how close he had come to getting his blue-haired head knocked off his shoulders, continued to pedal through the intersection.

Then I was left alone, clutching the fuzzy yellow gorilla, trying to swallow my heart back down my throat. I glanced around; no one else had seen How-hole almost get killed. The world continued turning for the ignorant.

I blinked a few times and swivelled my head, looking for his blue hair. I spotted him over by the main wharf. He had taken the road that wrapped around the back of the harbour.

If that was the way home, I wondered, why had he even gone up the hill to begin with?

A voice echoed an answer inside my head.

Reckless thrill-seeker.

My temples began to pound. I guess when you mix craziness with bad driving, your choices don't always make sense. Normal people don't careen down hills toward trucks for fun, right? A chill ran down my spine. Blaine wasn't the kind of guy who would plow into someone on a bike. He'd never drive recklessly. He'd only waved at me for a split second—it's not like he was texting.

Blaine was responsible.

I decided to walk home instead of calling for a drive. I needed to decompress. Besides, Blaine's truck might make another appearance and offer me a lift home. Francine would be proud. I was attacking "spontaneous chit-chat" with gumption.

But the only vehicles I noticed were a Stunder's Mercedes, a local in a banged-up two-door, and the shiny red SUV that everyone knew belonged to Frank Driscoll, high school dropout and local creep.

He lived with his mother and worked at the gas station, where he cleaned his car after every shift—inside and out. Harmless, but still able to produce skin-crawling comments on a regular basis.

He pulled up beside me and rolled down his window. "Hey, Kelsey," he said. "Need a drive?"

"No, thank you." I kept walking. "I need the exercise."

Friendly yet formal works for all kinds of situations.

His car kept pace with my steps. I noticed him incline his chin, like he was checking me out. "I think you look just fine. Girls are too skinny these days."

> When faced with an uncomfortable situation at a party you...?
> A. give a quick yet polite excuse and leave immediately.
> B. confront the reason for the discomfort. No one's going to spoil your fun.
> C. continue with your usual activity, hoping the situation will work itself out.

I quickened my pace.

"Are you sure?" he prodded. "There's a lot of strangers hanging around this summer. It's not safe to walk home alone."

"I get car sick," I told him. "I wouldn't want to vomit the Queen's Galley's famous fish chowder all over your nice upholstery. Think how hard it would be to get the smell out."

His smile faded. He started to say something, but a car right behind him blared its horn, making both of us jump.

"Bye," I called out, giving a wave for good measure. I pulled out my magazine, pretending to read. Frank's SUV moved on. I kept my head down as the rest of the traffic went by.

When I got home, Mom's car was gone. A weird, empty feeling pushed against my ribs.

"She's doing research at the library," Dad told me, not even looking up from the kitchen counter. He was wrapping fish in tinfoil, adding a sprig of rosemary on top of each fillet. "Supper will be ready in an hour," he said.

Chet was singing on the patio. His iPod shuffle was apparently playing Adele. Dad looked up. He had dark circles under his eyes. I stayed on the spot, one bare foot resting on the other. "What is it?" Dad asked.

I became interested in picking a hangnail. "Not much. I might be going to the beach tomorrow." I paused a few crucial seconds. "If that's okay?"

"Sure. Chet and I can make some plans. We need some man time."

I raised my eyebrows. "Man time" to Dad would probably consist of reorganizing his *National Geographic* collection. Still, I was relieved to have a clear schedule for tomorrow.

Dad wiped the counter and told me to join Chet and get some fresh air.

THE NEXT DAY was Saturday, and totally awesome for two reasons: I didn't have to take Chet to swimming, and I was meeting Chloe at the beach on our day off—okay, maybe that's three things.

I stared into my closet, then finally chose my two-piece with the Hawaiian print and white shorts. I loved that suit; it covered all the right bits. (And I didn't have to worry about it getting see-through when it was wet, since I never go in the water.)

I'd mastered the art of avoiding swimming. I loved the beach, not the ocean. I could wade up to my knees, but that was it. Any deeper and the ole stomach-heaving, heart-combustion dance began. *Go back to shore!* my cells would scream out.

I shoved sunscreen, my iPod, and the August issue of *Modern Teen* into my Kipling bag.

Mom slipped away from her computer long enough to interrogate me. I looked around her shoulder to peek inside her office. There were two apple cores, an empty glass, and an old coffee mug that had probably been filled three times already on her desk.

Then the questions started. Who was Chloe? Which beach were we going to? When would I be home? Would the boy from the restaurant be there?

That last one made me stumble a bit. Why did she care about How-hole?

After I convinced her I wasn't going to do drugs with the Hells Angels, I called out a "So long, smell you later" to Chet and hopped on my bike.

I usually prefer taking Mom's car, but today the blue sky and warm wind laced with the scent of wildflowers was promising a day of perfection. I loved biking the windy road to the waterfront. It was mostly downhill from my house, so I practically coasted the whole way there.

I smiled as I lazily biked along a row of clapboard Cape Cod-style houses. Tiny pink roses climbed up trellises while window boxes overflowed with bright red geraniums. I took in a deep breath, feeling like the sun was shinning just for me.

I paused when I came to the top of the hill above the Queen's Galley. I almost laughed; it didn't seem so steep today. Usually I tackled this beast of a slope with my brake-and-slow-release technique, but today was different.

I wiggled on my seat, then stared down the hill and began to pedal. I dared myself to keep going faster, ignoring my hands as they twitched, fighting the urge to squeeze the brakes.

The scenery blurred past me. I held my breath. The surge of adrenaline made me dizzy. I pressed my lips together, trapping an automatic scream. It was more terrifying when you could see how fast you were going. I should have worn a skirt.

I panicked and hit the brakes too quickly. The back wheel swerved to the side. I wobbled uncontrollably. This time the scream did come out. I'm sure a few Stunders turned in my direction. I steered the bike off the road, using the sandy shoulder to help slow me down.

I sucked in mouthfuls of air. Almost dying made me appreciate oxygen on a whole new level. I glanced at the hill. I'd been biking that slope for years. What the hell was I thinking?

Reckless thrill-seeker.

Stupid How-hole. I wish he'd get out of my head.

I needed to focus. Breaking enough bones to be in a full-body cast was NOT on Francine's spreadsheet.

When I finally got to the beach, Chloe had already established her spot. She had a blanket spread out and a picnic basket. I walked up slowly, suddenly nervous. Maybe she was expecting a whole load of people. Maybe she'd forgotten about me altogether.

She looked up from filing her nails and waved me over.

Hooray!

Two hunky guys ran past me, right up to her. A dark-haired one with a chiselled bod plopped down beside her. A tall blonde guy that looked like every girl's dream stood by, shifting his feet in the sand.

My stomach dropped. She hadn't been waving to me after all. My heart weighed a hundred pounds. I took a step backward and tripped. My butt hit something soft, and I heard a loud crunching sound.

"Hey!" A couple stared down at me angrily.

I quickly scampered off their blanket, leaving a flattened bag of chips where I'd landed. "Oh, geez," I said. "Sorry, Salt & Vinegar are my favourite too."

They didn't say anything. The girl let out a huff and lay back down.

Fingers curled around my elbow. "Kelsey?" Mr. Tall, Blonde, and Beautiful was beside me. He repeated my name again, then said, "Chloe is over here. We're waiting for you."

We're waiting for you.

Not only had Chloe actually intended to hang out with me today, but apparently two hot guys were part of the deal.

I hadn't forgotten about Blaine, of course, but a little practice in how to form a sentence with a suave-a-licious guy would be great preparation for our next spontaneous chit-chat.

Chloe had an umbrella set up. Actually, it came from the lifeguards' shed. Chloe, I soon discovered, gets a lot of stuff for free. People just want to do nice things for her.

Her blanket was a glorified girly spot. There was nail polish, snacks, drinks, coconut-scented sunscreen, fashion magazines, extra towels, even hairspray. The girl brought hairspray to the beach.

The dark-haired guy was named Sam. Officially he was a few blankets over, but Chloe let him stay and chat for a bit. He promised to get us some fries from the canteen. He introduced Mr. Beautiful as Ben, his friend from university.

"Kelsey works at Queen's Galley too," she told them. It was as if I were interesting or something.

"The uniform is hot," Sam teased me.

"I'm working it like Bo Peep," I said. They all laughed and I felt a surge of confidence. The nervous fluttering calmed a bit.

Soon Ben had to leave. He was one of the lifeguards, and his break was over.

"There must be an increase in the number of fake drownings when you work," I told him. I was feeling more confident now and my cockiness flowed easily.

He flashed me a smile, and then headed for his post. My eyes flicked back and forth between the waves and Ben's retreating back. I squinted at his shoulders.

Nope. Not worth it, I thought.

"It's so hot," Chloe said, peeling off her beach cover-up. "I'm going in for a dip."

"I'm more of a beach girl myself," I said. I waited for the questions, and even the prodding taunts, but Chloe stayed quiet and so did I. There's one thing I learned over the years: the less I say about my aquaphobia, the more quickly people leave me alone.

The day passed effortlessly. It was nice to just hang out and not worry about what time it was, or where I had to pick up Chet.

Over a bag of chips and two cans of iced tea, Chloe gave me the lowdown on every cute guy who walked by. She pointed out the good kissers, told me which ones texted back immediately, and smiled when she mentioned the guy who always complimented her outfit, no matter what she was wearing. I basked in her popularity aura. I had become cool by proxy. If she'd suggested that we get tattoos, I would have agreed that very second. I would have agreed to anything.

Sam eventually sauntered back. Chloe pulled back her sunglasses and gave his face a critical look. "You're getting a burn," she said, reaching for the sunscreen.

I peeked over the cover of my magazine. Sam had a goofy

look on his face that let me know he'd be all for getting a tattoo too. Delicately, Chloe dabbed a dot of sunscreen along his forehead. She rubbed it in, then let her finger slowly trail down his jaw. "Anywhere else need attention?" she asked.

Holy hormone machine. A live tutorial of "Are You Naturally Seductive?" was playing before my very eyes. Chloe was definitely a natural.

Sam didn't do anything, he just kept staring at her. I think he may have stopped breathing. "Maybe here?" Chloe asked, touching his chin.

Where was she going with this? I couldn't look away.

"Or here?" Chloe's finger grazed his lower lip. Then she leaned in closer. "I know," she said against his mouth, "right here."

I wasn't Bo Peep. I was a Bo-frickin'-Peeping Tom. I kept hidden behind my magazine when the kissing started. It didn't last long, though. Chloe was soon giggling and playfully pushing Sam away. I wondered if he was part of the good kisser group.

Chloe looked over my shoulder and her face broke out into a smile. I turned around and saw Tanner walking toward us. He was proof that looks and popularity transcended age.

I raised an arm, waving him over. Then I froze.

Blaine Mulder, my future husband, was right beside him.

My eyes hopscotched over Chloe's blanket of beauty products, madly looking for something that could instantly pizzazz me up.

A shadow fell over my stretched-out legs. "Hey, Kelsey." Tanner loomed over me. "What's up? I haven't seen you since Franny left."

Having a best friend with a hot stud boyfriend should have thrown me into the path of other hot studs—notably Blaine. However, the laws of high school state only one outsider at a time can break free from the pack and mate with a "cool dude." Blaine and I would have to solidify our romance in the summer, when the constraints of high school hierarchy weren't so strictly followed. Plus, there was Regan—*was*, as in past tense, I kept reminding myself.

"How's the job?" Tanner asked me.

I used all my willpower not to stare at Blaine. He was standing beside Tanner, smiling down at Chloe and me. He was also shirtless. "I look like Bo Peep," I said. This time it didn't get a laugh.

Chloe must have sensed my painful death about to play out in front of her. "You guys should drop in," she said, "for a Coke sometime." Then she added with a smile, "On the house, of course."

Blaine gave me a perfectly adorable grin, and said, "Oh yeah? All I have to do is ask for you?"

His tone was casual, but I could feel myself melting into the blanket. He took my breath away; everyone else disappeared. It was only me, Blaine, and his magnificent shoulders.

"That's all you've ever had to do," I told him.

He ran a hand through his hair, making the muscle on top of his shoulder bulge. The tease!

"Cool," he said. "By the way, my cousin's having a party tonight." He nodded to Chloe and Sam as well. "It's the big place at the end of Corkum Road. You know it?"

Chloe looked impressed. "Yeah!" she said. "We'll be there."

Tanner caught my eye. "I'll pick you up at eight, okay?"

"Yeah, okay," I answered, reaching into the bag of chips while my heart did backflips.

When I got home there was a note from Dad stuck to the fridge. He and Chet had gone into Halifax to see a movie. Mom was researching at the library and wouldn't be home until later. There was leftover chicken in the fridge with directions to make a pasta salad.

I rolled my eyes at his note. Pasta salad? Too much work. Instead, I made a peanut butter and Nutella sandwich, and took it upstairs with a glass of milk.

Francine's spreadsheet glowed back at me. I checked off "Spontaneous chit-chat #2." I even skipped one of the squares and checked off "Party." I felt a jolt of excitement.

Release the endorphins!

I scrolled down to the bottom. "Tell Blaine how you feel" was the second-last item. I read the final column and my heart did a tap dance. Since this morning I had moved two checks closer to "Have a simply amazing, neurotransmitter-firing, stomach-full-of-butterflies kiss."

FIFTEEN

B y the time I was ready, Mom still hadn't come home. I hated to admit it, but it felt weird to have the house to myself. There was an eerie quality to the silence that had never bothered me before. Maybe I had gotten too much sun today and it was making me loopy.

I stood in front of our living room window, watching for Tanner's beat-up Toyota. My red Toms were dancing on the spot. The tiny rip at the right toe was hardly noticeable. I should have been in my flip-flops, but they were too grungy. I had tried to straighten my hair but ended up with a weird ridge across the back of my head, so I'd had to put it in a ponytail and hope for the best. But I wasn't too panicked. Chloe had given me enough fashion tips to last all year.

Like, "Only one designer item per outfit, don't overload with brand names." Luckily, this wasn't a problem for me. My parents didn't budget for designer clothes. I wore my capris and the Tommy Hilfiger halter top that Francine had brought back for me from Florida last March break. I tucked the straps of my bra inside my armpits and I was good to go.

I left a note saying I was hanging out with Tanner and a friend from work. Since he met Francine's high standards, my parents approved of Tanner. They felt he was like my older brother, and therefore safe.

A loud muffler signalled my drive had arrived. I grabbed my Kipling bag and slammed the front door behind me.

Sweet holy rollers!

Blaine was sitting in the front passenger seat.

Don't pee your pants. Don't pee your pants. Don't pee your pants. I repeated my mantra as I walked in front of the car, knowing they were both sitting there watching me through the windshield.

Don't pee your pants. When I slipped into the back seat, my armpits were already sweating. The gorilla popped its thumb in its mouth all by itself this time.

"Are You A Fearless Flirt?"

Nope.

"What'd you bring?" Blaine tilted his chin toward the back seat. I was able to appreciate his perfect profile from this angle.

I flicked my hand at my bag. "Oh, um…like, stuff." I didn't think Blaine would be interested in what kind of lip gloss I'd taken for tonight.

"No," he said. "I mean for the party."

Francine had instructed me not to freak out during my spontaneous chit-chats with Blaine. She'd advised me to go with the flow and tell the truth. "Okay," I laughed nervously, thinking of the mints and tiny hairbrush I'd also stuffed in my bag. "Just a girl's survival kit."

Blaine's face instantly fell. The colour rose high in his cheeks. He turned forward again, staring out the windshield.

Holy frickin' bacon turds, I thought. *He thinks I mean tampons. I'm pretty sure Francine doesn't have that on the spreadsheet.*

Tanner, immune to my nerdiness, turned up the radio. "I brought the usual six-pack," he offered, his voice smooth and unaffected.

He meant booze, idiot, not tampons.

> ### When invited to a party, you make sure to bring...
>
> A. a gift for the host.
> B. your sense of humour. Everybody loves the life of the party.
> C. feminine protection. You'll always be prepared.

Tanner cut a corner onto the winding road that leads to the peninsula. I rarely took this route; it was a dead end with mostly big summer homes. I rolled down the window and the warm air blew in smelling of clover. I tried to relax.

"So," Tanner started, catching my eye in the rear-view mirror, "besides the Bo Peep uniform, anything good about being a busgirl? Are the tips decent?"

"It'll be good when I finally get paid," I said, looking down at my Toms, where the tip of my toenail peeked through.

"And you get to work with Chloe," Tanner added. "She's cool."

"Yeah," I said. I had to be careful. It was important to stay loyal to Francine, but a secret part of my heart was overjoyed that the cool girl was adopting me for the summer. "She'll be at the party tonight," I said, as if I were her personal events coordinator.

"The Queen's Galley, right?" Blaine asked.

Short-term-memory problems? Didn't he just wave to me the other day in front of the restaurant? "Uh, yeah," I said.

Blaine laughed. I guess he remembered now too. Sillypants. It would be one of those stories we'd tell our kids. "*And your father didn't even remember waving to me that day...*"

He turned around to face me again, then said, "You must know—"

"Dude," Tanner interrupted. "Which drive is your cousin's house, again?"

"Oh, next left," he said, pointing at the same time.

Why do people do that?

The woods were thick on either side of the car, and you'd never have known we were a hundred feet from the ocean. "Yup, this one here," Blaine instructed.

Tanner pulled in slowly to avoid hitting any of the cars parked along the side. "Man, it's jumping already," he said, his voice excited. I gave him a sideways glance. I wondered if Francine would be so excited to go solo to a party.

I leaned forward into the space between the front seats and turned to Blaine. There was a faint whiff of *Jake*. No one wore Hollister like Blaine. I wanted to bury my face in his chest. A wave of heat washed over me. I'm sure my hair follicles were blushing. "So, yeah." I started again. "The Queen's Galley is interesting. Oh, my God, the manager is outrageous. And the kitchen guy—"

"Whoa!" Blaine said to Tanner. "We're here."

I was momentarily speechless. I knew there were big fancy summer homes around, but I'd never been this close to one before. I didn't mix with Stunders often, and I'd never been considered cool enough to be invited to one of their parties before. This minor miracle called for two check marks on the spreadsheet.

"Wow," I breathed. The house we stopped in front of was a frickin' mansion, with Roman columns and everything. My house could easily fit inside of it three times.

Blaine grinned. "There's a tennis court, too," he said. "And a pool."

We got out of the car. Tanner walked on my other side, putting me between himself and Blaine. My heart swelled a little thinking of Francine. She must have left Tanner a spreadsheet too, with instructions to help me with Operation Tongue.

God, I hoped she hadn't told him the title.

The house loomed in front of us like a Gothic mansion from the south. "Your cousin is super rich," I breathed.

"Lucky," Tanner said. He had a six-pack in one hand. I knew these guys drank, but it was weird to see it happening. He offered me a can, but I waved him off. I'm not much of an expert, but I've seen enough episodes of *Gossip Girl* to know it's better to be the girl holding the puker's hair than to be the puker. Besides, if I was talking about tampons while stone-cold sober, what the hell would I say if I got drunk?

Blaine was carrying a bottle of some kind of hard liquor. He went ahead of us to the front door. "He's away with his much younger girlfriend," he told us.

"Your cousin?" I asked.

"No, his dad," Blaine said. "His girlfriend had to fly to Toronto to pick up her wedding dress." He paused and gave Tanner and I serious look. "My cousin's a bit pissed off about the whole thing. His mom took off for a spa retreat in Bali. So don't bring it up, okay?"

Tanner took a swig of beer. "Ouch," he said. "When my parents split, my dad just moved in with my grandma two houses down. He still comes over for supper sometimes."

Blaine grinned. "And stays for dessert?" he teased.

"Shut the hell up," Tanner sulked.

"Whatever." Blaine shrugged. "Anyway, my uncle's still a good guy. Plus, he left us a kickass house to party in." He opened the front door. Music blared in our faces. He stepped back and waved me in. "What do you say, Kelsey?" he asked. "Are you ready to party?"

SIXTEEN

B odies crowded the foyer, and the spiral staircase was dotted with couples either making out or laughing. Tanner immediately got his back slapped and hugged. "Oh my God, man. What's going on?"

I stood beside him, shaking like a church mouse. My fingers twirled around the fuzzy yellow gorilla. A cluster of girls strutted by with their perfectly straight hair and fresh lip gloss. I swear they left a trail of sparkly dust in their path.

One girl was wearing a crocheted sundress over a bikini. She squeezed Tanner's arm as she breezed by. "Hey," she said. There was a hummingbird tattoo on her shoulder. Tanner's eyes glazed over a bit.

He turned to me and said, "Come on."

We followed Blaine down a spacious hallway and ended up in the kitchen. The massive granite counter was covered in liquor bottles, plastic cups, and piles of beer caps. There was a sink full of ice, but no one was chilling their beer.

Tanner leaned against the counter and fell into an easy conversation with another jock. I smiled as he talked about scraping barnacles off boats. Then I smiled as Tanner talked about how the basketball team would have its best shot at the provincial title this year.

Everyone had a drink...everyone but me. My hands felt stupid by my sides. I craned my neck to find Blaine, but he'd been swallowed up by the crowd and spat out into another room. I was so nervous I was practically molesting my poor yellow gorilla. My eyes wandered to the plastic cups, several already filled—I could at least *hold* a drink.

My smile was stuck to my teeth. I needed a better plan than being Tanner's shadow all night. I grabbed one of the plastic cups and squeezed through the crowd, keeping an eye out for Blaine's perfect shoulders.

In the living room, a huge stereo pounded out music. The floor vibrated with heavy bass. Off to the side, a set of double doors led out to the patio. I was sweating like crazy. I took a sip of my drink. The second it was in my mouth, I knew I had made a mistake. It tasted like paint thinner.

"Kelsey!" Chloe called from the patio. She was surrounded by her usual supporting cast. About five male heads turned my way. I swallowed, feeling a burn all the way down my throat.

I stepped around people, fighting the urge to cough or spew all over the carpet. I wondered how much my Nutella and peanut butter sandwich had digested.

Chloe's smile melted into concern. "Are you okay?" She was wiping her hands on a towel. Sam and Ben were sitting on the deck railing.

I shrugged and tried to give her a smile; the real answer would take too long. She held up a bottle of gel. "I'm giving makeovers," she told me.

"Oh." I self-consciously smoothed a hand over my pony-tail.

"Just Luke so far," she laughed. "I thought he needed an updo for the party." Her eyes shifted slightly behind me. I turned around. How-hole's hair had been gelled into a faux-hawk, each spike ending in a perfect neon-blue point.

"What do you think, Kels?" he asked. I noticed the people around us stopped and listened. "Is this a *safe* look?" he nettled. "Or do I look like every parent's nightmare?" A few warbled remarks peppered the air from people around us, but he kept those blue eyes trained on me, waiting for my witty comeback. A warmth started to grow in my stomach.

I wet my lips, then tilted my head to the side. "I think you're afraid to look normal."

He waited a three-second beat, then slowly a grin spread across his face. "Brilliant," he said. "You must have a lot of experience analyzing people." It sounded like a compliment, but I could hear the snarky undertone. A bit cheeky coming from someone working under court order. He didn't look away, but neither did I.

How-hole didn't frighten me because I knew exactly what he was: a reckless thrill-seeker. He may have been teasing me, but he was right—I was good at analyzing people. I didn't spend all that time studying personality quizzes for nothing.

Chloe looked in my cup and wrinkled her nose. "What are you drinking?"

"Oh, this?" I stammered. I was afraid I'd have to take a sip in front of them and risk gagging. "Um…this isn't mine. I'm holding it for a girl. Yeah, the girl with the bird tattoo, she just handed it to me. So…yeah."

"A girl?" Chloe said. "With a bird tattoo?"

"A hummingbird tattoo?" How-hole looked alarmed. "Whatever Brooke's drinking is too strong for you."

I snorted at him, but he looked totally serious.

He took the cup from me and dumped it onto a plant in the corner. "I'm on safety patrol tonight," he told me, putting his hand over his heart. "A huge part of my job is prevention."

Was he serious?

"Cannonball!" a guy shouted from below. Seconds later we heard the splash.

How-hole let out a tired sigh. "Duty calls." Then he turned on his heel and disappeared back into the house.

I frowned at his retreating back. I hadn't expected to see him. How-hole must be friends with these other Stunders, or maybe Chloe invited him here tonight after we ran into Blaine and Tanner at the beach. It's weird, I'd never thought about it before, but if How-hole was a rich summer kid, then why was he working as a dishwasher? I thought all Stunders were snobs.

Nothing about How-hole added up.

"Here." Chloe took a bottle from a huge ice bucket, then untwisted the cap and handed it to me. "It's a cooler," she told me. Then she added for good measure, "Never take a drink from a stranger, Kelsey. And never leave your drink alone."

"Thanks, Mom," I mumbled. I was a newbie and it was obvious to everyone. I took a sip. It tasted just like lemonade. It couldn't be *that* bad if it wasn't assaulting my taste buds. I took a few more sips and found a spot on the railing. From this vantage point I could see the whole grounds.

Wowzers!

There was a tennis court, a pool, and a winding path through birch trees to a private wharf. Sailboats were silhouetted against the sunset.

"Cannonball!" A huge splash soaked a pair of girls lounging on the deck chairs. They squealed and covered their hair, then jumped up and hurried just out of reach.

I took another sip of my cooler and scanned the pool, but Blaine wasn't there. How-hole, I noticed, had sauntered up to the girls.

"Duty calls, my ass," I said into the bottle. That warm feeling in my stomach was spreading. I tilted back and finished my drink.

I plopped down my empty and picked up another. I double-checked the label to make sure I was still drinking the right thing. I scraped my hand twisting off the cap, but I didn't even feel it. In fact, everything felt a little disjointed. Not so much numb, just carefree.

I liked feeling carefree. Who cared about How-hole and his freaky super-secret life? Not this gal, that's for sure.

I walked through various rooms while taking sips of my cooler, leaving the noisy crowd behind. I stopped in front of a pair of French doors. I pressed my face up to the glass. The walls were lined with bookshelves and there was a big, puffy, leather couch.

I slipped inside and closed the doors behind me. It was much quieter in here. I tossed my Kipling bag on the floor. I realized the house was so huge that I might never find my way back to the party. "I should have left a trail of bread crumbs," I said, making myself laugh. I was so frickin' hilarious. Everything was suddenly hilarious.

I pulled out my magazine. "What Kind of Guy Do You Like?" I read. I laughed again. I should laugh more often, it felt so good.

What most attracts you to a guy?
A. His taste in music and movies is compatible with my own.
B. His attitude and strut make me weak in the knees.
C. He makes me feel special, like no one else can.

I took a long swig from my bottle and circled C. Yeah, definitely C. I finished the quiz and my drink in record time. At least, it felt like record time. Maybe I had been in here for hours.

I tallied up my score, but I didn't bother reading my result. I knew what kind of guy I liked. I started to scribble *Mrs. Kelsey Mulder* all around the page. My pen soon faded. I shook it and did that thing when you suck the tip, but it was bone dry—just like my bottle. I held it to my lips and blew out a tune. On a small writing desk in the corner I saw a cup full of pens. I let the bottle fall to the floor.

There was a picture frame on the desk. I stumbled closer. A man and a young boy were on the back of a sailboat with a perfect blue sky full of fluffy clouds behind them. The boy was squinting into the camera. I stared closely at the man.

This must be Blaine's uncle. This was the man who had divorced his wife and was now a sugar daddy to some dumbass beauty queen who had to travel to Toronto to get her wedding dress. I blinked a few times, then my eyes grew wide. This had obviously been taken years ago, but that handsome George Clooney face was still the same.

The frame almost slipped from my hands. The owner of the Queen's Galley was Blaine's uncle! Maybe that's why Mr. Deveau was being so fancypants about the upcoming wedding—it was for Edward and his much younger bride!

I thought about what Blaine had said about his cousin being angry with his dad, and how the mom was having some kind of mental breakdown in a tropical resort. How could someone do that to their family?

My dad would never betray us like that. Then again, socks and sandals kind of scream, "I'm off the market."

I sneered at the picture. "I will give you salt on purpose," I breathed against the frame. It was a weird *Scooby-Doo* moment—I finally had cracked the case. I had to tell Chloe!

I bumped my way down the hall and around the corner, trying to follow the music. I was totally lost. "Holy bacon farts," I called out. "This place is ridiculously huge." I stumbled and put my hand against the wall, knocking a few pictures to the floor. *Oops.*

I climbed a set of stairs to another landing, sucking in air. I had no idea I was this out of shape. A blurry vision of blue spikes came closer to me. "Hey!" I called out. My tongue felt thick.

I wiped a hand over my face. Chloe was suddenly in front of me. "Oh shit, Kelsey," she laughed a bit. "Are you drunk?"

"Nooooo," my head made some kind of movement.

She put a hand around my waist and said, "Let's get you some water."

I laughed and squirmed in her arms, "Don't," I giggled. "I'm ticklish."

"Uh-huh," she said, moving me into the kitchen.

I stopped in my tracks. "NO!" I grabbed her cheeks and put my face close to hers. "You're not going to believe this!" I sprayed her with my spit. "Edward is Blaine's uncle," I whispered loud enough for everyone to stop talking around us. "And he's marrying this homewrecking dumbass...*at the Queen's Galley!*" I squealed the last bit.

Chloe's eyes danced around the room. "Let's get you home," she said quickly. "Hey, Tanner," she called out.

Brooke, the girl with the hummingbird tattoo, was hanging off Tanner's arm, whispering in his ear.

My mouth fell open at the sight of another girl with Tanner. It felt like someone had punched me in the gut. How could he do this to Francine?

Tanner stepped toward me. Brooke's hand slid off his shoulder. "Where were you?" he asked me.

I glared back at him. Anger was quickly replacing my shock. "Not sticking my tongue in your ear," I said. "That's for sure!" Except my words came out slurred. They only made sense in my head.

He looked confused. He nodded to Chloe over my shoulder, "I'll take her home." He touched my arm but I pulled away.

"No," I pouted, crossing my arms in front of my chest. "I'm not going anywhere until I have another spontaneous kitty cat," I hiccupped. "I mean chit-chat."

Brooke started to giggle.

I singled her out. "You don't—*hiccup*—get it. You're too pretty to understand." I sniffed and wobbled on the spot, the kitchen floor had decided to tilt for some reason. "Do you have any idea how hards—*hiccup*—for a girl like me to get a—*hiccup*—guys to notice her? I hafta to use strategy and carefully—*hiccup*—laid out tactics. The Heptagon—*hiccup*—Pentagon did less during wartime…I'm exhausted!" My hand jutted out to grab the counter for balance.

Brooke backed up, looking perplexed.

I suddenly felt tired. I wish I'd stayed in the study with the cozy leather couch. The kitchen was totally quiet. I still had everyone's attention.

I took a breath, concentrating on making my mouth move the right way. In a rush of unexplained confidence, I had an unconquerable desire to speak up for every wife and girlfriend who had ever been cheated on. "What's wrong with this world?" I asked them. "Everyone makes out like frickin' monkeys—no one beli—*hiccup*—lieves in love. Not the guy who owns this house. Not girls—*hiccup*—with perfect makeup and hair." I looked at Tanner. My voice dropped to a sloppy whisper, "Not even your parents." My lower lip started to quiver, and I finally broke into tears. "So what's the point of a stu-*hiccup*—pid spreadsheet?"

How-hole stood in the doorway, the look of pity on his face was the perfect finale for my embarrassing monologue. You know it's bad when the crazy guy feels sorry for you. My stomach flipped painfully. Tanner's hand was on my arm again. I didn't protest this time. Even I could sense it was time to close the curtains on this disaster. He led me out of the kitchen. I blinked hard, keeping my eyes on the floor.

"Do you need any help?" How-hole's voice was behind us.

"No thanks, dude," Tanner answered. "Um…sorry about this." I knew he was talking about me. My stomach twisted again. I cupped my hand over my mouth and tried to speed up my steps, but I kept tripping on my feet. Tanner was practically carrying me by the time we made it to the foyer.

"You leaving already?" Blaine stood in front of us. He was holding a can of beer. He took a long swig and the sound was enough to trigger a chain reaction.

My guts heaved. What seemed like five hundred litres of Nutella and peanut butter lava erupted from my mouth and cascaded onto Blaine's feet.

SEVENTEEN

The neon light from the Shake Shack glowed off the hood of Tanner's car. He turned away from the order window with two paper bags. The driver's door creaked open. "Here." He passed me a bag, the top still rolled up tightly. The delicious smell of grease filled the car.

"Thanks," I said thickly. My stomach had finally settled. Once I'd upchucked all over Blaine, everything felt normal again.

Well, not everything. Tanner had only said a handful of words since we left the party. We'd been driving around Mariner's Cove, him silently fuming, me silently dying inside. Shame didn't even begin to describe what I felt.

Tanner had already finished his burger by the time I'd had a few fries. The salt made me feel a little bit more alive, less like the corpse Tanner had dragged out of Blaine's uncle's house. He crumpled up his bag and took a long sip of his shake.

He smacked his lips. "You know," he said, staring hard at the windshield. "I don't think anyone has ever insulted me *and* my parents in the same breath."

My mouth full of fries seemed like a glob of goo. I couldn't swallow. "I'm sorry," I whispered around the food. "I didn't mean to mention your parents…not like that."

He finally turned to me. "Jesus, Kelsey! What were you thinking saying all that stuff in front of everyone? You'll be lucky if you're ever invited to a party again."

I kept my head down, looking for an answer at the bottom of the paper bag. "I'm pretty sure my partying days are over," I said.

"You think?"

I groaned. There was no way to explain to Tanner about Blaine and the spreadsheet. Still, that wouldn't be enough for him to understand what it was like for me to be with those other kids tonight. How horribly out of place I felt, and how every pretty girl was a reminder of how plain I was.

He wouldn't understand because he's popular. All of the important stuff about high school came easily to him. I was sure Francine had never had to make a spreadsheet for him.

"I mean, you're Franny's best friend," he started, "and I promised her I'd look out for you this summer, but—"

"Look out for me?" I interrupted. I buried my face in my hands. God, Francine! She knew I would fail. She knew I was hopeless without her and that I'd need her boyfriend to bail me out. "I'm so pathetic," I whispered.

Famous last words.

Tanner stayed quiet, silently agreeing with my last statement. He took another long drag on the straw. Soon there was the gurgling noise you hear when you reach the bottom. As if that was his cue, he started the car and headed for my house.

When he pulled into my driveway, I noticed both cars were parked there. I suddenly panicked. "How am I going to get by my parents?"

Tanner gave me an unsympathetic look. "It's only nine o'clock," he said. "You smell like greasy fries. Just do a lot of yawning and head straight to your bedroom."

I stayed in the car, not trusting my legs.

Tanner relaxed. He reached out and touched my shoulder. "Hey, look," he said, his voice softer. "It's going to be okay. And when I see Franny next week, I won't mention a thing about tonight."

I stiffened. "What?"

"She invited me," he said. "I'll be there four or five days." He sniffed, then leaned back in his seat. "She figured you wouldn't be able to get the time off work. But like I said, I won't tell her about your screw-up tonight—you know, save you the embarrassment."

His tone struck a chord with my memory. An image of Brooke leaning in and whispering in his ear gave me a little backbone. I shook his hand off my shoulder. "*My* screw-up?"

"Kelsey." He said it long and laboriously, like it was tough for him to even explain the intricacy of the situation. "Never mind, you don't get it." He reached across me and opened the passenger door.

Holy geez, he had long arms!

I stepped out of the car and stood solidly on my two feet. The fact that I couldn't feel the rotation of the earth encouraged me. I leaned back into the car, still holding onto the door with one hand. I'm not sure if it was the need to avenge all the jilted women of the world, or if I was jealous of Tanner and wanted to lay claim to Francine. But the next words came out strong and clear, hardly the slobbering screw-up from the party.

"Actually, Tanner, I do get it," I said. "I wouldn't want Brooke hanging off *my* boyfriend's body. And it may have been totally innocent like you said, but Francine should be the judge of that. So you can tell her about my screw-up tonight and everything else, because you can be damn sure I'll be telling her about you."

I ended my speech by slamming the car door. I marched inside my house expecting to hear tires squeal down the street, but he simply backed out and drove away. Apparently I was the only one auditioning for drama queen tonight.

So much for my victim-impact statement. *Maybe I should just keep my mouth shut from now on.* Monologues didn't seem to be working for me lately.

Dad was sitting at the dining room table, making piles of paper slips. *Bit early for getting things together for tax time,* I thought. Dad barely lifted his head. "Chet just fell asleep," he said.

I waited for him to ask me how my night was. I even yawned, but he was already engrossed in some budgeting scheme. I wondered if this had something to do with the tutoring program at the library. Realizing I'd been given a gift, I went straight to my bedroom.

I could hear Mom clicking away on the keyboard inside her office. I blinked at my bedroom ceiling, unable to stop replaying all the catastrophes of the night. What the hell was wrong with me? A girl puts her hand on Tanner's shoulder and I accuse him of cheating on Francine?

Sleep wasn't coming easily. I pulled out my laptop and stared at the spreadsheet. Unfortunately, "Throw up on Blaine" wasn't part of Operation Tongue.

My eyes welled up. I had no chance with Blaine, I had pissed off Tanner, mortified Chloe, and Francine, my best friend, hadn't even considered inviting me up to her cottage.

A creak sounded outside my bedroom door. The doorknob started to turn. I slammed down the laptop, threw the covers up to my chin, and rolled onto my stomach.

Mom tiptoed in. She whispered my name. I did the long, slow breathing of someone pretending to be asleep. Her fingers gently combed through my hair, then she left, gently shutting the door behind her.

I wished I could tell her about my night. The words were in my head, all jumbled up. I opened my mouth, but only a creaking sound came out. All I needed was to hear her say it wasn't my fault and that things would be better tomorrow. But I knew she'd be upset about the drinking, and I'd get another lecture about responsibility. I pressed my lips together and cried into my pillow.

THE NEXT MORNING, I was woken by the roar of a lawn mower. It stayed under my bedroom window for longer than necessary. Mom must have smelled booze on me last night and told Dad, who felt the proper punishment was attacking my sense of hearing.

My head was throbbing and I was starving. I took some Tylenol and ate half a loaf of toast and peanut butter. Chet and Mom had already left the house for the Sunday flea market. The lawn mower finally stopped. I jumped in the shower to avoid crossing paths with Dad. By the time I was ready for work, the lawn was done and Dad had disappeared as well.

I pulled on shorts and a T-shirt, deciding to leave my wet hair down to dry. Who cares what your hair looks like when you can pile it under your nightcap at work? I could even have a mohawk and no one would know. The image made me cringe, remembering How-hole's pitying expression.

I wish I'd gotten drunk enough to forget everything. No such luck, though. I grabbed the bottle of Tylenol to take to work, then rummaged around my room looking for my Kipling bag.

Bacon turds!

My stomach took a nosedive. I had left my bag on the floor of Edward's study. My yellow gorilla! I could never get it back. The only—very small—consolation was that I hadn't had my wallet with me last night. Having the owner of the Queen's Galley arrive at work with my bag would be too humiliating. Mr. Deveau would probably set up a video camera to catch the whole thing live.

I grabbed an old backpack and dragged my sorry butt outside. My bike was waiting in the driveway, another form of silent punishment from my parents.

It was warm and sunny and the stupid birds were singing. Didn't they know how crappy this summer was? I paused at the top of the steep hill, the Queen's Galley waiting below. I used my brakes the whole way down. My hair didn't even flow off my shoulders, let alone fly straight behind me.

I locked my bike in the driveway by the kitchen. I frowned; usually How-hole's bike was there too, but this morning it was missing. In the kitchen, Loretta and Clyde were deep into Sunday brunch preparations.

"...that crazy dog, last night," Clyde said, whipping the scrambled eggs like they deserved it.

"Dog?" My heart rate sped up. Had Cujo-the-land-shark come back? What had it destroyed with its massive teeth and paws this time? The theme from *Jaws* played in the back of my mind.

Loretta had her upper body all the way in the fridge, reaching to the back. "The driveway was covered in shredded garbage this morning," she told me. She pulled out a long container of bacon slices, then closed the door with her foot.

"Maybe it's only a raccoon," I suggested.

"No," Loretta said, laying strips of bacon on the flat grill. She sprinkled a mixture of flour and brown sugar on top. "It's definitely a dog. Raccoons are cleaner."

"This beast roams freely throughout the night." Clyde had a flare for the dramatic too.

Maybe I should party with him from now on.

Loretta snorted. "It's not a werewolf."

"Werewolf?" I shuddered. Don't even get me started.

"Talk with Luke," Clyde ordered Loretta. "He must lock all the garbage in the shed from now on."

Music thumped from the driveway outside. I peeked through the kitchen window. A red sports car had pulled up. How-hole stepped out of the passenger's side. The mohawk was gone, and the usual ball cap was back in place. He waved at the driver as the car backed up and pulled away.

I couldn't see the hummingbird tattoo, but I still recognized Brooke. How-hole straightened up and looked in the kitchen window. I ducked back just in time.

I carried a weird hollow feeling around for the rest of the shift. I decided it was best to avoid the kitchen as much as possible. Whenever I had a tray of dirty dishes, I pushed through the swinging door making sure to keep my head down. I stared at the coffee-stained cups and smeared plates. How-hole moved in the corner of my vision. His hand reached out and helped me with my tray a few times, but other than that contact he seemed as reluctant as I was for us to acknowledge each other.

He must have been too embarrassed for me, or maybe he was like Tanner, bored with my outbursts and screw-ups.

Julia and Ronnie were the only other girls working. Chloe had the day off. My stomach tightened. I wanted to know if she hated me for being such a loser at the party. Tanner's remarks about never getting invited to another party had hurt me more than I'd let on.

Plus, I hadn't let him finish his sentence last night: *You're Franny's best friend and I promised her I'd look out for you this summer, but...*

But...what?

> When breaking up with a friend you say, "I promised to look out for you this summer, but...
>
> A.   you're killing my social status and I don't want to be seen with you anymore."
> B.   I'm breaking up with Franny to date Brooke so you can flounder on your own from now on."
> C.   I never liked you and I'm going to convince Franny to drop you as a friend."

Sometimes I hate having multiple choices.

EIGHTEEN

Brunch turned out to be crazy busy and the staff worked non-stop. It was a buffet where everyone served themselves, so I mainly brought out coffee and tea orders, and of course cleared away the dirty dishes. But I was grateful to have something to keep my mind busy instead of replaying last night's episode of *Kelsey's Moment of Shame*.

It was so hot I was downing ice water in the pantry after every table-clearing. More than once I thought I smelled vodka. I think it was oozing through my pores.

Yup, that's me: one classy lady.

After the shift, while Ronnie and Julia were counting up tips—and more importantly figuring out my ten percent—Mr. Deveau marched into the dining room where I was setting tables for the supper crowd. His outrageously bright coral shirt made me blink a few times. He started with the usual enquiries:

"Silverware polished?" he asked.

"Yes."

"Floors swept?"

"Yes."

"Napkins and tablecloths counted?"

I hesitated. "Um…no. Not yet."

He looked satisfied. "Good, I suggest you get started." He checked his watch. "The laundry needs to be ready in an hour for pickup."

I nodded curtly and made my way to the basement door.

Frickin' bacon turds! I hated counting the linen. Chloe usually volunteered for this task, but since I was the only busgirl today, the job was mine.

I went down the stairs to the basement where the laundry shoot emptied. I pushed open the heavy door and a wave of dampness escaped. Unlike the rest of the Queen's Galley, this area was untouched by a decorator's palette. I kept the door open with my foot while I stretched my reach inside the darkened room. I found the thin chain and pulled. A single light bulb glowed, bringing the creepy room to life.

The walls were the original stones used by Captain Bowsky's crew to build the foundation. The cool air was nice at first after having worked in a sultry restaurant in a long skirt, but one look at the huge pile of dirty linen overshadowed any silver lining.

I pulled a tablecloth from the mound and laid it out flat on the stone floor. Then I counted out fifty napkins, tossing each one into the middle of the tablecloth. I tied up the four corners of the tablecloth making a thick knot and then rolled the bundle to the doorway. I straightened up and heard my back crack.

Or was it a squeak?

I whipped my head around, squinting into the dark corners. Julia told me she once saw a rat down here. I tucked my skirt between my legs, then loudly cleared my throat. I read somewhere that rats don't like noise. I proceeded to stomp my feet, whistle, snort, and cough as much as possible while I counted the next batch of napkins.

It took longer this time since I kept stopping to look in the direction of every noise.

Rats like to attack from behind, I bet. First the ravenous dog and now this? I should get danger pay.

It couldn't be a rat, I tried to tell myself. Julia was just trying to scare me. Besides, a rat would be wary of a smelly busgirl, right? I glanced around the room again, hoping to find a stick or something, but there wasn't even a loose stone to throw.

Squeak.

One of the napkins moved.

I screamed and lunged for the bundle of linen by the door. I grabbed the thick knot and swung it over my head, ready to crush my assailant. I heard a *pop!* and the room suddenly went pitch black. Glass shards scattered on the floor around my shoes.

I'd hit the light bulb by mistake.

Squeak.

My fight-or-flight response kicked in and I started blindly whacking the floor. Something scratched my ankle. I swore with the gusto of ten pirates and pounded the ground even harder. "Die, die, die!"

I had no idea I was so brave.

The door burst open, sending a splash of light into the room. I froze, bent over with the linen bag spilling its dirty napkins. I squinted at How-hole's outline. Neither of us spoke; even the rat stayed quiet.

When it was apparent no one was being murdered—well, at least the two-legged variety anyway—he said, "Need help?" It came out so easily, like a commercial jingle that rolled off the tongue.

Ignoring his aloofness, I dropped the linen and pushed past him to freedom. Only once I slammed the door behind us could I find my voice. "Rat," I said breathlessly. Then I recounted my close encounter of the creepy-critter kind.

How-hole stayed quiet, letting me blabber on. It was hard to tell if he was taking me seriously because it was impossible for me to make eye contact. I flicked my gaze between his chin and his forehead. My insides were in knots, wondering what he must think of me. Two mortifying moments within twenty-four hours must be a record.

He simply nodded, then told me to wait. He returned quickly with a small tool kit and what looked like a humongous mousetrap. He'd taken off his usual white apron and was wearing a green T-shirt underneath. It had a logo of a giant "V" with two dudes in a canoe. "Nova Scotia Voyageurs" was written across the top.

Was How-hole part of a portage club or something? It didn't make sense for him to practice a serene sport. He seemed like more of a whitewater rafting kind of guy.

Within minutes, How-hole had replaced the light bulb and cleaned up the remnants of the broken one. There was a relaxed confidence about him as he fixed my mess. I found myself staring at his hands while he worked.

"Thanks," I said.

"No problem." Then he sat on the stairs and hung out while I continued working on my linen bundles in the safety of the well-lit and rat-free hallway. I had to admit, a calm sense of relief had settled nicely in my nervous stomach. We were talking again and it wasn't weird or forced.

"It's steaming hot today," he said.

"Seriously." I counted off ten more napkins.

He fiddled with a pair of pliers. "Looks like Loretta's curried chicken was a hit with the brunch crowd."

"Ronnie had to refill the heating pan *five times!*" I raised my voice at the end like I was giving him the most awesome news in the world. When had I become so excited about curried chicken? I realized this was the most fun I'd had all day.

It was nice being with How-hole this way. When I was around Blaine, I couldn't form a sentence without stammering. It was almost painful sometimes, the ache to impress him.

I pulled at the corners of the last tablecloth and made a tight knot. I surveyed my five bundles all ready for the laundry dude. How-hole joined me up the stairs, the tool box tucked under his arm.

I was grateful he hadn't brought up last night. I hoped my outburst wasn't as bad as I remembered. Perhaps someone else had done something even more embarrassing later, conveniently pushing my performance to the back of everyone's memory. The possibility gave me comfort.

We reached the top of the stairs and sauntered across the dinning room toward the kitchen. "You know what bothers me the most though," I said, now confident enough to look at him directly. "When people leave that one last bite on the plate. How could they not have room for that one last bite?"

He looked confused.

I continued, "Sometimes it's even on the fork. Why would someone put the last piece of chocolate cake, or baked potato, or even chicken curry on their fork, and then just leave it there?"

How-hole seemed to contemplate this as we pushed through the swinging kitchen door. Clyde had left, but Loretta was in the back corner, organizing tubs of condiments in the fridge. She was humming to herself, totally immersed in the task.

We stopped by the salad station. He leaned his back against the counter, one foot gingerly crossed over the other. "Maybe they've realized their limit and don't want to spoil a good thing," he said.

I put a hand on one hip. "There's no way one bite could ruin the whole meal," I said, unconvinced. "I think people who leave the last bite are masochists or something. It's like they're bragging about being able to deny themselves satisfaction."

A flash of mischief crossed his face. "Masochists?"

I rolled my eyes. "Geez, what is it with you twisting my words!" I fought the smile that was tugging at the corner of my mouth. I did a pretend huff to prove I was unaffected by his wit. "I feel badly for that last piece. Why wasn't it good enough to eat too? I mean, it's right in front of them, waiting to be taken."

"Maybe they're full," he said. "You're making it too complicated. The most logical answer is usually the right one."

I gave up. "Whatever."

He pushed off the counter and went over to a row of low cupboards by the window. "Or maybe," he started, "people don't want the thing that's right in front of them."

I crinkled up my nose. "That makes no sense," I said to his back. "If they didn't want it, why did they order it in the first place?" I added one of my snorts to prove my point. I'd won this argument. I glanced across the room. Loretta was on her knees, still singing into the fridge, totally ignoring us.

How-hole bent down and reached into one of the cupboards, then pulled out my Kipling bag.

My reaction was immediate and totally genuine. I took the bag from him and hugged it to my chest. "No way! Thank you!" I was so happy to see my fuzzy yellow gorilla I forgot to be embarrassed by the reminder of last night.

He looked pleased, his blue ocean eyes twinkling back at me. My stomach swooped a bit and I wondered if I still had some alcohol left in my system.

"I hope you don't mind," he said. "I tallied your quiz." He gave me a grin. "Interesting results." In his other hand he held up my magazine.

Happy feeling, gone.

I hugged the bag tighter. "You don't know anything about me," I told him. If anyone was a master at these quizzes, it was me.

He pointed to my face. "I know your nostrils do that weird thing when you get nervous."

I ignored his comment, but stayed quiet. I felt like we were approaching a potentially awkward moment. And I'd had my fill of those lately, thank you very much. I didn't want to talk about last night with him. I wished we could keep talking about dirty dishes or anything else that didn't make me sound like a total mess.

But How-hole wasn't dropping the subject that easily. "All the answers are in your magazine," he said. Then he flipped to the dog-eared page. He stared at me, waiting for my answer. "Aren't you even curious which kind of guy is your best match?" His tone was completely serious, not even a hint of teasing.

Even though I'd spent the last half hour in the cold basement, a prickle of heat moved over my skin. My mouth went dry. I hadn't realized how close we were standing. His Adam's apple moved up and down.

I nodded.

He cleared his throat and began to read: "*You are attracted to the guy who makes you explore the edge of your comfort zone, but you're no risk-taker. Only the guy who can make you feel safe and appreciated will help you conquer your fears."*

I frowned. That didn't sound like me at all. "I was drunk when I did that," I quietly defended. "Stupid thought process."

"More like uninhibited thought process." He rolled up the magazine and passed it to me. "This was your brain on truth serum."

Whoomp, there it is. Finally.

This is what I'd been dreading all shift. How-hole had been waiting to spring this little nugget of extra humiliation to make fun of me.

"No," I rebutted, a little more strongly this time, "more like moron serum. Besides, I couldn't care less what you think."

"Ah, but your nostrils tell a different story." He gave me a grin, then put his hands in his shorts pockets. "We can talk about it more tomorrow," he said. Then he made his way to the back door.

I stayed in place, watching him leave. He paused at the screen door, one hand resting on the handle. "Just for the record, though, Kels," he said, "I'll let you keep your name after we get married." Then he flashed me another grin and disappeared down the porch steps.

I looked down at the magazine and flipped to the quiz. I closed my eyes and groaned. I had written *Mrs. Kelsey Mulder* all over the page.

A new level of terror hit me in the gut.

Does he even know Blaine? Did he show the magazine to everyone at the party?

Warning bells were going off in my head. *I* was supposed to be the one who told Blaine how I felt, not some fellow partygoer.

Besides, I needed that check mark.

I raced out the back door. How-hole had just left the driveway and was walking toward the yacht club.

"Hey," I called out. I lifted up one edge of my skirt and jogged after him. He waited by the picket fence, looking more amused than curious. The white cap blew off my head and landed in the dirt by my bike.

I slowed down my last steps, coming up to him slightly out of breath. I was unsure how to word the next bit delicately, so I just came out and asked him. "Did you know most of the people at the party last night?"

"No," he replied without hesitating. "But that's the way most parties are."

"Oh." There were several beats of silence. But his answer gave me a little hope. "Okay, good."

He glanced over his shoulder toward the yacht club, then back to me. "What are you doing now? Are you free this afternoon?" He ran a hand through his bicoloured hair.

Free?

My stomach swooped again. *One minute he's making fun of me for doodling my pretend married name and now he's asking me out? Is he asking me out?*

My nerves didn't know whether to be excited or terrified.

He started to say something else, but a horn blared from across the street catching his attention. "Luke!" Brooke waved from her car, all smiles and designer sunglasses. "Need a lift?" she hollered out.

I self-consciously smoothed a strand of hair down the side of my face, hoping to disguise myself. How-hole turned to me, the question still written on his face.

Are you free?

Was he making fun of me or was he serious? This guy was so infuriating! Stupid How-hole and his stupid sexy eyes and stupid manly hands.

Focus, Kelsey! Friendly, yet formal.

I forced myself to meet his gaze. "Um…no," I said. "I'm not free."

He held my stare a few beats longer than was comfortable, then said, "See you around, then." He jogged across the street to his ride. I glanced quickly at Brooke, who was busy tapping out a rhythm on the steering wheel. She either didn't recognize me or had forgotten about my impersonation of a crazy local.

I dragged my feet back to my bike. My cap lay on the ground, discarded and forgotten. The sound of Brooke's car faded away behind me. My fingers were slow working the bike lock. Everything felt heavy.

"Who cares if he likes Brooke?" I said quietly. I picked up my bonnet and shoved it into my Kipling bag. "Blaine is my perfect match, not someone who…" I paused and dug out the quiz again, *"helps me explore the edge of my comfort zone."*

But no one answered. It was just me, standing alone in the driveway.

It sucks to be the last bite left on the plate.

NINETEEN

"Stretch out your arms," I said. "Pretend you're a starfish, just like your instructor told you."

Chet was floating on his back with his arms and legs wiggling for balance. My palm was gently pushing up on the base of his spine. We were hanging out in the shallow end of the lido, waiting for Mom to show up.

As long as I can see bottom and the water doesn't rise above my knees, I can keep my fear in check. This is how much I love Chet. I'm not sure if I'd even go into the pool for Blaine.

Chet's fingers and toes pointed outward. "Good job," I said. "Keep still." Then I slowly moved my hand away from his back. Chet's tummy sank into the water and he started flailing.

He garbled in the splashes. I had him in my arms instantly, wiping the drips from his goggles. He coughed a few times.

"No worries, Chetter-cheese," I said. "You'll float one day." I gave him a smile.

His wet, pudgy body tucked into mine leaving damp spots on my T-shirt and cut-offs. I carried him to the edge of the pool.

He hugged my neck, practically choking me. I was worried for him. There were only a few lessons left before badge day.

I'm not a swimming instructor, not by a long shot, but Chet looked like he wasn't going to get a badge. Mom said as long as he was having fun it was worth it, but I knew Chet wanted that badge. He told me stickers were for babies, and you know what, he was right.

I sat down on the bleachers by our stuff and wrapped a towel around Chet's shoulders. He put a hand on my cheek turning my face toward his. "I'm bad," he said. "I give up."

His tone broke my heart. "What happens when toad wants to give up?" I asked.

"Owed can swim."

"Of course he can, he's a toad. He just doesn't want people to see him in his bathing suit. But what about all the other times when Toad wants to quit or he gets all grumpy. What happens then?"

He poked his belly button with his finger. "Fwog," he simply answered.

"Exactly," I beamed. "And I'm your frog. I won't let you give up."

He looked unconvinced.

"Besides," I said. "Your bathing suit rocks, you're the coolest kid here." A little smirk played at the edge of his mouth. "I know a secret," I teased him. "The Shake Shack is giving away free triple-scoop ice cream for every kid with a swim sticker."

His eyes grew wide. Chet's kryptonite was ice cream.

"But you still have to finish your lessons before you get that sticker, okay?"

"Okay." He wiggled from my side, then dug into his backpack for a juice box.

I scanned the top of the stairs looking for Mom, but my eye caught the green-haired kid's mom. I could tell she'd been watching me and Chet the whole time. She waved and I smiled back. It was nice to be noticed while being good instead of caught in my usual screw-ups.

This week was a milestone for both Chet and myself. He would be finishing his first session of swimming lessons and I would be getting my first paycheque. It was hard to believe I'd been at the Queen's Galley for almost two weeks. The last few days alone seemed like a summer's worth.

There had been zero Blaine sightings. Although this was a fact I wasn't too upset about. The last time I'd seen the guy, I sprayed his feet with my supper. I hadn't thought of a witty excuse for my actions yet.

And How-hole seemed to be taking a page out of my own rule book by keeping things "friendly, yet formal." I couldn't figure this reckless thrill-seeker out. He almost, sort of, asked me out, then picked Brooke two seconds after I turned him down.

Her red car had dropped him off twice since then—not that I'd noticed…I just happened to be arriving for work at the same time. She always smiled and waved at me. I was sure they were both laughing their asses off, making fun of me when I wasn't looking.

And who could blame them? I was sure How-hole was waiting for my next disaster at work.

When Mom finally arrived at the lido that day, I had barely enough time to make it to work. "Where were you?" I asked her, throwing Chet's backpack in the car.

She tucked a stray clump of hair behind her ear. "The bank," she answered, making brief eye contact.

I stood beside the driver's door while she buckled up Chet. I'd been keeping things superficially complacent since the party. Mom and Dad hadn't said anything to me about it, and I was happy to fly under the radar and pretend I hadn't come home smelling of vodka. But this time I really needed Mom's attention.

She hurried over and opened the driver's door.

I took a quick breath. "Hey," I said. "Badge day is coming up."

"Yes." Her hand was on the door handle.

I dropped my voice and leaned in closer. "Can Chet have some private lessons? He's so close to completing his skills, but he just needs a little more instruction."

Mom's eyebrows knitted together. She hadn't put any makeup on this morning and her blouse was wrinkled. When had she become such a slob? At least she wasn't in slippers this time.

"Please," I begged her. "This is really important to him."

Her fingers tapped on the door handle. "How much would private lessons cost?"

"I don't know," I said. "Maybe twenty or thirty dollars. Does that really matter?"

Mom glanced at her watch, then peeked at the backseat. Chet was flipping through *Frog and Toad Are Friends*.

She let out one of her famous long, tired sighs. "Oh, Kelsey," she began, "he's enjoying himself. Don't set his expectations too high, he'll only be disappointed." She slipped into the car and shut the door. Her window rolled down. "If you're so concerned about it, why don't you teach him? What time are you finished work today?"

My face fell. A numbness overtook my body.

Mom read my expression. "I guess that's a no," she said. I stayed mute, shocked that she'd actually forgotten what had happened to me. "Call Dad if you need a drive after work," she instructed.

I stayed, zombie-like, staring after her hatchback as she turned onto the road and disappeared up the steep hill.

With a black cloud of gloom hanging around me, I made my way to work. I saw How-hole's bike up against the kitchen porch. The fog lifted a little. I trudged up the front steps of the Queen's Galley.

I came in from the bright sun and had to let my eyes adjust to the inside of the foyer. Someone giggled in the holding bar. I squinted at the couple in the dark corner. Their arms were around each other. His deep voice was soft enough that I couldn't hear his words, but the tone was enough to make me blush. My eyes grew wide. Chloe had already changed into her uniform and was up on tiptoe. He leaned down and met her kiss halfway.

I took a step back, partially hiding behind the corner. The floorboard creaked under my feet, but Chloe and her partner didn't even miss a beat. They were so entwined it actually looked like they were melting into each other.

It certainly seemed to be getting hot enough for things to melt. I was about to cough and pretend I'd just walked in when they finally parted. She whispered something in his ear, then he gave her a kiss on the forehead.

He stepped away from the embrace and made his way toward the front door. He caught my eye and winked when he passed by. "Hey," he said, not even a hint of embarrassment.

My cheeks, however, were flaming. "Oh, hey Sam," I replied, busy pretending to look in my Kipling bag.

Chloe came around the corner and joined me beside the massive flower arrangement in the foyer. I think "glowing" would describe her current appearance.

I had never glowed like that.

"Any chance you can stay late today?" she asked, her gaze trailing after Sam as he walked to his car.

My finger was twirling nervously around the fuzzy gorilla's tail. "Yeah, I guess so."

Chloe broke her attention away from Sam and smiled at me. "It would be great if I could get away early this shift." The smiled turned hopeful.

"You and Sam have a date?" I guessed.

Her eyes twinkled when she nodded. "We're taking his family's boat out to an island for supper." She started to look all dreamy, then she caught herself. "It's just a campfire on the beach with hotdogs on sticks, but..." She grinned again, ending the sentence.

"I get it," I said. "Sam is hot. Sure, I can cover for you."

Who am I to stand in the way of true love?

Chloe gave me a quick hug. "Thanks, Kelsey. I'll repay the favour."

Secretly, I was thrilled inside. Chloe was becoming a real bud. And I wasn't in awe of her because she was popular, but because she always seemed on top of stuff, confident, and smart.

I had been worried she'd never want to talk to me after my humiliating speech at the party, but the next shift we worked together she'd taken me aside and asked how I was doing. She told me not to worry, and that people had done much worse at parties. She then gave me a friendly lecture, emphasizing that if I ever go to another party, I have to promise to stick to beer, drink slowly, and never wander off by myself.

I told her she should write a handbook, then I mentioned I'd never party again anyway, so no worries.

"I wouldn't be so sure," she'd said. There was a coquettish tone in her voice that made me suspicious.

Now, as we were standing in the foyer basking in her post-makeout glow, I realized she was someone who probably had loads of tips on relationships. I bet she would score high on the "Are You Good at Giving Advice?" quiz.

The lunch crowd was steady. I must have refilled a thousand water glasses. Every one was ordering salads and lobster sandwiches, certainly nothing from the oven. Loretta's chilled, marinated pasta dish with olives and slivers of seared flank steak was the special. Mr. Deveau had suggested she call it "Bowsky's Bowl." Julia rolled her eyes at his back. There were tight-lipped expressions around the kitchen. Clyde's pencil-thin moustache twitched. We sold a lot of Loretta's special that lunch shift, but I never heard Julia utter the words "Bowsky's Bowl" once.

It was close to the end of the lunch shift, three tables were on dessert, and one group of middle-aged tourists were finishing up their main course. A travel guide to the South Shore was sticking out of one woman's purse.

I was hovering like a vulture, ready to clear away the dishes. Chloe had been hopping around all afternoon, checking her watch fifty million times. Mr. Deveau was strict about the staff:patron ratio. I wanted to clear out this crowd so she could leave early for her rendezvous with Sam. She had been so nice to me, this was the least I could do for her.

I puttered around the dining room, smoothing out table-cloths and placing candles on the tables for the supper shift, waiting for the signs that my table was done.

After almost two weeks as a busgirl, I could predict when people were ready for the bill: laying their napkin across the plate, leaning back in the chair, taking that last sip of water.

I approached the table of tourists with my busgirl smile firmly in place. "How was everything?" I asked, taking away their dishes.

"Just lovely," they praised.

"I'm so glad," I said. (Insert bigger busgirl smile.)

I stacked the dirty plates on the tray waiting on the stand against the wall. I glanced at the last plate. She'd left one olive. "Are you finished?" I asked the woman.

Her white visor turned up to me. "Yes, thank you," she said, leaning back so I could take the plate.

I stared at the olive, impaled on the end of her fork.

"Are you *sure*?" I nettled. A little sarcasm snuck out by mistake.

Julia came up behind me, and I felt a gentle nudge in my side. She took my place, offering them dessert menus. "You'll be sorry if you leave without trying the raspberry cheesecake." She winked at the faces around the table.

I sheepishly took the last plate away and carried the teetering tray of dirty dishes into the kitchen.

How-hole was wiping off the counter that ran alongside the massive industrial dishwasher. A half-filled tray of dirty plates and saucers sat on the stainless-steel track. He looked up when I plunked down my tray.

"This is the last of the main course," I told him. "A few tables are still on dessert, though."

"Thanks," he said.

I wanted to think of something witty. It had been so busy today, I'd barely spent any time in the kitchen.

I waved a hand at the lone olive. "Told you," I said, wondering if he'd remember.

He sadly shook his head. "That's unacceptable," he said.

"Exactly," I smiled. I helped him fill the dishwasher rack. Under his apron, I noticed he was wearing the T-shirt with the canoe dudes again. My hands were jammed inside my pockets fiddling with the bits of paper and peppermint wrappers. "So," I started nodding to his T-shirt, "you like the outdoors?"

He hefted the loaded dish rack into the washer, then slid down the door and hit a few buttons. How-hole was kind of on the skinny side, but the ease with which he moved those heavy racks around made me a little light-headed. He wiped his hands off with a dishtowel. "Sure," he said.

I counted to five in my head, hoping he would elaborate, but he stayed quiet. We had a staring contest, but instead of waiting for the other to blink we were waiting for the other to talk. A half grin was pulling at the edge of his mouth.

The Cellophane wrappers crackling in my pocket gave away my nerves. I focused on keeping my nostrils still.

"Here, Luke." Loretta plunked a half-litre container of what looked like "Bowsky's Bowl." "Make this disappear for me, handsome."

"Consider it done," he said. "Thanks."

"Anytime," she sang back, already moving to the salad station, focused on the next task.

I looked at the container and then at How-hole. His cheeks were rosier than usual. "Late lunch?" I asked.

He sniffed and pushed the container to the side. "Supper," he simply said. "My dad travels a lot."

"Oh." The silent staring contest was about to start again. "Well," I said, "it beats my dad's macaroni and cheese. It's always runny," I explained. "And sometimes the bread crumbs on top get scorched." I rocked back on my heels, wishing I hadn't started this topic. "Chet likes it though. So, yeah."

I don't think there has ever been lamer conversation in the history of lame conversations.

"He's cute," he said.

I smiled. "He knows it, too. He uses his charm to get whatever he wants." I paused. "Even scorched macaroni and cheese."

He bent down, leaning on his elbows, looking up at me. "So," he started, "what do you want?" He didn't say it in the way Julia or Ronnie would ask a patron what they would like off the menu. His suggestive tone hinted at something more than "Bowsky's Bowl."

My face grew warm. This was becoming a habit. How did he manage to turn the most innocent conversation into Confession 101?

The answer was on the end of my tongue, but I refused to say it out loud. My heart was pounding. I held my breath, clutching a fistful of wrappers. "It doesn't matter what I want," I said. I grabbed my tray and pushed through the swinging door back into the dining room.

Julia was serving a round of cheesecake to the tourists. I spied Chloe clearing the last of the tables in her section.

My hands were jittery. I swallowed a few times. "Hey, Chloe," I said. "Julia and I can handle that last table. I'll do the linen count and everything. You can take off."

"Thanks," she beamed. "I owe you." She stacked a couple of coffee cups on her tray.

"Um, hey," I said, scooping up the dirty flatware. "How did you meet Sam?" I asked.

She slipped off her cap. "He was a year ahead of me at school. We knew each other, but our paths didn't cross so much."

I frowned. Now that she mentioned it, Sam did look a little familiar. I guess my popularity radar only went up so many grades.

She lightly laughed. "He was kind of a jock in high school, but he's really filled out since he went to university."

"No kidding."

"Anyway, he's home for the summer and we just started hanging out again." She smiled then turned, ready to change for her date.

I jogged after her. "Wait," I stopped and looked around, making sure a certain dishwasher wasn't hanging out in the holding bar. I leaned in closer, "How do you know Sam is worth it? I mean, how do you know he's the right guy for you?"

God love Chloe. She didn't laugh or give me a look full of pity. She only said one word: "Butterflies."

My shoulders dropped. I didn't have the best luck with butterflies. When I was ten, I biked to a friend's birthday party. It was only down the road from my house. Where that butterfly came from, I'll never know, but that freak of nature fluttered right at my face and landed on my nose. I screamed and landed in the ditch, cutting open my knee. The scar is still there if you look closely enough.

"Butterflies?" I said. And I'd swear that scar on my knee stated to throb.

"You know," she laughed. "It's that funny swooping feeling you get in your stomach."

Chloe could tell I was disappointed. She put a hand on my shoulder. "The butterflies never lie," she said.

After Chloe left and the tables were cleared and prepared for the supper shift, I counted the linen in the basement, trying to remember the last time Blaine had given me stomach butterflies.

I changed into my cut-offs and T-shirt and left through the kitchen porch. How-hole's bike was gone. I glanced in the direction of the lido. A twinge of guilt pulled at my heart.

I should have taken Mom up on her offer to help Chet in the pool.

It wasn't his fault I hated the wet stuff. I could have at least helped him master the float.

Instead of calling Dad for a drive, I opted to walk home. I needed to clear my head. I was so confused about what I wanted. I needed to focus. I wished I could talk to Francine, but the thing with Tanner was too awkward to ignore and I didn't want to face that issue just yet.

Half an hour later, I was dragging my feet up our driveway. I noticed the flower beds at once. Perfect edging with fresh mulch? Who knew those marigolds Chet and I planted a month ago could look so good? Dad must have been getting his green thumb on. Chet was crouched down beside one of the shrubs, staring at a butterfly fanning its wings.

He jumped up and entwined himself around my legs. "How-hole," he said, pointing to the flower beds.

"Yeah, I get it," I told him. "I see the butterfly too." I ran a finger over my knee, looking for the bicycle-accident scar. Weird that Chet and I both think of How-hole now when we see butterflies.

Mom cleared her throat from the doorway. She'd changed into her usual overall shorts and ponytail.

Yes, overall shorts. Can you blame me for missing the fashion gene?

"Supper's almost ready," she said.

The house smelled like cheese…and burnt toast.

Great.

I slouched in my chair at the dining room table. My fork scratched around my plate while Chet bounced in his chair already asking for seconds.

"Kelsey, please eat," Mom said, not even looking up from her own plate.

"I'm not that hungry, I snacked at work all day." I pushed a few noodles around with my fork. Actually I snacked on peppermints all day, but that still counted as food to me.

Mom sighed, then took her plate out to the kitchen. She grabbed a chocolate pudding cup from the cupboard. Seconds later, the door to her office shut and the keys on her computer started tapping.

I glanced at Dad. The dark circles under his eyes would make an insomniac look radiant by comparison. He caught my eye and nodded to my neglected supper. "Just finish it, honey," he said tiredly.

I thought about How-hole and his little bucket of "Bowsky's Bowl." Was he eating by himself tonight? I pictured him hanging out on the couch in front of his television, the bucket of pasta in one hand and a fork in the other. My mouth watered.

The funny thing is I don't even like olives.

I suddenly had an idea. I shovelled the rest of my supper into my mouth—even the very last bite on the fork—and went straight to my room. I closed the door and opened my laptop.

Mom's keys had stopped momentarily. I heard the *squeak* of her office chair. I put my earbuds in and started listening to my summer playlist. Hedley came on and I turned it up.

The lyrics to "Kiss You Inside Out" filled the space in my head. I started my search engine and typed in "Nova Scotia Voyageurs."

After checking out the top sites it was obvious I was a dummy. The Voyageurs wasn't a canoe club; it was an old hockey team that was once based in Halifax. What the heck was a thrill-seeking risk-taker doing wearing vintage sports logos?

I went on Facebook and typed in "Luke+Nova Scotia Voyageurs." I had no idea what How-hole's last name was, but maybe he played hockey somewhere and was in a team photo.

I must have looked at a billion photos of guys named Luke, but none of them were How-hole. I rubbed my eyes with my palms. I pulled the earbuds out; the playlist was getting on my nerves.

My bedroom door creaked open. Dad stuck his head in.

"Does Chet want me?" I automatically asked.

Dad shook his head. "He's been asleep for a while. He's had a full day."

"Oh," I said, remembering all the yardwork they'd done this afternoon. "The flower beds look nice, Dad."

"What? Oh, they do don't they." He sounded confused.

What the hell was going on with him?

"Lights out, Kels," he said, nodding to my Snoopy alarm clock.

Lights out? What am I a baby or something?

"Yeah, sure. Good night."

He backed up and slowly shut my door. I stayed still. Mom's keyboard was quiet.

My eyelids were heavy. I glanced at the time.

Sweet bacon turds! Midnight!

My laptop glowed back at me accusingly. I'd spent my entire evening online searching for clues about How-hole and I hadn't even looked at my spreadsheet.

I fell back in bed and stared at the ceiling.

Oh my God, I think I'm in love with How-hole.

TWENTY

I changed into my uniform and filled the water pitchers with ice. It was going to be another stinking hot day. I'd helped Chet practice his float a bit after his lesson and was still enjoying the coolness of the lido. This time, Mom had been early and she'd watched us from the bleachers. She'd ridden my bike down so I wouldn't have to call home for a drive after my shift. It was an uncomfortable gesture. I'd never asked her to bring my bike. I wondered if she needed the car for something else and wasn't telling me.

Mr. Deveau paraded into the holding bar and handed out our paycheques. He was certainly dressed up for the occasion— white and blue-striped pants with a white crewneck sweater, topped off with a silk navy scarf, knotted twice in the front.

I ripped open my envelope.

"Don't look at the gross amount," Julia advised, "just the net. It's too depressing to see what you actually earned."

Mr. Deveau glared at Julia. "When you're done dissecting the tax system, give the brass bell in the bar a good polish," he said. "We want everything perfect when Edward returns."

We watched him make his way to the kitchen. "Aye, aye, Cap'n," Julia said.

Ronnie giggled, then gave me a nudge. "I remember my first payday," she said. "Are you going to buy something special to celebrate?"

I thought of my holey Toms. "Maybe shoes," I answered.

"Oh, excellent choice," Ronnie beamed.

Julia moaned about polishing the bell. "I swear," she complained. "Mr. D. lies awake at night thinking of extra mindless chores for us to do." She mimicked his voice. "We want everything perfect when Edward, my love, returns."

Ronnie laughed, but the image of Edward abandoning his family to start a new life with someone half his age gave me the queasies.

"I heard he left his wife," I said quietly. I folded my cheque and slipped it into my apron pocket, a little embarrassed by my ability to gossip so easily.

Julia was unaffected. "Meh," she said. "Whatever. I'm sure it wasn't a shock. Most people know when someone is cheating on them." She leaned against the bar. "My last boyfriend was always working late, then he started going to the gym more often. He'd pick fights with me about stupid things. Finally, I broke up with him. And that's when I found out he'd been seeing someone else. He called his other girlfriend and she came by and picked up his stuff."

My jaw was on the floor. "What? Weren't you furious?"

"Of course." She gave me a funny look. "But life is like that, you know, totally unpredictable. You can't plan anything because it turns on a dime."

"No one should ever get married," I said, more to myself.

Ronnie gave me an amused expression. "*You've* never been in love."

I rolled my eyes. "*You're* the romantic type," I said. "It's easy for you to believe in love when you've got guys falling all over you."

Ronnie and Julia shared a look, then started to laugh.

"What?" I said, feeling my cheeks heat up. "You're blonde and bubbly, any guy would date you."

Ronnie composed herself. "Well, my girlfriend would agree with you on that one."

I stared at Ronnie.

She only laughed at my dumb reaction. "Like Julia said," Ronnie reminded me, "life is unpredictable. I guess some things are more fun when you discover them on your own."

I spent most of my time that day re-folding napkins and making up excuses to avoid the kitchen. I'd seen How-hole earlier when I arrived at work on my bike. He was dropped off by Brooke.

I ignored how the sight of that red car burned like an ulcer in my gut. I took this as a sign from the universe I was taking the right path.

That morning, I'd woken up determined that I, in fact, did not love How-hole, but was rather intrigued by the mystery of him. I'd even convinced myself that the stomach swoops I felt when I pictured his blue eyes were NOT butterflies, but probably nervous gas bubbles.

Most importantly, I had this simple fact to rely on: Blaine was my perfect match, always had been. Chloe may think butterflies never lie, but neither do magazines. I was pinning all my hopes on the proven psychology of *Modern Teen* and *Cosmo Chick*.

Lunch went by quickly. I pictured myself biking back home way before I was ready to enter the gloomy zone.

Between Mom's reclusive pattern and Dad's chronic fatigue syndrome—or whatever he had going on—work was far more hospitable.

Thankfully, a flurry of reservations came in for the evening crowd, and Mr. Deveau asked me to do a double shift. Loretta made up plates for Ronnie, Julia, and I from the lunch left-overs.

We met in the holding bar and ate off our laps. I warmed up a basket of bread for us. I told them about Chet and the work Mom and Dad did. I didn't say too much after that; I had an uncomfortable ache in my stomach that had nothing to do with butterflies or blue eyes.

I pushed my food around, making patterns with the rice while Ronnie and Julia talked. I stayed quiet. Things were weird at home. Julia's story about her ex-boyfriend lurked around the back of my brain, colouring every thought with a sense of foreboding.

I called the house to say I'd be working extra hours. Dad tiredly answered the phone. His only concern was me biking home late at night.

"Dad, we don't live in Vegas," I grumbled. I pictured Frank's shiny red SUV, but I shrugged off the image. It wasn't like he trolled the streets or anything—at least not on purpose.

Dad didn't put up much of a fight. I could hear Chet in the background. "Mom home?" I asked carefully.

"Yes," he said, then after a slight pause, "in her office."

He stayed silent. I said goodbye quickly. The uncomfort-able tone in his voice was freaking me out. Home was becom-ing awkward and I didn't know why.

That evening, each time I went into the kitchen, How-hole was whistling a tune.

"Have a big date planned?" I asked, making sure I was busy with the dirty dishes, and avoiding those blue eyes. I hated that he had gotten under my skin. He looked confused, probably pretending not to catch on. "Brooke picking you up after work?" I prodded.

All he did was chuckle and shake his head. "You and Brooke are nothing alike," he said.

I snorted. "Anyone can see that."

There was a crash and Clyde cursed in French. Ronnie's flower vase had slipped and fallen on the floor. I jumped. My nerves were raw. Before Loretta could order me to clean it up, I raced out of the kitchen. I was becoming a pro at avoiding conflict.

It was ten o'clock by the time every table was cleared, the floor swept, and the front door locked.

I was a walking zombie. My feet were on fire and my back was a series of tight knots. I dragged my colonial, stinky self to the kitchen. How-hole looked up from his mopping. "Hey, Kels," he said, "what are your plans for tonight?"

"To die," I answered weakly. I emptied my apron pockets. Peppermint wrappers, nubs of candles, and little paper slips from the coffee and dessert orders soon littered the counter. I started counting my ten percent from the tip money Ronnie had given me. There were a few fives and even a ten among the change. This one little thing made me smile. I could easily have a new pair of Toms if I used some of my paycheque. Mom and Dad had insisted I put at least half of everything I earned this summer in my bank account, so spending cash on fun stuff took some organizing.

How-hole was quiet. "What?" I asked. "Is there something on my face?" I wiped a hand over my forehead. I had worked a double shift in the heat; there could be broccoli stuck to my face and I wouldn't care.

"No," he simply said. "I just wondered what you were doing after work."

I straightened up. Where was he going with this? He knew I was a social moron. I pictured Brooke wishing she'd caught my rant on her iPhone. She could have a billion hits by now. The only thing popular girls want more than clothes is to be more popular. Maybe she'd convinced him to invite me to another Stunder soiree.

That's why he's being so nice to me…

My paranoia was on high alert.

I pictured Brooke in her crocheted sundress, snuggling up to How-hole on his couch with a plate of Bowsky's Bowl untouched on the coffee table in front of them.

"I doubt we'll ever party together again," I said. I wanted to sound strong like Julia, but it came out weak and tired.

His face hardened, then he looked down and began mopping again. "Guess you have another hot night planned between the covers of your magazine."

That was cruel.

My pulse started to pound in my ears. I'd had enough of his confusing remarks and staring contests. In fact I'd had enough of a lot of things, like Mom ignoring me, Francine's empty spreadsheet, and how I was always expected to be responsible but never allowed to have any fun on my own.

I slammed my hand down on the counter. "I don't care what you're doing, and you shouldn't care what I'm doing…which is nothing. Okay? Happy?" I jammed all the paper slips into the nearest garbage bag and stomped away. Let him have his date with Brooke. She could have him *and* his piercing eyes.

Julia had changed out of her uniform and retired to the bar, planning on having a few beers with her boyfriend. Loud conversations seeped through the French doors. Most of the crowd came over when the yacht club closed. Some nights the bar at the Queen's Galley didn't shut its doors until two in the morning.

I caught my reflection in the window: frumpy nightcap, pale face, black bags under the eyes. I staggered into the sitting area and plopped into the nearest chair. All I needed was to close my eyes for a bit, then I'd change and bike home.

There was a knock at the front door. "We're closed," I yelled out, my eyes still shut. The knocking came louder this time. I grunted and pushed myself out of the chair. Probably some lost drunk looking for the entrance to the bar.

I peeked through the side curtain. They knocked again. "Fu—" I jumped back. It was Blaine! I pressed my back against the door, praying for lightning to strike.

There was another knock, then finally, "Kelsey?"

Okay, he'd seen me. I had no choice but to finally face my future husband. I pulled off my cap and stuffed it into my apron pocket. I rubbed my cheeks a few times, then unlocked the door.

He smiled at me and motioned to the door frame. "Thanks," he said. "I wondered if you'd be working tonight."

I could only nod. The ability to speak had suddenly deserted me.

"Look," he started. I noticed two other guys were behind him. They must have been Stunders from the yacht club. "My friends and I were hoping you could let us into the bar."

There was always someone checking ID at the real entrance to the bar. Blaine glanced back at his friends, then took a step forward. A warm breeze came up. He smelled especially amazing tonight. Hollister should really consider renaming their scent after him.

He took another step closer to me. "You told me all I had to do was ask for you." He lifted one eyebrow. I had no idea eyebrows could be that sexy. I stayed quiet, worried to say anything: the last time I'd brushed my teeth was eight hours ago.

He looked down and wiggled his toes in his flip-flops. "And you kind of owe me for last week."

I groaned inside. "I'm sorry," I said. "I think I had the flu," I added stupidly.

He bit his lower lip, and then did this kind of half-grin, half-shrug that made me melt on the spot. He reached up and squeezed my shoulder. "No worries. I'm just glad you didn't have pizza before the party."

He laughed, his friends laughed, and by God, I laughed too! And just like that, all my worries evaporated magically.

Blaine was that kind of guy.

During our grade six track meet, Blaine had sprinted for first place in the eight-hundred-metre race. Just before the finish line, the kid in very last place, who was being lapped by everyone, tripped and fell. Instead of jumping over the kid like a human hurdle, Blaine stopped and helped him limp across the finish line.

Someone that nice deserved a small favour. And yeah, I did kind of owe him for barfing on his perfect feet. What harm could come from helping a guy so forgiving and thoughtful?

I led Blaine and his friends to the French doors near the patio and unlocked them from my side. It was so crowded in the bar, they slipped in without anyone noticing—and I got a chance to enjoy Blaine's shoulders. "I'm finished my shift now,"

I said to his back. Thoughts of hopping on my bike for home had disappeared as soon as he smiled at me at the door.

He leaned into his friend. "Told you I could get us in."

The door closed and I was left looking at my reflection again. There were a few stunned seconds while my brain caught up to what had just happened.

I hated who I saw, but the ugly truth was staring me in the face: no matter where I worked, or how many spontaneous chit-chats we had, Blaine Mulder would never fall in love with me.

No one will ever fall in love with me.

"Boys suck," I said tearfully. It felt like someone had punched me in the heart. All I wanted to do was go home, bury myself under my Holly Hobbie bedspread, and cry for the rest of the summer. I grabbed my Kipling bag, muttering to myself.

I had taken this stupid job to be closer to Blaine.

Everything I did was for Blaine.

A rush of anger compelled me to start madly searching my bag. I wanted to rip up my paycheque—the meagre couple hundred bucks was like blood money to me now. I opened every compartment on that stupid bag, but my paycheque wasn't there.

Tears stung the corners of my eyes.

I must have thrown it in the garbage with the paper slips!

The kitchen was spotless. I almost slipped on the freshly mopped floor. How-hole's proficiency was maddening. A broken leg in a cast for the rest of the summer would probably be the next thing to happen to me. I checked all the bins, cursing under my breath. He'd already taken out the garbage. I went out to the shed and dragged all the garbage bags into the driveway.

I ripped each one open and started pulling out bits of kitchen scraps and soggy leftovers. Soon I was covered up to my elbows in pepper steak, melted ice cream, and congealed butter. I delicately unwrapped each piece of paper. I found a grocery list of Julia's, Loretta's reminder to call the vet, food wrappers, paper towels—

The kitchen door banged open. How-hole stood there in bright Hawaiian shorts. He was holding a baseball bat. "Oh, it's you," he said dryly. "I thought it was the dog again."

Cujo-the-land-shark was the least of my concerns at that moment. "Were you going to play baseball with it?" I had no time for chit-chat with him.

He took in the piles of categorized garbage. "What are you doing?"

"I threw out my paycheque by mistake."

"Not on purpose?" I could hear the grin in his voice.

I nodded at the baseball bat. "That for your date with Brooke? Which base are you hoping to get to tonight?" I didn't even try to hide the snark in my voice. To be honest, I thought it was a pretty clever remark to pull out of my butt considering my state of mind.

He didn't bother replying. Instead he went back inside the kitchen.

Whatever. I can do this on my own.

I glanced over at my bike, still waiting for me. Great, I still had that to look forward to. I could call home, but Mom wouldn't want to leave her office, and the sight of Dad's tired face was something my heart and head couldn't handle right now.

The kitchen door opened again. How-hole came over with several garbage bags. He worked silently, methodically sorting through the garbage. I noticed the bat hadn't come back out with him.

"Thanks," I said. "But you don't have to help me." I replayed the moment when I must have thrown away my paycheque. "It was my stupid mistake." I left out that I had been busy telling him off for teasing me about having no social life.

"Most mistakes are stupid," he answered, totally absorbed in handling potato peelings. He didn't even look at me.

Bacon turds to the tenth degree! I couldn't even compete with garbage for a guy's attention. It's like I only got noticed when I was messing up.

I wonder if I'm becoming self-destructive…

I waited for him to talk and maybe give some hint why he was being so nice to me. Was this about Brooke and another party or did he feel sorry for me? Neither one of those scenarios was desirable.

I wish I had a magazine quiz for this situation.

Still, he was helping me sort through this gooey mess. And suddenly being elbow-deep in garbage didn't seem that bad.

"Are you sure it's safe out here?" I asked him, partly testing the waters.

"Depends on what you're afraid of." He examined a piece of paper, then tossed it in a pile.

How-hole, king of ambiguous answers.

"I mean…" I scrunched up my nose as I pulled out a particularly gross piece of rare steak. "I read raccoons can be pretty bold sometimes. And, um…they have teeth, right?"

He only shrugged, intent on searching through more garbage.

Trying to talk with him tonight was torture. This was ridiculous, I had to find that damn paycheque and get home for my all-night cry-fest. I shoved my hand to the bottom of the bag. "SHIT!"

Pain shot up my arm. I pull out my hand, my fingers were covered in blood. "Something bit me!"

How-hole pushed me out of the way and stomped on the bag. We waited, but nothing moved inside. He flipped it upside down and dumped it out. Ronnie's broken vase hit the ground and shattered into even tinier pieces.

"Damn. I'm sorry," he said, kneeling next to me. "That's my fault. I should have wrapped it up before I threw it in the garbage." His fingers were cradling my hand, gently examining the cut. "We've got to clean that up."

His touch set off a nervous tingle over my skin. I met his gaze and our eyes locked. Our noses were almost touching. I held my breath.

"Kels, I—"

A threatening growl came from behind the shed.

We slowly turned. A dog the size of a pony came out of the shadows. It growled again, then leaned back on its haunches, launching itself toward us.

TWENTY-ONE

'm not sure if How-hole said it out loud or if we both thought, *Run!* at the same time, but when he grabbed my good hand, I was already sprinting.

How-hole pulled me through the garden, diving under shrubs and down the grassy slope. He shouted out directions every five seconds. "Jump! Faster! Duck!" I had no idea my legs could move so fast. I thanked God I was wearing the pleated skirt; I'm pretty sure the skin-tight, black pencil version I'd been wishing for wouldn't have stood up so well to this obstacle course.

I kept expecting a jaw lined with teeth to clamp down on my calves. We hurdled the last shrub successfully and crossed the road. We didn't stop to look back until we had gone the full length of the wharf.

I bent over with my hands on my knees, sucking in air. How-hole arched his back, equally out of breath. I took some satisfaction in that. He pointed toward the back of the Queen's Galley, where the dog had retreated into the shadows. "Hard…to resist…pepper steak," he said between breaths.

He took off his ball cap, ran a hand through his hair, and went down the small walkway to the float. I followed him down, simply because the dog could have been part ninja, waiting in the shadows to attack us again. I was, after all, covered in rare steak.

"Sit here," he said, pointing to the edge of the float. "You can soak your hand in the salt water."

The water was so calm, the float barely moved. I crossed my legs and dangled my hand in the cool water. It stung at first, but I kept it in, determined to be tough.

How-hole was still standing. He wiped his brow with his forearm. "God, we both stink," he said.

"Excuse me?" I pretended to be insulted. We had both worked double shifts and then played in garbage. Of course we stank.

He peeled off his T-shirt. There was a long scar on his right side, disappearing under his arm. I could see his nipples.

Why am I looking at his nipples? I don't even like nipples...I need to stop looking at his nipples.

I finally tore my eyes away. "Getting ready for your big date?"

"You seem pretty obsessed with my social life." His sneakers and socks were off now.

I swished my hand in the water. "I just need to know if anything else is coming off, so I can hide my eyes. Whatever, it doesn't matter to me."

He tapped his nose. "Your nostrils don't lie." He jumped in still wearing his Hawaiian shorts. He let out a *whoop!* and did a few strokes.

I sent a few splashes his way, but he couldn't feel them. Then he stopped and floated on his back, so still...so calm. I laid flat on my back, keeping my hand in the water. I looked up at the stars. I couldn't remember the last time I'd looked at them.

He started humming his song.

"What are you thinking?" I said.

"Huh?" He swam back toward the float. "What'd you say?"

"Nothing," I lied. I rolled onto my belly and took my hand out of the water. It was dark but I could see the jagged cut, white on the edges from the salt water.

How-hole brought his face closer. "You won't need stitches," he said, "just some Polysporin and a tight bandage for tonight. Make sure it's covered tomorrow too."

I gave him a look.

"People don't want to be served food by someone with a huge slash across her hand."

"Maybe I'll call in sick," I suggested.

"And miss all the fun?" he said. He crossed his arms, resting his elbows on the edge of the float. His hair was slicked back from the water. He looked normal without shaggy neon blue hair. "Mr. Deveau's outfits alone are worth getting out of bed for."

"I'm not a fan," I said. "He wants me fired, remember?"

How-hole pushed off and treaded water. I'd never seen him so relaxed. "I know why you're so upset," he said.

"I had to dig through garbage to try to find my missing measly paycheque and was chased by a mad dog to the wharf, where I am now soaking my sliced-open hand, which is probably infected."

He was quiet while he considered my answer. "Yup," he finally said. "You definitely need a guy to push you to the edge."

I made a *pfft* sound, a slight variation of my snort. "You don't know me," I said. The night was going downhill, but what did it matter? I was too tired to even care anymore.

"I don't even know me," I said truthfully. "I don't even know what I want, and you *definitely* don't know what I want."

"You're right," he said. "But I know what you need." His tone gave me goosebumps. He reached toward me. "Come on."

I looked at him in horror and jumped up. "Whoa, dude! The last thing I need is to go swimming…with you."

"Come on," he insisted. "Being on the ocean is my speciality. You'll be perfectly safe." He pulled himself up onto the float.

It rocked with his weight. I grabbed the handrail, probably getting more germs into my cut. "Then why aren't you teaching sailing instead of washing dishes?" I asked him. I was impressed I'd managed to think of a question to help solve one of his little mysteries.

He stood in front of me, dripping. I was too frightened to even give his nipples a glance. "All the jobs at the yacht club were gone by the time I moved down from the city." He reached for me again. "Don't be scared," he said. "The water is great."

"My blood will attract the sharks." I held up my prune-like hand as evidence, but he was unconvinced. "Look at my outfit," I pleaded.

"Take off your skirt," he suggested. "I'll be in the water, turned the other way." He stayed quiet, waiting for me to release my death grip on the handrail. "You'll feel better."

"No."

"We'll play Marco Polo."

"No."

"Why are you so determined to turn me down?" His voice had lost its teasing. He stared back at me, unflinching.

Dammit! I'm always the one to look away first.

"It's not you," I finally sighed.

"So you *do* like me," he smiled.

"I didn't say that." I sat back down. "Besides, you've got Brooke and her red car. Isn't she enough?"

He seemed to enjoy that last remark. "I already told you, you and Brooke are nothing alike."

This guy was like the Mad Hatter; he made no sense.

"I don't like the water. Okay?" I played with the end of my skirt.

"Sharks?" he guessed.

"No."

"Leeches?"

"No."

"Jellyfish?"

I huffed. "No. It's the water!"

He screwed up his face. "Seriously? Even in a p—"

"Yes, even in a pool!" I blew on my hand.

"Always?

"No. And that's enough questions, all right?"

He sat down beside me. I could see some kind of scrollwork along his scar. I tried not to stare at the tattoo. "What if someone was drowning?" he asked me. "Would you jump in then?"

"I'd call 911." I thought for a second then changed my answer. "Unless it was Chet, then I'd jump in and save him."

He nodded, then let himself slip back into the water. His head disappeared.

"Very funny," I said. I turned back to the Queen's Galley. The windows of the bar were open. The sounds of laughter and clinking glasses echoed down. I pictured Blaine leaning against the wall, a beer in one hand, his eyes roaming around the room. What if I changed into my clothes and slipped into the bar? Would Blaine notice me then?

He *had* smiled before I closed the door. It was so loud when I let him and his friends in through the French doors. He probably hadn't heard me say I was finished my shift. I closed my eyes. *I can't give up on him yet,* I thought. *Not after all the time I've spent dreaming about him.*

I glanced at my watch—maybe it wasn't too late to try. Besides, I'd thrown up on the guy and he'd still smiled at me. That was worth something, right?

"I'm going back up," I announced to the still water. I counted to five. "I'm going back up!" I shouted. No bubbles.

What had Julia said about him the first day?

"He's not dangerous, he's crazy."

I dropped to my knees and brought my face close to the water. "How-hole!" I screamed. I reached my hands in up to my elbows, blindly searching the water with my fingers. My heart was slamming against my chest. How long had I been daydreaming?

"I need help!" I screamed.

Something grabbed my wrists and pulled.

I tipped forward and plunged face-first into the black water.

TWENTY-TWO

was flailing, but moving nowhere. My fist hit something soft. I coughed out a mouthful of water.

"Kels!" His voice was urgent. "Calm down...ouch!" His voice was near my ear. Hands were suddenly pushing me up out of the water. I scrambled onto the float. My hair was plastered over my face. I pushed myself to sitting. My skirt was heavy and stuck to my legs, weighing me down.

I ran a hand under my nose and glared at How-hole through my stringy hair. He was sitting on the edge of the dock, staring at me intently, his eyes wild.

"I told you!" I blurted out.

"You told me you were afraid of water, not that you couldn't swim."

I was a soggy lump. "Same thing," I muttered.

"Hardly," he said. "Lots of kids are afraid, but they still learn." He watched me a little while longer. "How does someone who lives on an island—"

"Peninsula," I interrupted.

"Fine," he sighed. "How does someone who lives *very close* to the ocean, not know how to swim?"

"It's a long story," I told him.

He leaned back on his hands and crossed his feet in front of him. "I'm listening," he said.

I pushed the hair off my face and took some deep breaths. "My parents didn't put a lot of stock in summer sports. I was almost eight before they thought to put me in swimming lessons." I met his gaze, but this time I didn't turn away. I fixed my skirt and continued.

"I still remember how exciting it was to get that first sticker for putting my face in the water. I envisioned myself winning an Olympic gold medal. I couldn't wait to earn a real badge."

I paused and tried to read his expression. No hint of a sarcastic grin. He nodded for me to continue.

"Then Mom got pregnant, which was a total surprise, and when Chet arrived, what little time my parents had for me went straight to him. By the next summer everything had changed, but I hadn't forgotten about my Olympic dream. I begged my parents to sign me up for swimming again."

I hugged my knees to my chest. "I wanted that badge so badly. Most kids my age had at least three badges sewn onto their towels.

"The first few days went really well," I continued, trying to keep the quiver out of my voice. "Mom would be on the bleachers with Chet on her lap while I did my lesson. He was so busy, though, constantly wiggling out of her arms. Mom was terrified he'd topple down the stairs."

A loud explosion of laughter from the bar echoed down to us. I turned my head toward the noise, but How-hole kept looking at me.

"It's his nature to wander," he said, matter of fact. "Wanderlust," he smiled.

"Yeah," I said, remembering how I'd lost Chet only two weeks ago. "I don't blame Chet for what happened." My stomach began to twist. I let out a long sigh. "The class was doing this game called 'Bombs Away.' The instructor stands in the water and all the little kids jump off the edge of the pool. Then they have ten seconds to climb out and jump in again before the instructor calls out 'bombs away' again. Each time the instructor counts lower—until the end, when you only have one second to get out of the pool."

"How far did you get?" he asked.

"Four," I said proudly. "I was killing the other kids. But it was hard to tell who was in the lead because everyone was supposed to keep jumping in and climbing out. The water was a mass of kids splashing and screaming."

I took in a deep breath. "The thing is, when it happened, no one was watching me—not even my mom."

How-hole stayed quiet. He hadn't moved an inch. I don't think anyone but Chet had ever been so focused on my words.

I ignored the fluttering in my chest. "The last time I jumped in," I continued, "someone came down on top of me. All I could see were bubbles. It felt like my arms and legs were frozen. I wanted to swim up, but my head hit the bottom instead." I looked at him. "I remember that part so clearly. I thought I'd hit the pool cover or something. I was completely disoriented. I thought I was swimming to the surface.

"Then hands were under my arms lifting me out. I coughed at the side of the pool while the instructor made sure I was all right. I must have swallowed some water because my throat burned for the rest of the afternoon." I paused my story, watching the moon reflect patterns off the water.

"Mom didn't understand why I kept asking for ice cream that day," I said. "She never saw what happened, even when the instructor wrapped me up in my towel and was patting my back."

How-hole waited a few beats, making sure my story was finished, then he asked, "Why didn't you tell her?"

"I was angry at her," I said. "I almost drowned. Then I was too embarrassed to say anything. It would only sound like I was looking for attention. I thought it would go away by the next week, but the fear of being trapped under water stayed with me...Mom talked to the instructor, but by that time my incident in the pool had shrunken to a mishap that no one considered important. I hadn't been hurt, so Mom let it go."

How-hole tilted his head and studied my expression. It was unnerving to be listened to with such attention.

"And since I was dead set against going back to lessons," I explained, "that meant she wouldn't have to wrestle with Chet at the pool anymore that summer." Then I added bitterly, "It was an easy out for her. I never got back to the pool that summer. I never went beyond that sticker." I traced a line in the wood with my fingers. It was strange to share this with him, but I wasn't embarrassed or even ashamed.

How-hole spun around, letting his legs dangle in the water. We watched the phosphorous glow around the tiny waves. "So, yeah," I said. "I have aquaphobia. Now you know my big secret."

He ran a hand through his hair. It was starting to dry and the blue bits were sticking up. "But you're making your decision based on fear," he said.

"That's because I'm afraid of drowning."

"No," he said. "You're afraid of how the water makes you feel. Like you've failed at something."

I let out a very ladylike snort of indignation. "That sounds like something a psychiatrist would say."

"Maybe that's because I see one."

Water was still dripping from both of us. The night was hot enough to keep the chill off my skin. Oddly enough, How-hole had been right about the dip; I did feel better, less sticky. He sensed my mood had improved and shifted his body nearer. I leaned forward, taking a closer look at the scar that was partly covered with a tattoo.

He lifted his arm, letting me see the whole phrase. "*No one is to blame*," I read. My eyes lingered on his skin longer than necessary. My gaze slowly moved up his chest and met his eyes. "What does it mean?" I asked.

"It's from a song," he explained. "An old song. I heard it on the radio, when…" He shifted his weight again, letting the end of the sentence drift off.

"The one you were singing that day?"

He grinned sheepishly, and I knew he was blushing. "Yeah, but you should hear it properly, like on iTunes or something." There was an innocent quality to his voice that I found intriguing. I could've listened to him talk all night. "Anyway," he continued, "it's about when something doesn't seem fair and how to handle it. If you can't change it, then you just have to wait."

"Wait for what?"

"For the thing you're supposed to care about."

The air was so still around us, but it felt charged. I was afraid to blink and mess up the perfect simplicity of the moment. This boy didn't sound crazy or dangerous to me.

He leaned closer still, and faced me directly. "What do you want?" he asked, his eyes searching my face. "Like right now, more than anything in the world?"

I realized this was the second time he'd asked me that. It's a simple question, really. Only four little words. But coming from How-hole, the way his mouth formed the sentence, gave the question a weight that made me blush.

The words were in my heart, but the answer didn't come out. My lips trembled and I looked away. "I don't know," I lied. "For Chet to always be okay, I guess." I tried turning the tables. "And you?" I asked him.

He took a deep breath, then looked at the stars. "I want to make my dad proud," he simply stated.

We stayed on the float, listening to the crowd wind down at the bar. My skirt slowly dried. How-hole slung his T-shirt over his shoulder and gave me a hand up. "I could give you private swimming lessons," he said. "I'm pretty comfortable around water."

"Clearly." I fluffed out my white peasant blouse, extra glad I'd worn a plain white bra today for my impromptu wet T-shirt contest. "You know," I said, stepping onto the lawn, "we still stink. You'll have to shower before Brooke picks you up."

He stopped and asked, "Why do you think I'm dating Brooke?"

"She drives you around," I said. "And she wears crocheted stuff and likes flirting with guys." It had sounded much more sane inside my head.

"She lives close to me, that's all. Plus, I have a landscaping job she sometimes offers to drive me to." He smiled widely, like he was enjoying a secret joke.

"Convenient." I gave him my best "yeah right" face and continued walking up the green slope.

"She's only a friend," he called out, laughing at me.

My heart felt a little bit lighter. "Makes no difference to me."

I let him catch up with me. I tried to remember the tune to his song. We crossed through the shadow of the shed. I felt his hand on my elbow and I stopped. We were standing toe to toe. "Since we're talking about dating," he said. "There's this thing coming up and I want you to be there. I mean—"

"LUKE!"

Our heads snapped up. The kitchen door was wide open. The owner of the Queen's Galley, Blaine's soon-to-be-married uncle, filled the doorway. His face was the colour of beets.

"Edward?" I said, so surprised to see him I'd forgotten to address him formally. "I mean, sir," I squeaked.

His fierce expression made me wish I'd stayed quiet. This wasn't going to be a cozy conversation.

"Mr. Mulder is enough, Kelsey."

My cheeks grew warm. *Mr. Mulder it is*, I thought. Not that I'd ever want to be on a first-name basis with someone who treated their family like crap.

How-hole took a few steps ahead of me. His hands were out by his sides. "I can explain," he began.

"Please do!" Mr. Mulder said. He stomped down the stairs and waved an arm at the mess all over the ground.

"Oh shit," I repeated. The dog must have come back and feasted while we were contemplating each other's fears. All the garbage was strewn across the grass. The smell was putrid. I saw a pile of what must have been dog barf.

"I come off the plane and rush to get here," he started, "and the first thing I see is this mess."

How-hole and I were so fired. I didn't care so much about me, but what about his psychiatrist and jail work term or whatever? God! There was so much I didn't know about him.

Mr. Mulder tilted back his head and looked down his nose at me. His glare was unsettling. I looked at the dog barf and had to hold my gut, worried I would add to it.

Mr. Mulder broke off the stare, satisfied he'd scared the crap out of me. Cool and suave one second and lethal the next. I was glad my skirt was still wet, because I was in danger of peeing my pants any second.

He looked at How-hole and waved a hand at the mess. "Clean this up," he ordered. A box of garbage bags was on the ground by his feet. "You told me you were taking responsibility for your actions now."

"A dog chased us!" he said.

I nodded quickly. "He's right, sir." I gulped, then corrected myself. "I mean, Mr. Mulder."

Mr. Mulder focused on me again, his face softening this time. "You look like you've worked hard today, Kelsey." He remembered my name. I hated how special that made me feel. "But Luke knows this is his mistake to take care of." Then he reached out and patted my shoulder. "Time to get home," he said.

I snuck a peek at How-hole, but he was already moving toward the box of garbage bags. "You'll need gloves," I said softly. Mr. Mulder beat me to it and produced a set from his pocket.

I ran into the kitchen and ducked under the window. If Mr. Mulder was going to fire How-hole, I intended to say something—including all the crap he'd covered up for me.

Mr. Mulder began a lecture about garbage and responsibility. He kept on like a sergeant, but How-hole was silent until the very end. Then all he said were two words.

"Sorry, Dad."

TWENTY-THREE

I rolled onto my side and pressed the pillow against my ear, but I could still hear them arguing. Mom had been out when I came home still smelling of garbage in my damp uniform. Dad was sitting at the kitchen table, staring at an alumni magazine. I watched him from the doorway and gave a few standard lies about how well work was going.

I noticed that he didn't turn a page the whole time I'd been standing there. His eyes were fixed on the print, but he obviously wasn't reading. That uncomfortable feeling swirled around in my gut again. He finally looked up when Mom's car sounded in the driveway. For some reason, I didn't want to be there when she came through the front door. I had a quick shower and slipped into bed.

My head was pounding. Luke was Mr. Mulder's son, and Blaine's cousin. Oh, God! The things I had said that night at the party to Chloe about him, and all the while his son had been listening to every word. I'd had no idea how much of a how-hole I'd become.

Mom's voice was growing urgent. I couldn't make out the words, but I didn't have to. Dad sounded tired, almost desperate. What the hell was going on? I couldn't remember the last time the four of us had done anything fun together.

I'm never getting married, being in love sucks.

The voices finally stopped. Footsteps came down the hall. I heard Mom and Dad's bedroom door click shut, then the sound of Mom's keyboard tapping away in her office. I glanced at my Snoopy alarm clock. It was past midnight.

All I wanted was to fall asleep and forget all this mess. I threw my pillow onto the floor and took out my laptop, but instead of opening Francine's spreadsheet, I Googled the lyrics from Luke's tattoo. He'd told me it was a song about how to handle rotten stuff in your life that you couldn't change. The words to the chorus caught my eye. I soon realized Luke and I had completely different impressions of the music's meaning. For me, the ballad wasn't about dealing with change, it was a love song—a sad, hopeless love song.

After I got the title, I downloaded it from iTunes and added it to my summer playlist. I grabbed my earbuds from the bedside table and turned up the volume. Once the song was over, a tear rolled from the corner of my eye, down my cheek, and into my ear. I hit the repeat button seven more times. Finally, sleep dragged me under.

The float was completely still. The water was so flat, it perfectly reflected the night sky. I was convinced that if I put my hand in the water, I'd touch a star.

I mentioned this to Luke and he smiled at me. We were sitting side by side, our feet brushing against each other's in the water.

*He looked at me with those blue eyes and I felt like I was falling
into a crystal-clear ocean.*

*"What do you want more than anything else in the world?"
he asked me.*

*I leaned in closer, staring at his mouth. His kiss was soft and
warm. Slowly it took hold, sending tingles all the way down to
my toes. I wrapped my arms around his neck, unable to move
away. I was pressed against his chest like a willing hostage.*

*"Kelsey," he whispered into the kiss. I moaned and moved
against him. Suddenly he was shaking me.*

"Kelsey!" His voice rose an octave.

"What?"

I bolted up in bed. My Holly Hobbie bedspread came into
focus...and so did Mom. She said my name again, the cordless
phone pressed into her chest. "It's someone from the restaurant for you," she said. "It sounds important." She held the
phone out to me.

I waited until she left my room. My stomach knotted up.
Was Mr. Mulder on the other end, ready to fire me? Had Luke
told him what I said about his bride?

"Hello?" I said, unsure.

"Dude! Mr. Deveau is freaking out. Ronnie's sick and Chloe
can't come in until later." Julia paused to catch her breath.
"You've got to get down here. I can't do the whole brunch
myself."

"Brunch is only on Sundays." Julia wasn't making sense,
but her tone was enough to get me out of bed. I started opening drawers looking for something to put on. Julia never got
excited about anything. I kept the phone pressed to my ear.
"What's going on?" I asked.

Her voice became hard. "Mr. Mulder is closing the restaurant for the weekend. We're having the rehearsal party in two hours." She waited for a few seconds. "Just get down here," she ordered gruffly. "Like, now."

"Uh…okay."

Mom offered to take Chet to his swimming lessons, since I had to be at work speedy-quick. She only said a few words during the drive, and I suspected she was still wearing the same walking shorts and wrinkled top from last night. Chet was reading out loud in the back seat. I was thankful for his constant chatter; Mom's silence was unsettling.

"Owed always wands to give up," he told us, "but Fwog makes him keep twying."

"That's right, honey." Mom's voice was like gravel. My stomach twisted.

When we pulled up to the Queen's Galley, we could tell something was going on. Several delivery trucks were parked in the driveway by the kitchen. A florist's van was taking up two spaces, and, weirdly enough, a police car was also parked there. *At least there isn't an ambulance*, I thought, picturing Mr. Deveau clutching his heart with all the activity going on.

Chet gave me a big wave goodbye. Mom smiled at me, but I could tell it was forced. Like when you whack your hip on the corner of a school desk but you're so embarrassed you just smile through the pain.

I dragged my feet up the walk, glad to be out of the car and away from Mom's sullen expression but not exactly thrilled to face Mr. Mulder—junior or senior. The police car had me worried.

Was last night's screw-up with the garbage enough to get Luke in trouble with the police? What about his shrink and the jail?

My head started to throb again. I had started to call it my "Luke headache."

The foyer was full of huge bouquets. The dining tables were being taken out and white folding chairs were lined up along one wall. A mini arbour covered in white roses was set up at the front of the room. I glanced up at Captain Bowsky's portrait, half expecting him to roll his eyes at all the fuss.

"Finally!" Julia pulled me around the corner. Five tables had been pushed together, creating a long row in front of the windows facing the harbour. "We're seating twenty guests," she said, "two at the end and nine down the sides. Get the wine glasses from the bar while I polish the silverware and then we'll get started on the linen."

"Why the rush?" I asked. Her hair was still wet from the shower. She must have gotten an unexpected call too. "I mean…I get it, Mr. Mulder is the owner—"

"Just get the glasses!" She yelled over her shoulder, heading toward the kitchen.

This was shaping up to be a super-duper day. I went through the French doors to the bar, mumbling to myself. I stopped dead in my tracks. Mr. Mulder and a uniformed cop turned my way. I blinked back at them like a deer caught in headlights.

And we all know what happens to the deer in that situation, right?

TWENTY-FOUR

"Kelsey?" Mr. Mulder's voice had a slight impatient edge. "What do you need?"

My heart began to race. Oh God! Luke really was in trouble. The cop gave me a concerned look. The thought of him questioning me pulled words out of my mouth.

"Um..." I pointed at the bar. "Wine glasses. *Need them, I will.*" My Yoda impression had little effect on either man.

Lucky for me, Mr. Deveau breezed into the bar and put a hand on my elbow. "There you are!" He pushed two trays into my hands and started gathering wine glasses. "Pardon us, Edward," he apologized. There was a faint patch starting under the arms of Mr. Deveau's baby-blue dress shirt. At his throat was a white ascot with anchors.

It's like he's trying to look like Fred from Scooby-Doo.

But right now, he was my saviour, and we hustled out of the bar before you could say, "And if it weren't for those meddling kids..."

Julia had already set half the table. Mr. Deveau began to meticulously shine each wine glass. I grabbed a linen napkin and follow his lead.

"Lobsters just arrived," he mumbled to himself. "Flowers for the centrepiece are in the fridge. Loretta is mixing the ganache for dessert…"

I tried to catch Julia's eye as Mr. Deveau went through his mental checklist, but she was way too interested in placing the cutlery perfectly. I'd been hoping for an eye roll from her at Mr. Deveau's back. Her eye rolls always made me feel better.

"…photographer." Mr. Deveau stopped his list to breathe on one of the glasses. After he stubbornly rubbed it with his cloth, he held it up to the sunlight and nodded with satisfaction.

Mr. Deaveau may have been a mixed-up dweeb, but he certainly was devoted to the Queen's Galley. Inspired, I moved one of the knives a quarter of an inch so it lined up properly. He gave me a rare smile of approval.

I forgave him a little for yelling at me. "Thanks for rescuing me," I told him. "I didn't know Mr. Mulder was talking with a police officer."

Mr. Deveau's expression hardened. "He wasn't talking, he was being issued a fine. There were underage patrons in the bar last night. An off-duty police officer saw them sneak in."

The floor swooped out from under my feet. I leaned on the table, finally getting Julia's attention, but there was no smile or eye roll.

"The restaurant lost its liquor license for a *week*," Mr. Deveau continued, his voice cracking like he was going to cry. "All this plus the wedding tomorrow!" He loosened his ascot and blotted his forehead with it.

"But we're having the brunch today," I said weakly, hoping for a happy ending.

"Edward is the owner, silly girl," Mr. Deveau replied. "He can close the restaurant for his own private function."

Julia piped in, "As long as no one is *buying* alcohol, he can *serve* as much as he wants." I held her stare for as long as I dared. There was an awful drop in my gut. She'd been in the bar last night. She must have seen me let Blaine and his friends in.

I hadn't thought about Blaine since last night—that had to be a record. Had he gotten in trouble too? I was nothing but bad news for the Mulder men. My insides were so twisted it hurt to breathe.

"Oh, perfect!" Mr. Deveau clapped his hands. "You're right on time!"

A woman loaded down with a tripod and several black bags stood in the doorway looking overwhelmed. "Where should I set up?" she asked.

Mr. Deveau and the photographer roamed around the room, talking about lighting contrast and floral backgrounds. I snuck another glance at Julia, but she had decided to ignore me.

"Kelsey!" Mr. Deveau called out, waving me over. "We need you to stand in front of the window for a light check."

"Me?" No one had ever asked me to model before. "Should I smile?" I asked the photographer.

She shook her head, then took a few shots. She paused to look at the digital image.

"Mmm," Mr. Deveau said, leaning over her shoulder. "Too much glare."

People were rushing around now, setting up chairs for the wedding, placing flowers, assembling the microphone stand for the sound system. One guy with a crewcut wandered by

the doorway with his hands in his short pockets. He was wearing a white oxford shirt with the sleeves rolled up to the elbow.
I wondered if he was the photographer's assistant.

"It's off balance," Mr. Deveau announced, earning him a
huff from the photographer.

"I'm allowing extra space for the couple shot," the photographer explained. "Hey," she called out to her assistant in the
hallway. "Come stand here for a second. I need another model."

The guy turned and I was hit with a flash of tropical ocean.
Luke winked back at me. He pointed to his chest and gave us
a "Who, me?" expression, then sauntered into the room. Mr.
Deveau busily positioned him next to me, and then hustled
back to stand beside the increasingly red-faced photographer.

She pointed the camera at us. "Just a little closer," she
instructed.

Luke's arm slipped around my waist. I gulped. Of all the
times to be without a peppermint!

"So…your hair," I said through a smile, staring straight
ahead. All of the blue was gone. It was short, really short…
and really hot.

"Less maintenance," he said. There was a lyrical tone to his
voice, like we were sharing a secret. It gave me butterflies.

Butterflies!

I could feel the heat from his hand through my cotton
T-shirt. "Sort of a wedding present for my dad, I guess," he said.

"I just saw your dad with a cop," I dared to ask. "Is everything okay?"

"Now look at each other," the photographer ordered.

I stared at Luke's chin. The corner of his mouth curled up.
"Look at each other, please," the photographer repeated. I
raised my gaze and fell into his eyes.

"*Hey*," he whispered.

"*Hey, Luke*," I whispered back.

His crooked smile burst into a full-on grin. "That's the first time you've called me by my name," he said.

And I realized I hadn't thought of him as "How-hole" since last night. The butterflies were playing ping-pong now.

Everything must be okay, I thought. *He isn't in trouble with the police and he doesn't hate me.*

I smiled back and the photographer snapped like crazy. *Clink. Clink. Clink.*

Chloe was standing at the set table, tapping a fork against one of the wine glasses. She gave me a wink.

"Sorry I'm late, but I had to help deliver the wedding cake," she announced. Mr. Deveau clapped his hands and disappeared through the doorway. A burst of applause from the foyer seconds later proved that Jesse's mom had more than exceeded Mr. Deveau's expectations.

Chloe lightly clinked the glass again.

"Good idea," the photographer said, switching lenses. "I need a kissing shot."

I froze in Luke's arms. Chloe shrugged cutely, then resumed helping set the table. My heart was in my throat. I couldn't breathe.

"*What do you want more than anything in the world...right now?*"

The photographer aimed her camera at us again.

I couldn't feel my knees, and I'm pretty sure my teeth looked stupid. "Maybe in front of the fireplace would be bet—" My last word got caught inside Luke's mouth.

Before I could even register the pressure of his lips on mine, or even start to kiss him back, he was leaning away, already done.

"Great," the photographer said. "That's all I need."

I was still in Luke's arms. *Speak for yourself*, I thought.

"I was holding back," he said, slightly amused.

"Clearly."

Talk about always leave them wanting more. The faint taste of his mint toothpaste was still on my lips.

What a tease!

I stepped out of the embrace. I hadn't realized I'd been up on my tiptoes. My skin suddenly felt cool where he'd been touching me. I knew I was blushing like an idiot.

I turned away, afraid I was going to spontaneously combust. Luke matched my stride through the hallway. We were forced to stop in the foyer; a table was being rolled by with the beautiful wedding cake on it. Mr. Deveau leaped around us like a gazelle on Skittles and Red Bull.

Luke ran a hand over his new hair. I wondered what it felt like. Julia hustled by us on her way to the holding bar. She shot me a look out of the corner of her eye. A brand new, horrible idea came over me. What if Julia had told Luke about me letting Blaine in?

He must be waiting for me to confess.

The knot in my stomach grew. I knew I had to tell him, I knew it was the right thing to do.

I focused on the little polo player on his shirt, trying to build up my courage. "I have to change into my uniform," I said, totally chickening out.

"Not yet, Kels." He reached into his back pocket and handed me an envelope. "I believe this belongs to you."

I opened the clean envelope. My stinky paycheque smiled back at me.

"I found it after you left." He dropped his head and looked at the floor.

I felt the rush of a blush as I remembered the scene from last night with his dad. I lovingly tucked the envelope into my Kipling bag. "Thanks," I said.

He lifted his eyes and smiled back. There was a silent moment and I began to wonder what was going to come out of his mouth next. Clearly he wasn't in a hurry to leave me. He reached up and touched one of the flowers from the huge bouquet, already drooping in the heat. "I wish I was working," he said. "But it's a family rehearsal brunch so I kind of have to attend."

"Right," I said slowly, deciding to pretend I'd known who he was all along.

Play dumb. I love a safe option. Nothing bad can happen if I just stay quiet.

He tapped the baseboard with his Docksides. I guess smelly Converse wasn't the proper footwear for today. "So," he began, "um...about last night—"

Oh God! That was it. He knew. I had to confess.

"I'm sorry," I said, quickly. "Look, it was totally stupid, but I had a good reason—not that it seems good now. But I never would have let those guys in if I knew what could happen. Please don't hate me for messing up your dad's wedding plans."

"Messing up what?"

A big gong sounded inside my head. He truly had no idea what I was talking about.

He leaned in with a half smile on his face. "I was talking about asking you out."

"What?" I felt my back press up against the wall. My knees had turned to water. "Asking me out?" The mix of relief and surprise on my face made him smile even wider.

"I don't hate you." He took a step closer. "I mean, it's hard to be angry with the girl who scribbles your name all over her magazine."

"Magazine?" I'd become Chet, the human repeater.

The toes of his Docksides lined up with my holey Toms. He smelled nice today, salty and fresh, just like the ocean. "That's right, *Mrs. Mulder*," he whispered. "Although if you want to keep your name, that's cool with me."

The magazine.

That weird little valve over my throat opened and closed a few times. My brain couldn't decide if I should breathe or throw up. I had no idea what my body would do next.

The colour was high in his cheeks. "Don't be embarrassed. You're kind of goofy and adorable. I like that."

"Thanks." I loved that he found my goofiness attractive. I loved that even though he'd seen me at my worst, he still wanted to date me. I loved how he never looked away when we talked. What I wanted more than anything in the world at that moment was to go up on tiptoe and kiss him again and again, until I got breathless and dizzy. I wanted Luke. And amazingly enough, he wanted me.

The easy thing would have been to pretend that I had been thinking of Luke when I'd scribbled all over that magazine. We could fall into each other's arms and maybe find a dark corner of the restaurant to pick up where we'd left our kiss. The memory of his lips against mine had made me light-headed.

"Luke," I began, then I paused. Something was missing, or rather something had changed. I knew what it was immediately. The butterflies were barely fluttering. Another sensation had overwhelmed my senses. A stone had lodged itself inside my heart, creating an ache that was heavier than any longing I'd ever had for Blaine.

The guilt was killing me, even the butterflies knew.

Butterflies don't lie.

And in this case, they weren't going to let me lie, either. Because even a goofy, lovesick mess-up like me knew Luke deserved better. I couldn't do this to him. I had to tell him the truth. I was responsible for the restaurant getting a fine, and I had already let him take the blame for so many of my screw-ups this summer.

I forced myself to look into his blue eyes—another ocean I was terrified of drowning in.

Please, let him understand, I prayed.

"It wasn't about you," I said, hating the sound of the words. "It was about someone else."

Luke tilted his head and gave me a crooked grin; slowly his eyebrows furrowed. The front door squeaked open. Blaine walked in with his parents—here, obviously, for the family brunch. He raised a hand to us and smiled. Luke followed my gaze. His expression caved.

"Oh," was all he said to me.

One syllable was all it took to break my heart.

TWENTY-FIVE

Chloe and I cleared the first course as Julia refilled the wine glasses. Blaine and Luke were only drinking Coke. I watched as Blaine used a piece of baguette to sop up the dressing from his spinach salad.

"Excuse me," I said softly, staring at the tablecloth. I had to reach around Blaine's shoulder to take his plate. I glanced at my old obsession; his shoulder didn't seem so interesting today. The plate shook in my hand and I knocked over a salt shaker.

He righted it, then threw some over his left shoulder. "Thanks, Kelsey," he winked. "A little luck never hurt anyone." I smiled and my upper lip stuck to my teeth.

Luke was sitting opposite him. He hadn't looked my way since we'd spoken in the hallway. I kept trying to get his attention, desperate to explain my side of the story. A little part of me hoped Luke still might like me, but the bigger part couldn't stand the thought of him hating me. I could try and at least explain why I'd acted like such a moron.

Meet me in the holding bar, my eyes kept trying to say.

I certainly couldn't lean over the back of his chair and whisper in his ear, *"Okay, so I used to like your cousin, but now I'm totally into you. Forget the stuff I said about your dad in front of all of your friends at your party. I just really want to make out with you. Oh, and by the way, I'm responsible for the restaurant losing it's license. So…we cool?"*

Yup. Epic. I'd sweep him right off his feet. Who was I kidding? I didn't stand a chance. I was meant to only like guys who ignored me.

At the beginning of the summer I would have been thrilled to have Blaine talk to me, but now all I could think about was Luke and how much he must loathe me.

Thanks, irony. You rock.

I snuck another glance, but it was impossible to catch Luke's eye. In fact, he was busy answering questions from his soon-to-be stepmom. The future Mrs. Mulder wasn't the blonde runway model I'd envisioned. She looked more like Ms. K. from the library—pretty, but in a plain, simple kind of way. She wore a modest sundress with a thick waistband. There was no huge diamond ring, either.

Our trays stacked with greasy salad plates, Chloe and I rushed back to the kitchen. Twenty demitasse glasses were lined up for the sorbet. Julia breezed in with a pitcher of iced tea for Clyde and Loretta.

"How's Joe?" Chloe asked Julia. "I saw him the other day giving someone a ticket."

"Oh, yeah," Julia grinned. "Who?"

"My mom," Chloe laughed. "She's always badgering me about my driving, so it was nice to witness her being lectured for a change."

Julia placed paper doilies on the tiny plates waiting for the sorbet. "I hope he was nice, though. Sometimes cops can be dickheads." She loaded up a tray with the sorbet, then used her butt to push open the swinging door.

"Who's Joe?" I asked Chloe.

Chloe emptied a few more scoops into the tiny glasses. "He's Julia's boyfriend," she said in an obvious tone. "You know, the hot guy with the motorcycle."

All the air left my lungs. When Julia saw me let in Blaine and his friends, she must have pointed them out to her boyfriend...*an off-duty police officer.*

I looked around the kitchen. Clyde and Loretta were still doing their dance behind the counter—passing each other, reaching high for a hanging pot, then swinging low to open the oven.

Did Julia tell anyone it was me who let Blaine in? Maybe she told her boyfriend and he's still building a case against me.

I shivered, picturing myself in juvenile hall. I'd be dead in the first week.

Between Julia's accusing stares and Luke doing his best to pretend I was invisible, I decided once and for all that Blaine wasn't worth this much effort. I was going to quit this close-to-the-yacht-club job as soon as this brunch was over, spreadsheet be damned.

I ignored the knot that started to grow in my stomach at the thought of never seeing Luke again. I had no choice. Leaving all of this mess was the best option, the safest option.

Once the sorbet was cleared it was time for a parade of Clyde's famous seafood specials. Personal-sized casserole dishes were filled with steaming lobster meat and grilled potatoes topped with a cream sauce. Chloe and I made half a dozen trips bringing out heaping platters:

Scallops smothered in caramelized onions. Shrimp sprinkled with lemon and cilantro nestled among bowls of fettuccine. Oysters on the half shell lying in a bed of ice. There were more fish on that table than in the whole ocean.

I had begun dispensing my tray of tiny dishes of melted butter when Mr. Mulder announced that Luke could take their boat out that afternoon. Luke looked surprised. His dad laughed and then motioned to Blaine. "Take some of your friends, too," he encouraged.

Blaine immediately pulled out his phone. He said to Luke, "Hey, man. Who do you want to invite? I'll send out a text."

Luke only shrugged. "I can't think of anyone."

I died a little inside.

"No phones at the table," Blaine's mother insisted. Blaine conceded easily, but he caught Luke's eye and gave him a wide grin.

"Sorry," I said to Mr. Mulder, my voice low. "I just need to…" I reached across him to place the tiny dish of melted butter on the table.

"Hey, Kelsey," Blaine said all of a sudden.

I jumped and almost spilled the melted butter on Mr. Mulder's sleeve. "Yes?" I asked, waiting for him to ask for another glass of water or more bread.

"Why don't you come with us?" he asked me. "You'll know mostly everyone."

I was stunned. Blaine Mulder was asking me to go sailing. On the ocean. The huge, great, big, ginormous, bottomless ocean. He mistook my silence for reluctance.

"Come on," he urged. "This boat is gorgeous. And you'll have time, we're not leaving until after lunch. You'll be finished work, right?"

I felt a nudge in my ribs. "Of course she will," Chloe confirmed.

Still I gave no answer. Luke finally spoke up. "Kelsey's not such a fan of the open ocean," he said, twirling his glass of Coke. He met my gaze and I couldn't breathe. "She doesn't like to take chances. She likes the safe option."

His cutting tone made me bite back tears. Suddenly all the weird stuff at home and the stress from the last twenty-four hours piled up and threatened to spill out of my eyeballs.

I still hadn't answered Blaine. Luke gave him a curious look that bordered on exaggeration. "I can't believe there are still people in this place who've never been on a sailboat before. Seems pointless to live by the ocean."

The reference about me was lost on most of the table. No one noticed my shaking hands hovering over the next dish of melted butter.

Why was Luke being so mean? I thought he was being especially cruel for someone who regularly sees a shrink. What ever happened to "no one is to blame"?

Anger was slowly seeping through the heartache. I couldn't believe he was mad at me for having a crush on his cousin. He had no idea how many things I'd done to screw up his summer. I began to channel the wisdom of May's issue of *Cosmo Chick*.

Are You A Fighter Or A Crier?

Your friend buys the exact same dress you've picked out for the prom. You...

A. laugh about the coincidence and decide to match your jewelry as well, knowing that you'll be the story of the prom and friends will applaud your good sportsmanship.

B. say the dress suits her better anyway, so you stay at home on prom night crying into your pillow.

C. complain about it to everyone on Facebook and demand she return the dress since you bought yours first.

With a dish of melted butter as my witness, I made a vow. I'd done enough crying these last two weeks.

From this day on, I am a fighter. No one messes with this busgirl.

How-hole, indeed!

I flared my nostrils at Luke, then gave Blaine a sweet smile. "Of course," I agreed. "I love to sail. I appreciate the invitation."

"Good," he smiled. Then he dropped his voice and draped an arm over the back of his chair, leaning toward me. "I kind of owe you. I'm sorry about—" he motioned to the French doors that lead to the bar.

"No worries," I quickly interrupted. Luke was listening too closely.

I escaped to the kitchen and took turns with Chloe peeking through the glass panel. When the photographer took Mr. Mulder and his soon-to-be bride to stand by the windows for some rehearsal-brunch shots, Mr. Deveau shoved us out, our cue to start clearing the table.

With all the emptied shells overflowing everyone's plates, it looked like low tide after a storm. Some people had wandered onto the patio. Luke stayed in his place, leaning back in his chair. I stared at him, willing him to look at me. When he did, all the blood rushed down to my feet.

Being a fighter takes practice, apparently.

I started stacking plates like crazy. I loaded up my tray in record time. All I wanted was to escape those eyes. My peasant blouse was smeared with bits of fish and sauce. I hefted the tray up and rested it on my shoulder, creating a block against Luke's stare.

I kept my eye on the kitchen door. My long skirt snagged on the toe of my shoe. I flicked it free and quickened my pace.

A flashbulb suddenly went off in my face, blinding me. My feet caught again, but this time I couldn't get my foot free in time.

In horrifying slow motion I saw the tray fly out of my hands, directly into the path of the photographer. Lobster bits and rivers of melted butter careened across the wooden floor. There was a crash, followed by complete silence.

Loretta came flying out of the kitchen, perhaps expecting to see the front of a car embedded in the wall. She slipped on the mess and fell. Her foot was trapped against the wall at a nauseating angle.

The silence was finally broken by Mr. Deveau braying like a mule. I slowly made it to my knees. Mr. Mulder's face was as red as the lobster shell still spinning at his feet.

TWENTY-SIX

• • • • • • • • • • •

Chloe helped me clean up the mess. My plan to quit after this shift was probably moot now, considering I was going to be fired. Clyde finished the dessert while Mr. Deveau gave Loretta a ride to the clinic for an X-ray. Then I hung out in the pantry with Chloe, watching the clock and praying for the day to end.

The kitchen door swung open. Julia passed by with an empty breadbasket in her hands. "When they're finished with the cake," she told Chloe, "we'll take out the champagne for the toast." Then she turned to me, holding the basket. "This should have been taken off the table long ago, Kelsey." There was an edge to her voice.

"Thanks," Chloe said, taking it from her. She flounced back into the kitchen, completely oblivious to our conflict.

"Yeah, thanks," I replied deadpan, doing my best to attract zero attention. I wished I was invisible. Since my latest busgirl catastrophe I'd taken up a new philosophy:

I am not a fighter, I am a zombie.

Julia's mouth was a tight line.

A knot burned between my shoulder blades. I hated guilt. And considering I'd be fired at the end of this shift, I figured a little confession was in order to try and salvage the day.

"I get it, Julia," I said. "You hate my guts for letting Blaine sneak into the bar. But please understand that I had good reasons, and I had no idea the restaurant would lose its license." I clasped my hands in front of my chest. "And please, please, please talk your boyfriend into not arresting me and sending me to jail."

The last bit I threw in spontaneously. I didn't think I was in the position of asking Julia for a favour, but I guess having a shirt covered in fish guts made me...well, more gutsy.

Julia took in my speech without even blinking. She wiped her hands on her apron, her expression almost bored. "Dude," she finally said. "You knew it was wrong. You knew you could lose your job. Why the hell did you let those guys in?"

I was put off a bit by her casual tone. I'd thought she was ready to report me. "They're my friends," I said.

"All of them?"

"Well, no. Just one."

"The hot one?" She motioned to the glass panel. "The same hot one who happens to be enjoying the chocolate ganache right now?"

I dropped my head, ashamed, embarrassed, depressed, exhausted...take your pick.

She let out a long sigh. "It was stupid."

I sniffed. "I know. And everyone will hate me because I closed down the Queen's Galley."

Julia rolled her eyes. "It was stupid to do something for a guy when you knew it was wrong." She stared at me. "That's why I'm pissed at you. You're a strong woman, act like it."

That was a surprise. No one had ever called me strong *or* a woman before, let alone both at the same time. Coming from Julia, the compliment was tenfold.

I must have looked even more pathetic than usual. Her expression softened and she gave me a smile. Then she messed up my white cap. "Chill," she said. "No one knows you let them in. I didn't say anything to Joe, either. One of his friends was with us, and it was pretty obvious the baby-faced trio at the bar had snuck in."

My heart sped up. "So Mr. Mulder doesn't know I let Blaine in?"

She gave me a critical look. "Blaine," she said, "is the only one who knows, plus me and you. And I won't say anything."

I felt like I could breathe for the first time that day. "But what about the restaurant being closed?" I asked her.

"We'll be open, we just can't sell alcohol." She loaded up a tray with champagne glasses. I reached for it but she stopped me. "I'll carry these," she told me. "You seem a little shaky today."

"No kidding," I said. "Um…Julia? Thanks. You know, for not telling and like, well everything, I guess."

"Wow," she said. "That was poetic. You should write for Hallmark."

I smiled back at her and we left it at that.

Since Luke wasn't working, I volunteered to be the dishwasher. I had no idea a full tray of dishes was so frickin' heavy. I remembered Luke's ease with it and the ache started fresh and raw. No matter how many other things I tried to resolve, today kept coming back to me disappointing him.

The industrial dishwasher got everything clean in under an hour. By the time I was done, Chloe was waiting for me.

She ushered me into the bathroom and methodically started giving me a makeover for my sailing date.

"Seriously?" I asked, dumbfounded. "Even after I made that whole mess?"

Chloe zipped open her hot pink satchel and pulled out a makeup bag. "He's waiting for you in the foyer," she said.

"Oh," I said, surprised.

Has Luke forgiven me? I wondered.

The butterflies began to stir awake.

Even if he isn't interested in dating me, I'll at least get a chance to try and explain my side of everything.

I felt hopeful for the first time that day.

Fighting a grin, I played the part of a fashion experiment as Chloe rummaged through her bag, mostly talking to herself about colour, and using terms like "sporty-natural."

I stood in front of her in my white tank top and jean cut-offs. "Here." Chloe handed me a top. "It should fit you."

It was a chunky-knit turquoise sweater. I slipped it over my head and waited for her critique.

She puckered her face, then made a few adjustments. It was thick, but light enough that I felt like I was wearing silk. "Do you have a statement necklace?" she asked.

I shook my head. All I had was my yellow bag, and it only held my stinky uniform, some sunscreen from our beach date, and a magazine.

"There." She twirled me around to have a look in the mirror. After a bit of lip gloss, some bronzer, and her designer sunglasses, I was ready to go. She also let me borrow her flip-flops, even though they were a size too big. "No one's going to know," she laughed. "They're supposed to flop around. Besides, you can kick them off when you go on board."

My stomach did its own flip-flop.

On board. A boat. In the ocean.

I took a deep breath. Luke was worth it.

I hesitated at the doorway, sneaking a peek. My hopes at patching things up immediately vanished. It was Blaine who was waiting for me, not Luke.

Again. Irony, you suck.

Chloe's hand was on my back. "Go on," she whispered, sensing my nerves.

I closed my eyes, imagining the spreadsheet. Francine's little columns and rows were comforting in a strange way. I was completely floundering today; maybe all I needed to get things working in my favour was some organizing. If anything, I was determined to check off at least one more box. I could finally tell Blaine how I felt, or rather how I used to feel. And then I could concentrate on Luke.

His feelings couldn't have changed that quickly, I thought. *He must still like me in some way...*

I had to move forward: first confess to Blaine, then confess to Luke.

Fantastic plan.

Mr. Deveau's shrill voice pierced the air. He was in the kitchen and heading our way. A new kind of panic began to set in. That was the kick in the drawers I needed. If Mr. Deveau was going to fire me, he could do it over the phone where there were fewer witnesses. I swallowed down my fears and stuck out my chest.

"That's the ticket," Chloe giggled behind me.

Blaine gave me one of his perfect smiles and bounded down the steps, already bragging about the boat his uncle was letting us take out.

I silently prayed as we walked past the gazebo to the yacht club. *Please let the boat be broken. Please let there be a problem with the sails. Please let the sky open up and a downpour of crickets plague Mariner's Cove.*

"Isn't she beautiful?" Blaine waved his hand. The sailboat was docked right alongside the wharf.

I pushed back Chloe's sunglasses so I could see it with my own eyes. "Wow" was all I could say. It must have been forty feet long.

"Yeah," he grinned. "I know. Everyone is totally jealous I get to sail this baby."

Someone cleared their throat. Luke was already on board, sitting on the edge, keeping his eyes—and his condemning stare—hidden behind sunglasses.

Blaine winked at me, then nodded to Luke. "Well, with help from my cousin, of course."

A wooden set of steps on the wharf made climbing up onto the boat a ton easier. Blaine stepped on board, lifting each leg over the safety tie that encircled the boat. He gave Luke a fist-bump, then disappeared inside the cabin. I licked my dry lips, then grabbed the safety tie and hoisted myself up. I swallowed a scream as I felt the boat list, certain I would drop face-first and become trapped between the boat and the water.

Luke reached out and grabbed my free hand. I stumbled in Chloe's flip-flops. He caught me and said, "Are you okay?"

My heart faltered. "Yeah," I said. Then I quickly added, "Well, no. I'm not okay. I need to talk to you."

He stepped back, letting go of my arm. "I meant being on the water." He said it low enough that Blaine couldn't hear, but his tone was patronizing.

"I'm fine," I said. We were rocking back and forth and I had adjusted my footing a few times.

"Really?" he looked pointedly at the safety line. "Because your white-knuckle death grip tells another story."

I began to doubt the butterflies. I wanted to tell Luke I'd listened to his song and cried. And that being with him made dealing with killer dogs, emotional bosses, dirty dishes, and creepy rats seem like a good time. But it was clear from his inflection that he wasn't interested. And I'd had my share of chasing after guys who weren't interested in me.

I glanced longingly at the wharf. "This was a mistake," I said. I was becoming an expert on those this summer.

"What?" Blaine popped his head out of the cabin, huge grin on his face. "You brought steaks?"

"We just ate," Luke said in a much less snippy tone than he used with me. He nodded to the front of the boat. "I need you to check the jib sheets."

Blaine bounded to the bow with effortless ease. He dropped to his knees checking the ropes. Luke turned back to me, he wasn't smiling. "What are you doing?" he probed. "You hate the water, remember?"

Did he really expect me to answer that? Of course I remembered! His sunglasses never wavered from my face. My tiny reflection stared back, small and scared. I'd been trying to get his attention all morning, and now that I finally had it I'd clammed up.

"What's so important?" he prompted.

More than anything else in the world?

He leaned closer. "This seems like a dangerous outing for someone like you," he said. "I was under the impression you liked the safe option."

I narrowed my eyes. Was he really making fun of my aquaphobia? I couldn't believe he was teasing me about my greatest fear! This was ridiculous. I needed to set things straight. I had to explain how I'd been crushing on Blaine forever, even though we'd never been more than acquaintances. I had to convince him that he was the "Mr. Mulder" I wanted…and needed.

The quiz had been right all along, but I'd never noticed because I was so busy staring at Blaine's shoulders. Luke was the guy who pushed me to the edge of my comfort zone. He was the one who made me feel safe and appreciated. He would help me conquer my fears.

That's what I knew in my heart to be true. And that's why I was on the boat. I had to tell Luke.

Instead, this was what came out of my mouth: "The magazine," I blurted. "That's why I'm here."

A confused expression played over his features. Blaine hollered something from the bow, but the wind stole his words.

Luke's shoulders caved a bit. "Oh, right," he said. "Your future husband invited you. Don't let me get in the way of your big plans." He dropped his chin, then started to tidy various ropes that already looked tidy to me.

I rolled my eyes. "It's not like that," I said. "Blaine and I are only friends." I took a quick glance at the front of the boat. Blaine was still messing around, clearly out of earshot. I let go of the safety line and stepped closer to Luke. I had his full attention now.

My face grew hot in spite of the cool ocean breeze. "I mean, I used to like him…in the more-than-a-friend kind of way." My voice was shaky. Nerves started to speed up my words. "It's been going on for a while," I said. "It's weird because I've known him since we were little. He's always been the super-nice guy, and then he turned into the super-hot guy. But he still managed to stay really nice, even though he could have turned into an idiot like most hot guys do…" I was rambling on like a runaway love train on a roller coaster of mixed-up hormones.

Luke turned away from me, lifted one of the seat covers, then reached in and pulled something out.

I continued talking to his back. "You can ask anyone in town about Blaine," I said, "and they'll all tell you the same thing: Blaine's the kind of guy that all the girls want to date and all the guys want to have as a best friend. I don't think I've ever heard a bad comment about him. Even the teachers think—*oof!*"

A bright orange life preserver hit me in the chest. "There," Luke said. "Put that on."

I held the bright neon vest at arm's length. I was momentarily jarred from my monologue about Blaine. "I don't think so," I said indignantly. What was the point of wearing Chloe's sweater if I covered it up with this thing? I was more likely to fall overboard if I had it on—it was bulky and horrible. I might as well have stapled "loser" to my forehead.

Blaine scrambled along the top of the boat, then jumped into the cockpit beside me. I crossed my arms in front of my chest, unsuccessfully trying to hide the flotation device. But Blaine didn't even notice. He disappeared down the ladder and into the cabin.

Luke caught my eye. "Who do you think is going to jump in after you fall overboard?" he challenged.

I hated how I kept getting sidetracked from my confession of love. Words were failing me. I needed to grab the collar of Luke's shirt and lay one on him. But he seemed so pissed right now that he'd probably push me away—or even worse, laugh at me. I was beginning to fume at his self-righteousness.

I plunked myself on the long bench opposite him. "I plan on staying on the boat, actually," I said, crossing my legs. Then, for good measure, I took the life jacket and sat on it, using it as a cushion. "If you fall over, I'll throw this your way, though."

The corner of his mouth twitched. "You're all heart, Kels," he said. There was a smile, but I could hear his underlying tone. It wasn't hurtful, it was worse: he was disappointed.

I silently wondered if he got tips from his shrink or if he had a natural talent for making people feel guilty. I tried to think of something to say that would get a reaction out of him. I wanted the old How-hole back, not the reserved safety guy he'd become.

He busied himself with checking the wheel and whatever other technical things needed to be done to get this monster out on the sea.

A chill ran over my bare legs. I smoothed a hand over my cut-offs, wishing I'd stayed on land after all. This was all wrong. I was supposed to be telling Luke how I felt, not arguing about a stupid life jacket.

Blaine came out of the cabin and started hopping over the top deck, untying the sails. "Are we putting up the spinnaker today?" he asked excitedly.

Luke turned to the horizon and tilted his nose up into the air.

"What are you, like, smelling a storm or something?" I said.

Luke ignored my comment. He gave Blaine a nod. Apparently this was the signal for Blaine to pump his fist into the air and give a whoop.

Seriously? It's sailing.

Luke and I traded looks. I guess we were thinking the same thing. Then he smiled at me. And that's all it took to make everything all right again.

I madly went through every quiz in my head for tips on how to romance Luke back into my arms.

"Are You A Natural Flirt?"

I grinned back at him. *Okay,* I told myself, *we're both smiling at each other, say something sexy.*

"Your head looks good," I said.

Bacon turds!

"I mean, your haircut is good. It's good."

Luke's smile got bigger. And so did mine. Then he raised his hand, waving at someone on the dock.

A group of Stunders were all decked out in their designer shorts and tops, eagerly making their way toward the boat. One was a bikini-clad girl with a hummingbird tattoo.

TWENTY-SEVEN

The boat listed and I held my breath. I concentrated on the perfectly fluffy white clouds in the sky, not how fast the water was rushing by. Four feet was all that separated me from my death. I hadn't moved from my perch on the bench; I suspected an imprint of the life jacket was becoming permanently etched onto my butt.

Brooke was light on her feet. Miss Twinkle-Toes easily hopped from one end of the boat to the other. There were half a dozen other kids on the boat with us. I only recognized Brooke, but thankfully she didn't mention my rant at the party.

Forgettable. That's me.

Blaine was Mr. Popularity as usual. He laughed and socialized with everyone, even me. "Come up here," he called out. A row of legs dangled over the high end of the boat. Brooke was in her bikini. Her hummingbird tattoo was mocking me: "*See how quickly I can move about the boat? I'm fearless!*"

"On the way back," I told him, flaunting my best fake smile. I don't think he suspected I hadn't breathed since we left the yacht club. I hugged my elbows, freezing in the wind. I guess when you're waiting for the next wave to take you to your death, the sun doesn't feel so warm.

I hate sailing.

I couldn't believe how much of a loser I was turning out to be. Francine would have had a stroke if she had seen me wimping out like this. "*Think of the spreadsheet,*" she would remind me, prompting me into action. "*Think of the check marks!*"

But fear kept me welded to the bench. It's hard to seduce your crush when he's getting all the attention and help he wants from Brooke, the professional good-times, party girl. She knew all the boat's thingys' and doodads' real names.

Luke was mostly at the helm, giving her instructions. "Tighten the jib. Pull in the sheet on the other side."

Brooke did all of this to his satisfaction while laughing and looking gorgeous. Pretty much the opposite of me. Then she hopped around, offering to put lotion on the shirtless guys. I looked away when she began to lotion Blaine's shoulders.

My sunscreen stayed unused inside my Kipling bag, forgotten and unnecessary—just like me.

Luke reached over, undoing the rope for the main sail. "I'll get it," I said, eager to upstage Brooke. I jumped up and wobbled a bit. My legs were like jelly. He eased back on the tiller, changing our direction, taking us out of the wind. We slowed down. My shoulders unglued themselves from my ears.

"Better?" he asked. There was genuine concern in his voice. We were the only ones in the cockpit.

I noticed the tips of his ears were getting red. I took the sunscreen out of my Kipling bag, then pointed to his ears. "You're getting a sunburn," I told him. He only shrugged. I unscrewed the top for him. "Trust me," I said. "When I was thirteen I had a pixie cut and my ears were blistered all summer. It was gross."

He made no movement to take it from me. The wind played with his shirt—it was unbuttoned to mid-chest. I could see the last two letters of his tattoo, "*me*." His hands were on the wheel, relaxed and confident. A rush of heat that had nothing to do with the weather pulsed all the way down to my toes.

I studied the sun sparkling on the waves, trying to clear my head. "And everyone thought I was a boy," I continued my story, "so it was twice as bad." He said nothing. I pushed the bottle closer, almost under his nose. I gave it a tiny squeeze and a dollop of cream bubbled on the top. I stared at it, trying to ignore the way his shirt kept opening and closing. "You'll be all blistered for the wedding," I finally said. Okay, that was a last-ditch effort.

He stayed quiet.

This guy was so frustrating. I didn't understand why he was so upset about me crushing on Blaine. I mean, everyone with a pulse had a crush on Blaine—even some guys, I bet. Besides, I'd never even kissed Blaine...but I'd kissed Luke, and I wanted to kiss him again. Why couldn't I just tell him that?

I was swaying in the cockpit, alone with Luke and a bottle of sunscreen. This moment called for action. I couldn't wait any longer.

"Are You A Natural Flirt?"

No. But I knew someone who was.

"Here," I said. Then, before Luke could protest, I began to lightly dab the tips of his ears. He stayed very still, then he inclined his head just an inch so I could reach in front of him to get the other ear. Even though I couldn't see those blue eyes, I felt his stare. The scene of Chloe on the beach with Sam played over and over again in my mind.

My finger left his ear, then trailed down his jaw. The words were out of my mouth before I lost my nerve. "Is there anywhere else that needs attention?" I asked.

He took off his glasses, then slowly moved in close. His lips brushed against my earlobe. I couldn't breathe.

"*Don't mess with my head,*" he whispered.

Then he pulled away, sunglasses back in place. He was looking ahead, already forgetting me.

I dropped the sunscreen and clambered down the tiny ladder into the cabin. I raced to the bathroom and locked the small door. Then I put my face in my hands and started to cry.

I hated how he got under my skin. I hated how everything I'd ever said or done had been nothing but a disappointment to him. I hated how I cared what he thought of me.

When I was done, I ran the tap and splashed some cold water on my face. I looked in the mirror. Chloe's lip gloss and bronzer had worn off. "What's the most important thing to you, right now?" I asked myself.

Getting the hell off this boat, I thought. *Enough of this.*

Determined to make it to dry land, I opened the door—and ran right into the bare chest of Blaine.

"Hey." His arms went automatically to my waist as we wobbled against each other. "Coming up top?"

This is it! My brain screamed at me. *This is it! I'm in Blaine's arms, pressed up against his chest. When will I ever have this opportunity again?* Francine's voice was inside my head: "*Kiss him, Kelsey! Kiss him now!*"

But I didn't. I stepped back.

Footsteps squeaked down the ladder. A pair of legs came into view. One calf boasted a long scar. Luke ducked his head and turned to us.

I wrapped my fingers around Blaine's neck, pulled his mouth down to mine, and kissed him right on the lips.

Blaine made a surprised noise at the back of his throat. I peeked to the side, but Luke had already started back up the ladder.

I let go of Blaine. Neither of us said anything. It was dead quiet. No butterflies. No standing on tiptoe for another kiss. And certainly no neurotransmitters firing.

"Okay," he said slowly. I was ready to apologize, but he smiled and took my hand. "I think you need some fresh air," he said. He led the way up top. I didn't even glance over at the wheel.

We walked along the deck, then he lifted me, placing me in the main sail. "Just lean back," he said. It was like an upright hammock. He stood in front of me. "That was a nice surprise," he said.

"It's been a weird day," I said quietly.

He laughed, then patted my knee, and turned to look out over the water.

I stared at the back of Blaine's head, thinking of all the times I'd kissed him in my imagination. Maybe I'd built it up so much that the real thing, or at least the first time, wouldn't be able to compete. I should have been shaking with excitement. But there wasn't even disappointment, only a hollowness.

Butterflies don't lie.

I didn't even have a sense of accomplishment at finally getting to check something off Francine's spreadsheet.

I closed my eyes, wishing I'd never set foot inside the Queen's Galley, thinking of the heartache I would have been spared if I'd decided to spend my summer mowing lawns instead.

"Coming about," someone said.

"Hmm?" I kept my eyes closed. The rocking sensation of the boat was surprisingly soothing.

Yes, I'll just go to sleep. Wake me up when we're back at the wharf.

"Coming about."

I took in a deep breath, letting the salt air fill my lungs.

"Kels!"

My eyes flew open. Luke was at the wheel, pointing at me. "Coming about! Get out of the sail!"

Brooke stood in front of him, then did a mock salute and began to undo the sheet for the jib. This made him smile—that or watching her bend over, giving him a nice shot of her butt.

"Coming about." Stupid sailing terms. Why can't they just say, "We're turning now, everyone, watch yourselves."

I hopped out of the sail. I still had Chloe's flip-flops on. They made me stumble forward.

I grabbed the safety stay, but I was already moving too fast.

I tumbled headfirst over the edge and hit the water.

The last thing I remember seeing was Blaine's shoulders. He was turned away, as always, with his back to me.

TWENTY-EIGHT

Water was all around me, even above me. I was in the ocean.

THE OCEAN.

My head popped above the waves. The back of the sailboat was quickly getting smaller. I pictured it turning around, but it kept moving away. No one had seen me fall in.

A wave crashed over my head. Chloe's sweater sucked up the water, weighing me down. I sank again, trying to move my arms and legs, but it felt like I was moving in mud.

I slipped lower and everything grew darker. Where was the surface? I expected my head to hit the rocks below any second. How deep had I gone? My fingers clawed at the water.

The last few bubbles escaped my mouth.

This didn't feel like that time at the pool. Gone were the shouts of other kids and the white water blinding my vision.

I was suspended in a dark infinity of space. No sound. No vision. No direction.

And unlike the last time, I wasn't swimming to get to the top. I was sinking.

I knew I was going to die. The weirdest things started going through my mind. I imagined my parents and Chet weeping as they went though my room after the funeral. I pictured them finding Francine's spreadsheet on my laptop. I was surprised to find I wasn't upset about dying; I was mostly upset that I wouldn't get the chance to tick off all the squares.

Maybe Blaine would tell them at the funeral that I'd kissed him. I would want Francine to know that even at the bitter end, I was dedicated to Operation Tongue.

I was weightless.

How did I get here?

I didn't know what I was supposed to do. It was so quiet.

A roar exploded beside me. Pain seared the top of my head. Suddenly, I was moving up.

Air.

Someone was yelling in my ear. I was coughing and spitting. I flailed again, punching everything around me.

"Quit it!" The voice was right beside me. My orange cushion was thrust into my chest. "Hold this." Strong hands roughly pulled my arms through the holes.

Life really does turn on a dime, just like Julia said. I was supposed to be dead, slowly floating down to the bottom where the lobsters hide, but there I was, bobbing on the ocean, breathing oxygen, staring into Luke's blue eyes.

He shouted out orders to Blaine and the others on board, who looked totally helpless without him. While they manoeuvred the boat back to us, Luke treaded water and swam forward with one hand grasped onto my life jacket's belt, tugging me back to the boat.

Trust me. Nothing is more embarrassing than almost dying in front of the guy you are secretly in love with.

Luke kept mumbling under his breath, frustrated with Blaine's lack of finesse with the tiller. Several Stunders clambered to drop the sails. The jig was loose and fluttering wildly. Brooke managed to get the motor started. The boat turned around and headed back toward us.

I watched the on-board antics with a sense of numb detachment. I felt like I was in a movie theatre, innocently watching from the safety of my seat, rather than the person who had caused all this calamity.

Luke and I were two little soaked heads bobbing in the waves.

I should be screaming right now. I'm in the water. I can't see the bottom—and let's not even think about the wildlife circling under my feet, ready to start nibbling...

But the funny thing was, I didn't feel scared. I could have waited in the water with Luke forever—if it were the Bahamas.

"It's cold," I finally said, my lips quivering.

"It's the Atlantic Ocean," he replied.

"Thanks," I said weakly.

A waved crashed into his face. He spit out the water to the side. Even drenched and coughing up sea water, I still found him sexy.

"For Christ's sake, Kels," he groaned. "You almost drowned."

I could read the tension in his features. He was either extremely scared or completely pissed with me—probably a little of both. I had no defence, so I stayed quiet while he treaded water for both of us.

Brooke slowed down the motor and Blaine threw us a rope. Luke kept a hold of me while he grabbed the line with his other hand. We were quickly pulled to the boat. The small ladder on the stern had been extended to reach the water's surface. Luke pushed me up first. My legs had zero muscle memory. I had to be pulled in by the others.

When Luke and I were safely on board, one of the Stunders said, "Holy shit. I've never see anyone fall overboard before!"

"Luke, you're a hero." Brooke gave him a hug, then squealed and stepped back quickly. "And you're freezing," she teased.

Luke peeled off his shirt, and I had to look away from the tattoo. The song played in my memory. I blinked away the prickle of hot tears.

"Dude," Blaine said, handing him a dry T-shirt. "I had no idea what was going on. One second you're at the wheel and the next you're diving off the boat."

"I didn't even see you fall in," Brooke said to me.

I shivered on the spot, a puddle of sea water growing at my feet. All heads turned to me, including Luke's. "I owed Kelsey," he said. "The first time we met I almost ran her over." He grinned at me and I knew it was fake. "We're even now, okay?"

There was a smattering of laughter. A few Stunders began raising the sails again, anxious to continue their cruising. Luke gave a few orders, organizing everyone.

Luke didn't say anything else to me for the rest of the trip. Someone wrapped a blanket around me and Brooke even gave me a towel for my hair. I took inventory: Chloe's flip-flops had gone overboard with me, plus her designer sunglasses.

Oddly enough, my falling off the boat hadn't dampened the party mood. When we docked, everyone made plans to continue the festivities at Brooke's summer house. No one bothered to invite the pale, pruned-up corpse under the blanket in the corner.

Blaine helped me off the boat. He laid his hand on my shoulder. "Are you sure you're okay?" he asked. It was in his usual "I'm everybody's best friend" voice.

I guess his neurotransmitters didn't fire either.

I shrugged off the blanket and handed it back to him. "Yeah," I lied. "My mom is picking me up."

He pointed to Chloe's sweater, now stretched out of shape. "Next time just wear your bikini," he joked.

I pictured my paycheques going straight to Chloe for the rest of the summer. I didn't even register that Blaine had kind of insinuated he might take me out sailing again—or that he was imagining me in a bikini.

It was sunset and the wind had picked up. I was freezing and all I wanted was to get home and pull the covers over my head. I started up the wharf toward the yacht club.

"Hey," Blaine called out. "See you tomorrow."

Sweet bejesus! Was he actually asking me out? Like, right now?!

"You're working the wedding, right?" he clarified. "Make sure you save the biggest bacon-wrapped scallops for me!"

"Sure. I'm all about the big scallops," I wanted to tell him. *"In fact, I could be getting real close with all the scallops right now if Luke hadn't jumped in while you were gazing at the ocean, butthead."*

But instead I gave him a fake smile.

I was learning to master the fake smile.

There's nothing like walking barefoot though the back roads of your village with someone's droopy designer sweater slapping against your knees. Whatever I'd messed up this summer, I would say this was proper punishment.

My feet were numb, and I was so cold my goosebumps had goosebumps. At least my Kipling bag was dry. Halfway home I took out my magazine and started to read, just so people wouldn't think I'd escaped from the insane asylum.

Who the hell was that about? I read the other descriptions and was just as confused. I fit none of the answers. In fact, I didn't seem to fit in anywhere. I took the magazine and flung it into the ditch.

How To Know You're Really In Love

You're a romantic at heart, and find something sensual in everyone you meet. Guys gravitate to your warm personality. You usually have many offers, but your deep commitment to true love prevents you from ever totally trusting someone until you're sure he's just as romantic as you.

What's the point of being in love if no one loves you back?

It was dark now. I hugged my elbows, wishing my house would come into view. A stone dropped in my gut. What would Mom and Dad be arguing about tonight? Poor Chet, he was worried about his badge and I was literally falling for all the wrong guys. I suddenly felt so stupid for what I'd done. Did I care so little about myself that I had risked dying because I didn't want to look stupid in a life jacket? How could anyone have explained that to Chet?

Tears streaked down my face. Lights crested the hill behind me, casting my long shadow on the road. I moved to the side and kept my head down.

A car slowed down and came up alongside me. Shiny red paint crept into my peripheral vision.

"Hey, Kelsey. Need a drive?"

"No thanks, Frank," I said.

He leaned out of the window. "Are you crying?" he asked.

I stayed quiet and tried to hurry my steps, which was stupid since I couldn't outwalk an SUV. The shiny red paint stayed right beside me.

"Did you and your boyfriend have a fight?" Frank's tone was laced with perverted enthusiasm. I shuddered at whatever images were swirling around in his head.

"No," I said. "And no, I don't need a drive. I'm fine on my own." I turned around, praying for another car to crest the hill. Frank seemed especially tenacious this evening.

"Going all women's lib are you?" he teased. "Maybe that's the reason you and your boyfriend broke up. Don't be stupid, beautiful." He patted the door with his pudgy hand. "You better hop in, I'll take good care of you."

When faced with an uncomfortable situation at a party you...?

A. give a quick yet polite excuse and leave immediately.
B. confront the reason for the discomfort. No one's going to spoil your fun.
C. continue with your usual activity, hoping the situation will work itself out.

"Come on, Kelsey," he pleaded. "I don't bite." There was a deep chuckle then he added, "Unless you want—"

"FUCK OFF!" I screamed.

He stopped the car. I pointed my finger right at his face. "I don't want a drive with you. I don't want to do anything with you. So put that creep-mobile in drive and get the hell away from me before I start screaming. I swear to God, I will tell my parents and call the cops if you don't leave right now."

Frank wiggled his shoulders back into the cab. "I'm only offering you a drive," he said. "Fine, get kidnapped. See if I care." He pulled away, hitting the gas hard. Bits of dust and tiny pebbles sprayed in my direction.

I stood in place, trying to catch my breath. I'd never told an adult to fuck off before. (I don't think I'd ever said it to anyone's face before, actually.) I found it oddly gratifying. Maybe I needed to start making my own spreadsheets.

I started waking again. A new-found sense of calm took over. The crickets serenaded me from the shadows alongside the road. I appreciated their soft and non-judgemental murmurs—it made nice background music. I planned on downloading some nature sounds from iTunes that night. My summer playlist could use some meditation pieces, I reasoned.

A blinking light came through the darkness over the hill. I wondered if Frank had circled around. My insides steeled for another round. But as the single light approached I realized it wasn't a car, but a bicycle.

"Kels!" I heard a breathless voice call out.

Luke biked toward me, the front light blinding me. I put up an arm to shield my eyes. I didn't bother to wipe my face of my latest bout of tears. I'd had enough of being fake for one day. He pulled up beside me, then switched off the light. He'd changed into a hoodie.

His face was blotchy. "Why did…you leave all…alone?" he asked between breaths.

I stared at him, trying to figure out his angle. This guy was so confusing. What did he expect me to say? The weight of the day suddenly settled on my shoulders. If I wasn't going to hide my tear-streaked face from Luke, I wasn't going to lie to him either.

"I thought that would be obvious, Luke," I said. "Everyone else was invited to Brooke's house."

He wasn't sure how to respond to that one. I was pleased to have stumped him. "Why did you follow me?" I probed. Suddenly I didn't feel so cold anymore.

Luke had the strangest expression on his face. "I would think that would be obvious," he said, adding with emphasis, "*Kelsey.*" He glanced down at my bare feet, then back into my eyes. He frowned. "It would have been useless to save you from drowning and then let you get hit by a car on your walk home."

"I thought we were even," I said, reminding him of his declaration on the boat.

He shrugged. "You seem to get into a lot of sticky situations. I should at least make sure you make it to your driveway. "

A warm rush spread over me, but I was in no mood for flirting—just ask the magazine I'd cast into the wilderness. I tucked a stringy bit of hair behind my ear and started making my way up the road again.

Luke stepped off his bike and walked alongside me, keeping the bike between us like some kind of chaperone.

He cleared his throat. "I guess swimming lessons don't seem so useless now, huh?"

His cavalier tone bristled my nerves, disturbing the serene attitude I had won by yelling at Frank. I was irritated and pushed to my limit. "Look," I said, my voice echoing sharply against the lazy summer evening. "All I want is to go home, be ignored by my parents, have a nice, hot shower, then snuggle with Chetter-cheese in front of *The Sound of Music*. All I want is for everything about this horrible day to melt away."

I breathed heavily, too exhausted to cry anymore.

Holy bacon turds, I was messed up.

His expression was pained, but he didn't look embarrassed or try to tell me to chill out. He simply kept walking beside me.

When I calmed down, he finally told me his story.

TWENTY-NINE

"Four months ago," Luke began, "I had this whole summer planned out. I'd be moving down here, working at the yacht club and partying with Blaine every weekend." He paused and let out a sigh. "Or weeknight, if the opportunity presented itself."

He sniffed. "Then my dad comes home and announces to my mom that he's moving out and wants a divorce. I spent the whole night listening to my mom scream questions. It turns out he's in love with someone else, and not only does he want to marry her, but he's going to be a new dad...all over again."

"Oh my God," I whispered. It was so quiet the only sound was our footsteps and the clicking of the bike's spokes. Even the crickets had stopped chirping to listen. "What did you do?" As if there were anything he could do.

"I took off in the middle of their fight," he said. "I got in my dad's BMW and drove around. I had no idea what I was doing. Then I hit a long stretch of road with no one else around. I pressed the gas pedal to the floor, daring myself not to slow down."

My mouth fell open. "Were you trying to kill yourself?" I felt sick to my stomach,

"No." He shook his head slowly. "Well, I don't know. I mean, I wasn't really trying. I guess at that moment I didn't care. I was mad enough to destroy something. All I was thinking about was hurting him the way he was hurting me and my mom."

We walked a little further in silence. He absentmindedly touched his side where the tattoo was. "I don't remember the accident. I ended up going off the road and slamming into a power pole. I must have chickened out, though, near the very end." His voice was sterile, unfeeling. "The police told my dad there were brake marks fifty yards before the crash site. Any faster and the scar under my arm would have been stitched up by the coroner."

I hugged my waist, fighting the chill from his words. I had been so concerned about finding out all his secrets, and the shock of finally hearing the real story behind all the mystery made me ashamed. I'd never considered the reasons behind his circumstance would be so tragic and painful.

He cleared his throat again. "When I came around, the fire department was trying to cut me out of the car. The radio channel was programmed for my dad's music, and that song was playing."

"'No one is to blame'?" I asked.

"Yeah. It's weird, though," he told me. "I don't think I turned the radio on."

I shivered, but he didn't notice; he was staring straight ahead. "Does it still hurt?" I asked.

"The scar or my dad?"

"Both, I guess."

"Not always, but yeah, it still hurts. I had to see a shrink for a few months," he said matter-of-factly. "Our family doctor suggested it. You know, suicide risk and all that. And when my dad bought the Queen's Galley, he figured working there would be proper punishment and a way to keep an eye on me at the same time."

He let out a heavy sigh. "My job teaching at the yacht club went to Blaine. He was supposed to be on the maintenance crew, painting handrails and tendering boaters back and forth to shore. But after my screw-up he got promoted."

And there it was: No jail time. No prison sentence. No work order. Just a sad and angry kid with a dick for a dad.

"That's so unfair," I said. "I'm sorry. You'd be a great sailing instructor."

"Don't be," he sniffed and tapped the handlebar of his bike. "You kind of saved me."

"What?" That was the last thing he should be saying to me.

"Being a dishwasher while my cousin has a blast at the yacht club was not part of my summer plan. I didn't know how I was going to survive. I considered running away or totally messing up on purpose to get fired, just to let him know he didn't control the whole planet."

He paused and looked up at the sky. "But I couldn't make any more mistakes or my dad would send me to a treatment facility for 'troubled teens.'" Luke made finger quotes in the air.

"He told you that?"

"Oh yeah," he said. "As pissed as I was, I knew the Queen's Galley was a much better prison than the hospital."

I didn't know what to say. My mouth opened and closed a few times, like a mute marionette.

A half grin curled up the corner of his mouth. "And then you came along," he sighed.

I smiled back cautiously. "Yes?"

He chuckled. "At first I thought you were the icing on my dad's imprisonment: a girl who couldn't stand the sight of me. But then…" He wet his lips and shrugged. "Then you started screwing up all over the place. I couldn't believe there was someone at the Queen's Galley more of a train wreck than I was."

"Oh." My face fell.

He put a hand over his chest. "No, not like that," he explained quickly. "I had no idea what you were going to get into next. I actually started looking forward to going to work."

"Because my disasters were so entertaining?" I asked tiredly. The truth sucked.

"No." It was a complete sentence. The word hung in the air between us. His tone became serious. "Every time I helped you it made me feel important, like I was a hero instead of a screw-up. I was someone worthy, someone to be proud of. Someone," he paused and used my own words back at me, "someone who all the girls wanted to date and all the guys wanted to be best friends with."

My description of Blaine stung my ears. Had I been that blind? "You're nothing like him," I said.

"No kidding." He looked away.

I bit my lip, wishing I had Mom's panache with words. Her brain was a frickin' thesaurus.

What's another word for hero?

The crickets grew bored and started to sing again. Our footsteps scuffed along the road. "I mean, *he* never would have jumped in after me," I finally said. "That was very brave."

When he turned to me, his face had paled. "Seeing you fall over was the most terrifying thing," he said.

"Even more terrifying than waking up in a car full of blood while firefighters cut you free?" I asked incredulously.

He nodded, then started to pick at the tape on his handlebars.

The weirdest image, of Luke biking back to that huge summer house, popped into my head. Would his dad and his fiancé be waiting up for him? Would they make sure there were leftovers to warm up or even a smoothie for him in the kitchen?

"What about your mom?" I asked. He'd been silent about her so far. I couldn't imagine either one of my parents giving the other complete control over me.

His cheeks reddened, and for the first time he actually looked uncomfortable. "She's on a month-long retreat thing for divorced women."

"I'm sorry," I said. My summer suddenly seemed like a dream compared to his life.

"Yeah, well, it gets worse," he told me. "I'm best man at my dad's wedding, so that means I have to give a speech tomorrow."

The cruelty knew no bounds. "This is like Dickens," I told him. That got a smile out of him, and I felt like I'd done at least one good thing today.

We stopped at the end of my driveway. I looked up at my house. Only the living room light was on. I noticed Mom's car was gone as well. "This is me," I told him.

"I know," he said.

My heart skipped a few beats. The butterflies rejoiced that Luke somehow knew where I lived.

We traded weak smiles. I held his stare and wished the moment could go on forever. How could I tell this guy how

I felt when he was dealing with so much? The last thing he needed in his life right now was a screw-up like me.

"What do you want more than anything in the world...right now?"

I wanted Luke. And I wanted him to forget what an idiot I'd been on the boat trying to seduce him with the sunscreen, and especially my non-kiss with Blaine, which was only to make Luke jealous in the first place. And most of all I wanted Luke to want me.

But the words would not come.

I couldn't tell him the truth. Considering all the stuff I'd done to get him in trouble over the past two weeks, the best thing for Luke was the opposite of what I wanted. I wanted him to keep being my hero. But he needed to be far away from me before I messed up his life even more.

Instead of spilling my heart at the end of my driveway, I took the safe option.

"Thanks," I told him. "We're even now."

THIRTY
· · · · · ·

Mom looked up when I came in. She took in my appearance and I waited for the barrage of questions. Instead, she was the one who shocked me. "We have to talk," she said.

Her tone sent a chill down my spine. I glanced down the hallway. "Where are Dad and Chet?" I asked nervously.

"I sent them out," she answered.

I was frozen to the spot. She patted the space beside her on the couch. *Oh my God, it's a sit-down talk.* Suddenly everything made sense...horrible sense.

I shook my head. "No," I said defiantly. "No! You are not moving out and splitting up the family. I will not let you hurt Dad and Chet like that. Who is he?" I demanded, mentally flipping through the faces of men in our village. "Someone from the library?" I almost gagged. "The pharmacist? The guy who owns the deli store on the corner by the old highway? The one who always offers me free gum?"

Mom scrunched up her face. She put up a hand, interrupting me. "What are you talking about?"

"You're never home anymore. Dad looks tired and sad. You only spend time in your office. You never ask how I'm doing…" My voice was rising so high that the neighbours probably thought I was a cat in heat. "I fell into the ocean today and almost drowned! Do you know why I almost drowned?" I didn't wait for her to answer. "Because I can't swim!"

Mom blinked a few times. She stood and reached for me. "Kelsey, honey, calm down." Her arms enveloped me. "I'm not having an affair." She squeezed me tightly, then pulled back. "You're freezing. Have a warm shower and I'll tell you everything."

"No," I sniffed. "Tell me now."

She read my face, then nodded and pulled me down onto the couch beside her. "I know I've been absent a lot lately, and I'm truly sorry for that, but I've had to work for both Dad and I this summer."

"Dad is tutoring at the library," I said, not completely understanding.

Mom let out a sigh and her shoulders crumbled. "He got laid off from the university."

"What?" I was not expecting that. "When?"

"A few weeks ago," she answered. "And because he won't have a job in the fall, I have to work on my thesis and continue working full-time in September to support all of us." She paused, allowing me time to digest what she was saying. "That's why I'm trying to work as much as I can on my thesis this summer."

"But the late nights?" I asked her.

"Sometimes it was research, and sometimes," she tilted her head and focused on my shoulder, "well, sometimes I was checking up on you."

"Huh?" My tone dropped.

She pressed her lips together like she was fighting to get the next sentence out. She was usually full steam ahead, a no-nonsense kind of gal. To see her struggle with words was freaky. I swore she was going cray cray. I could almost hear the spooky violins playing in the background.

"I wanted to make sure you were safe," she finally confessed.

"Huh?"

"I only followed you a few times," she said quickly. My expression must have conveyed my growing horror. She gave me a defiant look. "I just wanted to make sure you got home all right," she defended. "Occasionally, when I finished researching at the library, I'd wait outside the Queen's Galley until you'd finished your shift. Then I'd follow you home."

She sat straighter and looked down her nose at me. "One time I saw you talking with Frank Driscoll and I almost rammed the back of his truck." She paused and gave me a stern look. "I don't want you socializing with him. He's older, and his character is too suspect in my opinion."

"Don't worry," I said, putting up my hands. I decided to keep my recent fight with Frank a secret, though. My head was hurting with all of Mom's revelations. I wanted to know everything and not get sidetracked by talking about the village creep.

"I also hired Luke to cut the grass," she said, matter-of-factly. "I liked how you both worked at the same place, and it was clear the day I met him, after he found Chet, that he could be trusted."

"Huh?" I was becoming stupider by the second.

"Actually, he came over the first time and more or less offered to help for the rest of the summer. You know how your dad's herniated disc can pop out so unexpectedly.

Plus, he's really good with Chet." She was using a voice that seemed to come straight from her days on the university debating team. Even though it never would have entered my mind that Mom had been checking up on me, when she explained it point blank, it made logical sense. To know she'd been spying instead of ignoring me was strangely comforting.

"But that's not important." Mom waved her hand, erasing the subject of Luke off the board. "I wanted to tell you that even though things may seem bleak, your dad and I will always be there for you and Chet. And we will do everything to make sure there is enough money for you after graduation. We don't even need that second car. Dad and Chet are actually at the dealership now, discussing pricing for the hatchback."

She put her hand over mine. "Dad wanted to tell you from the beginning, but I was adamant we keep it from you. We argued about it a few times. Now, of course, I see I should have listened to him. I wish I had told you earlier, but I didn't want to spoil your summer." She squeezed my hand and got a little misty-eyed.

Mom doesn't do misty-eyed. I felt like I was being fooled.

Maybe I should start searching the basement for alien pods.

"I don't get it," I said. "You're always in your office or doing research. If you were so worried about me having a good summer, why didn't you confide in me about Dad? I mean, things could have been so much better if I'd known what was going on. Do you have any idea how stressful it's been around here for me?"

Mom dropped her chin, looking guilty for the first time that night. "I know," she said. "And your dad argued the same point, but I convinced him that we shouldn't involve you in our financial worries. You already have a job, and you take care of Chet so much."

I stayed silent, trying to reorganize my brain. Mom took in a deep breath. "I appreciate that this is a lot to hear at once. There were times when I wanted to tell you everything, but you seemed to be having a good summer. You met a new friend at work and Luke says everyone enjoys your company at the Queen's Galley. He says you make the shift so entertaining that the time flies."

I couldn't argue with that. "Entertaining for others, I guess," I said.

Mom's voice sounded tired, but she made sure to look me right in the eyeballs. "This may be a poor excuse for not telling you about your dad's job, but sometimes it's hard to tell the truth to someone you love, especially if it's something that will hurt them."

Yeah, been there, I thought.

"What about having to take Chet to all his stuff?" I asked. "That always gets dumped on me."

Mom looked surprised. "He loves you the most, Kelsey. Dad and I have no choice but to let you be his first pick."

And just like that, life turned on a dime. How could I complain about being the most-loved person of the most loveable person in the world? Suddenly, being Chet's chauffeur and personal cheering section was an honour, something my parents coveted.

I'm not sure if it was relief that my mom wasn't having an affair or the fact that she was acting like a mom again, but the floodgates opened, and I spilled out all my secrets.

She listened without interrupting as I explained about the salt fiasco, getting Luke in trouble with the messy flower garden, the dog, and my big screw-up of letting Blaine and his friends into the bar. And then finally, my epic adventure from that day, starting with the spilled seafood on the floor and finishing with my sloppy spillage into the high seas.

She was right, it's hard to tell the person you love the truth sometimes, but I was learning that life only gets harder if you keep it a secret.

She made me a cup of hot chocolate, then told me to have a shower and get some sleep. In the morning everything would seem better, she promised. Then she added, with a tone that left no room for doubt, "I'll make sure of it."

After I showered I put on my warmest pyjamas, opened my laptop, and stared at Francine's spreadsheet. Only two boxes were left: "Tell Blaine how you feel" and "Have a simply amazing, neurotransmitter-firing, stomach-full-of-butterflies kiss."

I thought back to my so-called sailing date. I couldn't really check off either box. It was unsatisfying, just like Blaine's kiss.

THIRTY-ONE

· · · · · · · · · ·

The next morning, Mom drove me down to the Queen's Galley. She had washed and ironed my uniform. It lay neatly folded on my lap. I was pretty sure Mr. Deveau would be adamant that I stay far away from the guests, and the dishes, and also the food. I didn't know what Mom thought she could do to save my job, but at that moment I had no other plan than to follow her. She had assured me that she would take care of everything.

Vague much?

We walked into the foyer. The large dining area to the left had been transformed into a wedding room. Rows of white chairs were getting trimmed with organza bows. Jesse's mother's wedding cake was on a pedestal in the corner.

I suddenly felt guilty complaining about my two parents when she'd just lost her dad. I hoped her summer at camp was shaping up better than mine.

Mom marched through and headed toward the kitchen. She had swapped her usual bun and frumpy denim walking shorts for a French braid and pencil skirt. She was on a mission.

I trailed behind, wishing she had let me quit like I had wanted to this morning. My Kipling bag bounced off my hip, but I didn't reach down for my gorilla. Clyde and Mr. Deveau looked up when we walked in.

I nervously glanced around, but it was only the four of us here this morning.

"Mr. Deveau?" My mother smiled and held out her hand. "I'm Kelsey's mother, we spoke on the phone earlier."

Earlier?

My armpits got sticky. I had no idea what was coming next.

"As I told you during our conversation," Mom began, "last night Kelsey confided to me what transpired the other evening when she let the underage boys into the bar. She will, of course, apologize in person to Mr. Mulder."

Mr. Deveau stiffened his shoulders and tilted up his nose. He wasn't in a suit jacket today, but his white shirt was embroidered with mermaids. "I contacted Mr. Mulder following your call this morning. He has been informed, and he has left the decision up to me." He paused and scanned me as if his eyes were lie detectors. "In this case, firing Kelsey is an appropriate course of action."

Even though I'd wanted to quit that morning—and I figured I'd be fired anyway—his words still cut through me. I winced.

"Because the restaurant has lost its liquor license for a week?" Mom clarified.

"Yes," Mr. Deveau answered.

"Because she let her friends into the bar area?" she continued.

"Yes." Mr. Deveau was sounding more European with every confident yes.

Clyde stayed quiet, watching the conversation like a tennis match. I'm not sure who he disliked most, me or Mr. Deveau.

My mom continued. "Please explain to me why she was left alone in a restaurant, supposedly under your supervision, where anyone could have come to the door and assaulted her."

Mr. Deveau faltered this time.

Mom's best teacher voice was in full swing now. "Is it customary for a young girl to be in charge of deciding who gets access to the bar through the dining room?"

"Well, of course not," Mr. Deveau stammered.

"Oh!" my mom said with exaggerated surprise. "So she *did* receive specific instructions about never opening the front door after the restaurant has closed?"

Mr. Deveau fumbled. His fingers flitted over the embroidered mermaids. "It goes without saying, Mrs. Sinclair."

"Is it typical training protocol to have the underage staff also work as bouncers for the bar? I looked at Kelsey's paycheque and her hourly rate does not indicate that she is responsible for any duties other than being a busgirl." Mom paused and waited for Mr. Deveau to swallow whatever part of his stomach had risen into his throat.

The corner of Clyde's mouth slowly curled up. He reached for a cigarette from the breast pocket of his white smock.

My mother was some kind of bizarre enigma. I was rapt, hanging on her every word.

"What…" Mr. Deaveau began, then he cleared his throat. "What do you think would be proper action in this case, Mrs. Sinclair?"

His question was sincere.

Mom looked at me. My eyes widened. Holy sweet bejesus! I hadn't had a chance to look at the script; I had no idea what to say.

"Well, Kelsey," Mom started. "Have you had enough of being a busgirl?"

Talk about a loaded question. "Yes," I answered truthfully. "But I want to keep working here." This came as a surprise to me, but weirdly enough Mom didn't look shocked.

She nodded, then looked at Clyde. "I understand Loretta will be non-weight-bearing for a few weeks." Clyde nodded. We both looked at my mother with amazement—how was she privy to a stranger's medical condition?

"Her son is tutored by my husband at the library." She beamed. "Kids find that kind of thing so exciting to talk about." She put a hand on my shoulder. "And since you'll be short-handed, perhaps Kelsey can work in the kitchen?" Then she added with a smile for Clyde, "Under your supervision, she'll really reach her full potential."

Mr. Deveau forced a smile.

Nice burn, Mom.

Clyde placed the unlit cigarette between his lips. "I'm short a dishwasher," he said. "I'll need her for the wedding this afternoon."

"Perfect," she said. Then she gave me a questioning look.

"Oh, yeah," I stammered. "Perfect."

My mom shook hands with them, thereby officially ending the business transaction. Before she left, she added one more tidbit. "Oh, yes, and Kelsey will need to leave early this afternoon," she explained. "Her little brother is going for his swimming badge and he insists that she be there to cheer him on."

"This afternoon?" I frowned back at her. "But Chet's lesson is in an hour." For a second I thought I ruined some part of her elaborate plan to overthrow the Queen's Galley.

But Mom didn't even miss a beat. "I spoke to his swimming instructor," she said. "Chet will be having a private lesson this afternoon." Then Mom smiled. "She'll give him something special even if he doesn't get his badge."

"Thanks," I said.

She gave me a wink and we both smiled again.

Mr. Deveau's face was as red and greasy as the lobster special. Clyde merely raised a shoulder. "I'll make sure she gets out on time," he grinned, "mademoiselle."

Then, I swear to God, Mom sashayed back out to the dining room. Mr. Deveau made to leave, but then turned and walked out the back kitchen door, as though he were afraid to run in to Mom again.

I thought about my discarded magazine lying in the ditch at the side of the road. There was no quiz on the planet that could have accomplished what Mom had just done for me. She might not know what an ombre hair treatment is or what the top five hottest fashion trends for the summer are, but she'd came through for me in a major way when it counted the most. I was in awe of her ability to stand up and fight for me.

I discovered more in that five minutes listening to Mom's slick logic as she debated with Mr. Deveau than I'd learned all those years doing stupid quizzes. Growing up had absolutely nothing to do with makeup and clothes. It was about taking care of the people you love.

Clyde and I stood by the window, watching my mom back out of the parking lot. "I like your mother," he said, the unlit cigarette bobbing up and down in his mouth. "She's got fire in her heart."

"Nah," I said, blushing with pride, "she's got me and Chet in her heart."

THIRTY-TWO

The reception was in full swing. I was whirling around the kitchen in my T-shirt and shorts, sweating like a pig. But I didn't care. I was hidden in the kitchen, and Clyde was turning out to be a pretty cool guy to hang out with. He even made me the most amazing cheese omelet I had ever tasted.

Chloe flitted in and out, giving us gossip about the guests. Julia told me I was doing a great job and that maybe the kitchen suited me better, since I was already a pro at dumping food. Ronnie was waltzing around as if the heat and constant smiling at strangers weren't exhausting.

I managed to sneak a quick look through the glass panel. Luke was in his tux, leaning against the wall with a few other guys I guessed were his friends from the city. He looked uncomfortable. No, wait: he looked amazing, but I could tell he was hurting.

I wanted more than anything to whisk him away from this ridiculous wedding. I'd wrap my arms around him and tell him everything was going to be okay. I thought about how my mom had come through for me, and how she'd been trying to protect me by keeping dad's job a secret. I didn't think Luke had anyone looking out for him.

This time I want to rescue the hero for a change.

My palm pressed against the kitchen door. I wished I could march into the dining room and tell his dad off for being such a selfish turd head. Couldn't he see how miserable he'd made his family?

My chest tightened at the thought of Luke having to give a speech. I don't even like giving oral reports in front of classmates. But Luke had to give a toast in front of all these stuck-up adults to his cheating dad. I'd be so angry. What the hell was he going to say?

I let myself have one more look. Luke was shuffling around, hands in his pockets, head tilted downward. *"Everything's going to be okay,"* I whispered. If only I'd had more courage last night, I could have said it to his face.

Since my talk with Mom, my life didn't seem so pathetic or disastrous. But I'd wasted my chance with Luke, I was sure of that. When Mr. Deveau called Mr. Mulder that morning, he'd probably told Luke all about my part in the Queen's Galley losing its license.

He must think I'm the biggest schmuck on the planet. I purposely made out with his cousin in front of him, then hardly offered any kind of empathy when he told me about his car accident.

I thought about his tattoo.

Except in this case, I'm the one to blame.

Chloe came back to load up another tray. I helped Clyde remove a fresh batch of broiled scallops and bacon from the oven. "Awesome," she smiled. "I love being the most popular."

I twisted a tea towel in my hand. The day, it seemed, was made for confessions. When I told her about her flip-flops lying at the bottom of the Atlantic Ocean, she gasped. "I'll pay you back," I sputtered. "I promise."

She looked shocked. "Who cares about flip-flops? You fell off a sailboat...like, into the ocean."

"Luke saved me," I said, looking down, feeling the blush grow hot.

Chloe made a sound between a giggle and a knowing sigh. "Listen," she said. "Don't worry about the flip-flops, they were knockoffs. And so were the sunglasses."

"But I still need to pay you," I offered.

She grabbed a fresh batch of napkins. "Chill," she laughed. "You can pay me thirty bucks, okay?"

I nodded, but I was still unconvinced she was telling me the truth.

She picked up on my hesitance and put down the tray. "Listen, it's all right. Friends swap clothes all the time."

Friend!!!

I immediately brightened. "Is there anything of mine you want to borrow?"

She gave my ridiculously plain T-shirt-and-shorts combo a quick up-and-down glance. "Um...not yet. Let's see what your school wardrobe is like in September." She picked up the tray and moved toward the dining room.

I leaned over the counter. "You mean you'll talk to me in the hallways and stuff?"

"I always talk to my friends." She stopped and laughed a bit. "You kind of remind me of Jesse when she was younger, but without all the jock stuff." She looked me up and down. "Yup, you're a little Jesse. I'm calling you L. J. from now on."

I pictured myself jumping over the counter to hug her. I had always wanted a nickname. And now I had one from the coolest girl in school.

Julia burst in and slapped her empty tray on the counter. Clyde and I moved into action, sliding the mini crab cakes into place. I added a few sprigs of parsley for decoration. Julia and Clyde shared a look.

"What's so funny?" I asked them.

"Nothing," Julia said, clearly smirking. "Absolutely nothing."

When things slowed down enough, I was able to put a load of wine glasses through the washer. I wandered over to the window. Blaine was standing in the driveway, hanging out with a few other guys who'd been with Luke earlier.

His hands were in his pockets. He looked very handsome… well, from behind. I suddenly realized I had been so in love with Blaine's shoulders because that was the part of him I saw the most. I hardly ever saw his face; he was always turned away from me.

I thought of Francine's spreadsheet. I may have failed at Operation Tongue, but I had learned a lot. Like how the best advice is from people who know me and care about me, and not from a magazine trying to sell me lip gloss. And that the right thing to do is usually the hardest. Francine would be proud of me.

Blaine threw his head back and laughed. I folded my tea towel and left it on the counter, then made my way out the back kitchen door. At least I could check off one more box on the spreadsheet. The guys turned my way. I didn't hesitate, but walked straight up to Blaine. I smoothed my hands over my dirty apron. "Hi, Blaine," I said. I was surprised my voice sounded so level. I wasn't the least bit embarrassed to look so grubby in front of him.

He smiled but kept his hands in his pockets. "Hey," he said. "All dried off?" he joked.

I didn't even bother asking the other guys to give us some privacy. I handled it just like Mom had, truthfully and simply. "Blaine," I started, "I've been in love with you for the last year and a half."

His face fell. I ignored the snickers from his friends and continued. "Actually, I was in love with your shoulders—I sit behind you in math class," I explained. "But here's the thing, it turns out I only *thought* I was in love with you. I didn't even know you. And I wanted this summer to be the chance for that to happen."

Blaine rubbed his chin, maybe trying to conjure up a memory of us in math class. Or maybe he was stalling until I got called back into the kitchen. "Well," he started. "I'm not really into starting a new relationship right now. I mean, I just lost Regan, and…" he slouched as a way of ending his sentence.

I shook my head. "No, it's okay. I don't want to date you or start a relationship. I just had to tell you that."

"Okay," he said, uncertain. His eyes darted around the driveway as if he was waiting for someone to jump out and yell, "gotcha."

I wondered if he was a bit insulted when nobody materialized. "It's not that I don't enjoy staring at your shoulders," I explained. "I finally figured out I don't want your shoulders."

"Uh-huh," he nodded.

I started to back up. "So, enjoy the rest of your summer."

He gave me a confused wave. One of the guys punched him in the shoulder. By the time I opened up the kitchen door, their conversation had moved on to sailing.

I walked over and started unloading the dishwasher. Clyde asked me why I was smiling at the sink.

"I'm a sucker for check marks," I told him.

Chloe and Julia rushed into the kitchen. "Quick!" they said. "The toasts are beginning."

I helped pour champagne into their glasses and load up their trays. They teetered out, fighting to balance the delicate glasses. I gave silent thanks NOT to be carrying those around. Ronnie waltzed in with a white orchid in her blonde braid. "I love weddings," she beamed.

Clyde and I shared a look and laughed.

When the last tray had gone out, Clyde checked his watch. "Fifteen minutes until your brother's swimming lesson, Kelsey," he reminded me.

I pretended to clean up the salt and pepper shakers in the pantry. I wedged my toe into the kitchen door, leaving it open a bit so I could hear better.

My heart was smashing against my ribs; I was so scared for Luke.

I peeked through the glass and he was standing at the microphone. He cleared his throat and the room went quiet.

Everyone leaned forward, probably anxious for a delicious bit of gossip about the groom's son.

Luke began, the paper shaking slightly in his hands.

"How do know you're really in love?" he read.

"A. You wander around with a goofy grin on your face.

"B. You start saying things like, 'Aren't the clouds especially fluffy today?'

"C. You're consumed with singing every song that pops into your head."

As Luke read off the list, the smattering of nervous laughter turned into true appreciation. There were even a few claps. I'm sure Mr. Deveau was behind one of them.

When Luke was finished, he finally raised his eyes from the page and looked around the room. "For my dad," he announced, "it was all of the above."

A smile spread across my face. *"That how-hole stole my stuff,"* I whispered.

Luke raised his glass, "A toast to my dad, the guy with the goofy look on his face."

There was a round of cheers and a standing ovation. I was so proud of him. Tears swelled in the corners of my eyes. His face was blotchy, making his eyes bluer than ever, even from all the way across the room.

"What's the most important thing to you in the world...right now?"

I wanted him to look at me. I stared at him, willing him to see me like he always does. The way no one has ever seen me before.

Look at me, Luke! Look at me!

What had he been thinking when he wrote that speech? Had he found my magazine in the ditch on the way home? He'd spilled his story to me and all I'd said was, *"Thanks, we're even."* He must have thought I was unbearably selfish.

He started to turn my way. My heart pounded out a staccato beat. What would his expression be when he saw me? Would it be full of disappointment or hate? Or worse, aloof and uncaring, just like Blaine?

At the last second I turned away and pressed my back up against the wall. If he'd looked for my face and only saw an empty glass pane, I would never know.

THIRTY-THREE
· · · · · · · · · · ·

Clyde tapped me on the shoulder, then nodded to the clock on the wall.

"Oh, bacon turds!" I untied my apron and flung it on the counter, then raced out the back kitchen door. I ran through the intersection, dodging a few people as I pushed my way to the pool.

I scanned the water. There was Chet, splashing and laughing. Only five minutes were left in his private lesson. I made my way to Mom and Dad, sitting on the bench, towels and backpacks strewn around their feet. Dad turned and said something to Mom. She smiled and gave him a kiss. Normally I'd be gagging, but the sight only warmed my heart today. I flopped down beside them.

"How's everything going?" Mom asked, keeping the finer details out of the question.

"Good," I answered, out of breath. She leaned in and inspected me. "Yeah," I insisted. "It's okay. Actually, it's much better. Um…thanks, Mom."

She patted my knee.

"So," I squinted at the pool. "Do you think he's getting a badge?" I asked.

"I'm not sure." Mom sounded worried. "He seems like he's done so much better this week. But when I spoke to his instructor she thought he'd need another two full weeks."

"Doesn't matter." Dad adjusted the video camera. "Chet will be happy with a sticker, too."

I kept quiet, not wanting to disrupt Dad's wishful thinking. Chet knew the difference between a sticker and a badge. I wish I had spent more time with him in the pool. Not that I could have helped with his swimming. I thought of Luke; if I hadn't been so busy trying to make him jealous or check off my stupid spreadsheet, I could have asked him to give Chet private lessons instead of teaching me.

Whoa! Lose that dream, loser.

I wiped that thought bubble away.

Mom squealed and stood up. Chet's private lesson was over. The instructor gave him a hug and passed him his report card. Chet bounded over to us, his little paper booklet for swimming already soggy. Dad gave him a high-five. I blinked a few times, certain I could see a bright sticker stapled to his sheet.

"Kowsey!" he hollered. "Just like Fwog and Owed!"

"Frog and who?" I teased, crouching down, getting ready for my "That sticker is awesome, let's get a free triple-scoop ice cream to celebrate!" speech.

"Owed always wands to give up, but Fwog makes him keep twying. So I keep twying!" His chubby hands held open his booklet.

That little stinker. His beautiful badge made me cry—and Dad got it on video.

Chet pulled away from me and pointed to the top of the bleachers. "How-hole!" he cried out.

I slowly turned. Luke was coming down the stairs toward us. With his sunglasses and his tux, he looked like James Bond. Several heads swivelled in our direction.

My brain was firing out orders: *Run. Stay. Smile. Cry. Hug. Pee your pants.*

Fortunately I stayed, but I chickened out and smiled at the ground.

Luke crouched down and gave Chet a high-five. Chet babbled for a while. I snuck a glance at my mom; clearly these two had been putting in time together.

Mom pulled me off to the side. "He'll be a big brother in a few months," she said. "Chet is more than willing to help him practice."

I frowned at my mom. What the heck else had she been cooking up behind my back?

"Everything all set for this afternoon, I hope," Mom smiled at Luke. "We'll expect you two at eight o'clock tonight. We like to eat later in the evening."

You two? As in Chet and Luke? Is that why he's here, to take my brother for ice cream?

My mouth fell open. "He's taking Chet?" I asked her. I felt a bit put out. If anyone was going to celebrate with Chet, it should be me, his favourite person on the whole planet.

Mom gave me a look that mimicked Francine when she's trying to explain a simple math rule. "No, Kelsey," she said, "I arranged for Luke to give you some private swimming lessons."

And there went the ground, plus my stomach.

"Huh?" I'd been falling back on that phrase a lot lately.

Mom picked up my backpack and handed it over. "Your bathing suit and towel, plus capris and a top that still had the tag on it."

I couldn't move.

Luke reached out, taking the backpack and shouldering it over his tux. He pulled his glasses down a bit, just to give me a quick peek at those blue pools. "I hope you don't mind," he said, putting a set of keys in my hand, "you're going to have to drive."

Driving to Luke's house without going off the road was the most difficult thing I've ever done. I can drive a stick, and yeah, when he put the top down, it was impressive. And driving a Mercedes E-Class Cabriolet was a nice change from Mom's hatchback, but all I wanted to do was pull over and attack him.

I kept sneaking sideways glances. Luke had undone his tie and the first few buttons of his shirt. His arm was over the back of the seat, his fingers inches away from my shoulder. I remembered the first time I'd seen him in the kitchen.

When faced with the guy you'd like to kill, you...

I had chosen C.

Play it cool and attack him later when there are no witnesses.

My hands clenched and unclenched the wheel as I thought about our first kiss.

We were the only car in the driveway. "Dad and Monica are heading straight to the airport," he told me. This was the first time I'd heard him mention his new stepmom's name.

Maybe we were both getting better at this "no one is to blame" philosophy.

I tried to read his face. Was he just doing this because he felt sorry for this loser who didn't know how to swim? Was he doing Mom a favour? Or was he genuinely just a guy who did nice things for people?

I walked through the house, my blush growing hotter.

Oh, here's where I threw up.

Oh, and here's where I insulted you and your dad.

Oh, and here's the library where I cursed the picture of you and your dad.

Luke didn't mention any of that, though. He showed me a bathroom where I could change, then he disappeared down the hallway.

I slipped on my black two-piece, then wrapped my towel around my shoulders. Luke was already by the pool. He sat on the side by the steps.

Sweet and sour bacon turds!

He had a life jacket out. Clearly this was a lesson, and not a chance to see me in my super-cool Snoopy beach towel.

I sat down beside him, my eyes skimming his scar.

"No one is to blame."

He stared across the pool. We lightly kicked our feet back and forth. The sun was hot on the top of my head.

There were no distractions. We were alone. Now was my chance.

I'd chickened out last night, but I'd learned that keeping secrets only makes things worse. Luke probably already knew, but since I owed his dad a personal apology when he returned from his honeymoon, I thought I should start by first confessing to Mr. Mulder, junior.

I took a few quick breaths, then held the last one. "I'm the one who let Blaine and his friends into the bar," I said quickly.

"I know."

"Oh. I wondered if your dad might have said something—"

"Blaine told me after the sailing trip last night." Luke stared across the pool's surface and over the tips of the spruce trees. The water on the harbour far below us glistened in the sun.

I dropped my chin. The scar on my knee was a faint white line. "I didn't think such a mess would happen," I said. "I'm sorry."

"You already apologized, remember? In the hallway before the rehearsal brunch."

And after our first and probably last kiss, I thought.

"Although I was clueless about what you were saying," he added. He didn't need to remind me that he'd been about to ask me on a date.

The butterflies started to swirl at the unexpected memory.

"Oh," I replied. This was followed with several beats of torturous silence, then I brilliantly added, "Right."

We stayed quiet. Luke scooped up a handful of water and let it trickle out. The only noise was the gentle motion of the water.

"I heard your speech," I finally said.

He tilted his face, squinting at me. "Yeah?"

"It was good." I splashed my feet a few times. "Really good."

"Thanks. I was nervous. I think I read once that people fear public speaking more than shark attacks."

"I don't know of anyone who ended up on *Real Life in the ER* because of public speaking, though." I laughed a little too long at my own joke. This was followed by more silence. So far, I was totally acing the swimming lesson.

He hopped into the water. It came up to his waist, and I had to pull my eyes away from his torso. He took a step closer, putting his hands on either side of my thighs. He looked up at me. "I have something to confess," he said.

"Really?" My pulse picked up. The butterflies began to circle my stomach. They liked the slight tease to his voice.

"I don't have any badges to hand out," he told me. "Do you still want swimming lessons?"

Yes, there was definitely a flirtatious edge to his question.

The butterflies started doing the cha-cha, but my head made me hesitate. Common sense would argue he was just making it clear that there would be no reward system with these lessons.

This was Luke, not some made-up crush I'd concocted during math class. He was a real guy with real feelings. And the last thing I wanted was to mess up any chance we might have to be more than swimming buddies and co-workers.

I decided to ask him one of his favourite questions. "I'm not sure," I finally answered. "What do you want?" My mouth was dry.

He gave me a safe answer: "I don't want to have to jump into the ocean after you every time you fall off my boat."

I squirmed under his gaze. "That's not what I meant."

Something in the air between us felt electric. He slipped the towel off my shoulders, then put his hands on my waist, gently pulling me forward.

"Wait." I resisted.

"Nope." He picked me up, lifting me into the pool. The water crept up past my waist. I kept my elbows out of the pool. "Relax," he said, now taking hold of my hands.

"Far enough!" I screeched, trying to dig my heels into the slippery pool bottom. My bathing suit top was still dry. I took some deep breaths, trying to keep calm. "Water," I sighed. "It's, like...everywhere."

"You weren't this bad on the boat."

"No, I behaved very badly on the boat," I said, thinking of Blaine.

He let go of me, then ran a hand over his face. A droplet of water clung to one of his eyelashes. He had one freckle to the side of his Adam's apple, and when he smiled, he had one dimple. It suddenly occurred to me I had no idea what Luke's shoulders looked like—he'd never turned his back on me.

My breathing had calmed. I was in the water and I wasn't dead. Maybe as long as I was with Luke, everything would be okay.

> How do you know when you're in love with the right guy?

"How do you feel?" he asked.

I could have given him the long answer, about his eyes, and how he always sees me, and how his speech made me cry. Instead, I gave him the short version.

How do I feel when I'm with Luke?

"Perfectly safe," I smiled.

"And we both know you like the safe option," he replied. His hands lightly squeezed my waist. He stepped closer, closing the space between us. Our bodies were touching all the way to our feet. I wondered if he could feel my heart thumping madly against his chest. He stared back, content to let me make the next move.

I reached up and linked my fingers behind his neck. "When you were giving your speech," I started, "did you see me spying on you through the kitchen door?"

Luke stayed quiet. A smile played on his lips, then he leaned down and kissed me. And when I closed my eyes and kissed him back, I felt the rush of a thousand butterflies taking off at once, filling the sky above us.

EPILOGUE
· · · · · · · · ·

That night before bed I opened up my laptop and grinned the biggest, goofiest smile at Francine's spreadsheet. I'm amazed at her genius. I hadn't noticed before, but Blaine's name wasn't in the last box; it only read, "Have a simply amazing, neurotransmitter-firing, stomach-full-of-butterflies kiss."

I closed my eyes, replaying that afternoon with Luke in the pool. When he kissed me, I melted into his arms. There's something about kissing a boy when you're both in your bathing suits, pressed up against each other. The skin-to-skin feeling sends a cascade of tingles all the way down.

But Luke was determined to fulfill his obligation as my instructor, and by the time we had to go for supper at my house that night, I could tread water. Luke was a great teacher, and we both discovered that I was more motivated to learn when rewarded with kisses rather than stickers.

It's been three weeks since that first lesson, and my life has improved in so many ways. Working in the kitchen turned out to be the best thing ever. Since Loretta is still off with a sprained foot, Luke has taken over her post with salads and desserts. He actually has a knack for that kind of thing, and Clyde is more than happy to taste-test any of Luke's new dressing recipes.

I'm the dishwasher, and I get to give Luke googly eyes all day. I never tire of seeing him. He spends a lot of time at my house, making marinade for Dad's BBQ, and of course hanging out with Chet. I'm not jealous, though; I still get to have my private lessons in his pool. Although, since I'm such a quick learner, we do more making out than actual swimming.

When Luke's mom returned from her spa retreat, he went to the city to spend the weekend with her. I'm joining him next time.

Francine called me after Tanner visited her. She cried when I told her everything that had happened. She said it was all her fault and that I never should have taken her stupid spreadsheet seriously.

I reassured her that stuff happens, and that no one was to blame. She also confided that Tanner had told her about the party and flirting with Brooke. She was pretty cool about it and asked him point blank if he wanted to still be her boyfriend.

Francine's voice lost its matter-of-fact tone when she spilled that he'd told her the L-word. Yup, Tanner was all lovey-dovey for my Fran-man. And she told me they made out like crazy.

Then we talked for another hour about how awesome our boyfriends were at kissing, and how the fireworks in your heart and stomach go on and on until you think you're going to explode.

My favourite part about working at the Queen's Galley is the end of my shift. I wear my bathing suit under my shorts all the time now. Luke and I lock up, and then run down the green slope to the wharf.

I jump off the edge, and when I surface he's always there with his arms open wide, ready to take me around the waist. Luke makes this deep moan when my finger traces his scar. It's very sexy. Then we kiss until we both get dizzy from all the heavy breathing.

We found out that when you make out in the water, one of you needs to be touching bottom or at least holding on to something. Like Ronnie told me, some things are more fun when you discover them on your own.

Then we float on our backs, looking up at the stars. Luke points out the constellations sailors would use to find their way home; something tangible that would point them in the right direction.

Nothing is ever planned the way you expect it to turn out—Chet's extra chromosome, Dad losing his job, Tanner's parent's divorce, and yeah, me and Luke finding each other. I guess Jesse's grandma was right: when I stopped chasing the thing I thought I wanted, the thing I really needed caught up with me.

> How do you know when you're in love with the right guy?

When you're too busy enjoying the present to wonder if you're following the right plan for the future.

I'm not sure what will happen when the summer ends and Luke goes back to the city. For now, though, I'm content and safe watching the stars twinkle down on us, satisfied that I'm exactly where I should be.

ACKNOWLEDGEMENTS

Butterflies Don't Lie is loosely inspired by my summer job experiences at The Captain's House in my hometown of Chester, Nova Scotia. It was originally written as a featured novella for Wattpad. I have to first thank Pamela Odina and her wonderful staff for giving me the opportunity to share Kelsey's story on such a far-reaching platform.

Writing is a solitary venture and I've been lucky enough to find kindred spirits along the way. Many thanks to fellow writers and critique partners Jen Swann Downey and Ann Marie Walker. Navigating the publishing corn maze has been much more enjoyable with you both.

I'm grateful for my dearest friends and beta readers extraordinaire, Barbara MacDougall, Tricia Dauphinee Bishop, and Shannon Macgillivray. Thank you for reading my books from the very beginning, helping with edits, and for talking about the characters like they were real people. You're better than a gingerbread latte with extra whipped.

This book wouldn't exist without Penelope Jackson, super-star editor and angel in disguise. Your keen eye and passion for this story created some of its best moments, and were essential in helping it evolve into a novel.

A gigantic slice of gratitude goes to Patrick Murphy and his team at Nimbus Publishing, especially Whitney Moran, who took this project under her wing and gave it the last bit of spit and polish, turning it into the shiny version it has become. I'm more than thrilled to have *Butterflies Don't Lie* in your care.

Thank you to my parents, Eric and Ethel Bishop, for creating a loving home where a good sense of humour was held in high regard. A nod also goes to my siblings, Brad Bishop and Cynthia Flack. Growing up with you two was never dull. Thanks for giving me so much material for future books.

And finally, I'm most thankful to my husband, Ken Myers, and our children, Ruth and Adam. Nothing I ever put on paper will compare to real life with you. Thank you.